FANG

VOLUME 3

Edited by Alex Vance

Bad Dog Books

2007

FANG Volume 3
First publication 2007
First revision 2010

ISBN: 978-90-79082-15-5

Edited by Alex Vance
baddogbooks@gmail.com

Published by Bad Dog Books
www . baddogbooks . com

Printed by FurPlanet
www . furplanet . com

TABLE OF CONTENTS

Preface

It's been a long time coming.

Work on this volume began in 2005, part and parcel of the enormous success of the inaugural volume.

When FANG was just a fresh new idea and submissions began streaming in it soon became clear that even with this editor's strict demands for quality, a very great deal of excellent material would have to be scrapped to prevent the first volume from becoming too thick to carry.

Then a pattern emerged. The finest stories showed a clear division: roughly two-thirds were contemporary fiction, and the others were fantasy erotica.

Fantastic.

All fantasy stories were summarily removed from the line-up for FANG Volume 1 and saved for the next volume. It seemed a perfect solution.

However, at the time, Halloween was around the corner and there came a clamoring for a new quick fix of FANG. This was originally intended to be a slim little special issue, but some authors couldn't restrain themselves and even after a gruelling editorial process, that issue grew enough to become a Volume 2 in its own right.

So the fantasy stories were relegated to Volume 3. Those familiar with the history of Bad Dog Books know what happened next.

Alex Vance, your humble editor, suffered nerve damage to his fingers and announced that FANG could no longer continue. Ben Goodridge, whose contributions to Volume 2 were numerous, didn't take kindly to that news and bullied his way into the ranks of what was to become Bad Dog Books.

Now, nearly two years later, the dust has finally settled and FANG Volume 3 is ready to go, with a slightly different line-up than it originally had.

Kyell Gold had written a short story that bridged his novels 'Volle' and 'Pendant of Fortune' (both available from Sofawolf Press), which was removed from this volume after it was published in his collection of short stories, 'The Prisoner's Release'.

New submissions had come in, and therefore a story I'd penned for Kyell, a darker piece set in the world of his novels, had to be cut out to make room for the new material. Those interested in this piece can find a revised, trimmed version in the ninth and tenth issue of FurNation Magazine, titled 'A Constellation of Black on Black'.

A longer piece by Teiran, 'The Hero' had to be cut simply on account of its length, which was a terrible tragedy. I was deeply charmed by its honesty, its straight-forwardness—I'm always impressed when an author has the balls to write something conventional, something that's been done before. In this age of novelty and innovation, writing something deeply ordinary shows great courage.

I'm therefore pleased to report that, while this story had to be cut from this volume, Teiran worked at it for a year, and 'The Hero' is now a full-fledged novel with illustrations by Ayame Emaya, Kamui and Satinka, available from Bad Dog Books.

Volume 3 has aged well. The authors have, as is typical for the authors who submit their works to Bad Dog Books, taken massive liberties with the genre; Whyte Yoté's 'Coming of Age' tells the tale of a young primitive cast out of his tribe, 'Fall' by Mwinzi is set in the feudal era of Japan.

Some authors stayed true to the notion of fantasy, though. Swords and dragons and magic and all that lark.

A lot of work has gone into this volume. More than any other, so far.

On behalf of the authors, who have been tremendously patient, always ready to make revise their work over and over again, I invite you to read, and to enjoy.

Sincerely,

The Editor.

The View from the Ivory Tower

K. M. Hirosaki is an old standard of FANG. A prolific writer, whose works have appeared in every volume of FANG to date.

He is a master of anguish—not outright angst or pain, but of the sensitive, shallow cuts that life makes.

In 'Sanguine and Clockwork', he tells the story of a wizard who, despite being loved and revered by the community he serve, feels trapped by his status.

Loneliness can drive a man to make dreadful decisions.

Sanguine and Clockwork

K. M. Hirosaki

Vico was a good fox: he was dutiful, he never complained, and he was good at what he did. Never during the course of Florian's studying, experimenting, transcribing or tinkering did the coyote ever meet with a single interruption from Vico, and the fox was always whisper-quiet as he went about his work. All in all, he was the perfect house-fox for someone like Florian, whose vocation called for things like peace, quiet, and orderliness.

Of course, Vico wasn't a *real* fox, which is what made all of that possible to begin with. A homunculus was created in order that it might serve, after all, and so it was no surprise that Florian, whose day-to-day work would otherwise leave his house a complete mess, would want something to help him with that.

Florian could conceivably have used magic to clean his dwelling in between different tasks, but that would have been awkward, more time-consuming, and, frankly, a waste of his abilities. Besides, the coyote was rarely *between* tasks, and was more frequently dealing with two or three (or more!) things at once, with a great deal of overlap. An already invaluable tool like Vico then became even more so, due to how much that constant assistance meant to Florian.

There were times, however, when Florian would look up from whatever tome he was poring through, or stop grinding up ingredients, or take a break from whatever he happened to be doing, all so that he could just quietly look at Vico as the fox puttered around the house. While the artificial fox was certainly a marvel of wizardly craftsmanship, that aspect of his being was all but matter of course in Florian's mind; the coyote was more just shamefully indulging himself in the ability to look upon and stare at a fox from whom he wouldn't need to hide his gaze.

In the strictest sense, Vico wasn't male at all, but rather was androgynous, like all homunculi. (A magician, sculpting the form of a drone helper to include such superfluous parts? Imagine it!) Still, the form of the fox's body was nominally masculine, in that 'he' was fully grown, lacked breasts, and had a boyish face as opposed to a girlish one, and so Florian considered the creation a 'he' all the same.

Besides, while Vico was clothed, it wasn't immediately apparent that he was lacking in gender definition, and when he was moving slowly or standing still, he even looked like a real, live fox. Only when the homunculus moved at full speed (which was rather clumsy), or when one were to look into its empty, soulless eyes, was it really apparent that Vico was an 'it' and not a 'him.'

Getting closer to a homunculus like Vico blew the illusion right out of the water, though: he couldn't react with anywhere near convincing enough a response to a stimulus like someone approaching or waving their paw in front of his face, and once someone *got* that close, they'd likely notice that he didn't breathe or blink (unless one who held control over him specifically directed him to). Touching Vico's skin or fur would be another telltale sign: the body temperature of a homunculus was markedly cooler than that of a real living being, and even if he looked and felt like flesh and blood on the surface, there was also the matter that the pulsing of veins was instead replaced by the barely audible whirring of a wonderful clockwork heart.

The heart of a homunculus was a truly maddening contraption, made possible only by the graces of wizardry. Clockmakers and tinkers had tried for centuries to build one without the aid of magic, but only once had anyone ever succeeded: some eight centuries prior, Laurent the Mad, whose most famous achievement up until that point had been the construction of a chamber-sized orrery for the Fifth Earl of Hangknave, had managed to create a functional heart, but its implementation resulted in a rapid turn of events that history texts stated was "rather unfortunate for all involved."

When Florian had finally reached the level of mystical skill necessary for creating a homunculus' heart, he had leapt at the opportunity to do so. The coyote had worked ceaselessly in crafting the body, barely sleeping for a week as he prepared the material components for the spell that would bring his creation to life. The decision to cast Vico into the form of a fox was a simple one, yet the choice itself was nothing that would bring undue suspicion upon him.

Vico may have been Florian's very own special little fox, but while a homunculus could make a fine surrogate for a houseboy or a maid, it could never come close to filling a more special position in a real person's life.

An Excerpt from "On the History of Spellcraft, Volume II," by Simon Canopus Artyle

The very earliest homunculi date back to several millennia ago. In the beginning, laypeople and the magically-inclined alike were wary and fearful of them—rightly so, perhaps, since in these beginning times, the creation of a homunculus was much more closely tied to the realm of black magic and necromancy. It is quite possible, in fact, that the homunculi of this time period were created from the dead themselves (although records that remain from this time do not go into the specifics, and so this point is a matter for much speculation and contention).

Perhaps it was because wizards the world over saw the inherent usefulness of a homunculus that the clockwork heart was invented: in this way, one could be sure that it was the power of magic itself that animated an otherwise entirely artificial construct, and therefore was far less abhorrent a prospect. Of course, the Magicians' Charter was quickly edited to codify just what made for an allowable homunculus, specifying the permissible components and even the number of homunculi a single person was allowed to create. Details changed, over time, but the standard concept changed very little.

It was just about sunset by the time that Florian was done with his alchemical experimenting for the day. He had missed the festival itself, he knew, but that didn't bother him all that much. If it wasn't full on into evening yet, then that meant that the follow-up celebration hadn't started, and so the coyote knew that he had time.

"Vico," he said, as he drew his mantle over his shoulders. "Clean my workspace while I'm gone." There was no commanding tone to his voice, but neither was he *asking* Vico to do as he said.

The artificial fox gave a small nod of acknowledgement, and immediately headed over to one of the cabinets in the far corner. Knowing that his house was in good hands, Florian closed the door behind him and started down the path to the town.

Even from a distance, the signs of the festival were obvious: townsfolk were still scattered about the fields and streets, but for the most part, people were reconvening at various points around town itself. The streets were strewn with trash from what looked to have been a raucous celebration, and Florian knew that more than a few merchants in town were already gleefully counting their profits from the day.

As the coyote made his way along the streets themselves, the few people who weren't too busy bustling about to notice his presence turn to him and bowed their heads, greeting him with polite reservation, holding still until he had passed. "Master Innswick," they addressed him, most seeming happy to see him among them.

Finally, Florian arrived at the Grass and Moonlight Tavern, and from the sound of it, the place was packed and bustling already. Slipping in through the front door, the coyote could see that not only was the place packed, but also that all eyes were fixed on Lord Rentell.

The young fox was standing on top of a sturdy oak table off to one side of the bar, ready to address the crowd that had assembled. Florian shuffled his way to an open spot near the wall, and watched eagerly along with everyone else.

"Ladies and gentlemen, what a wonderful day it has been," Rentell called out, silencing the crowd's murmurs and assuring that all attention was fixed on him. "I'd like to congratulate the good people of Honeybrush on their bountiful harvest: you all worked very hard, I know, and I'm very happy to see that the world has responded in kind with its richly-deserved rewards."

Cheers and applause broke among the crowd, and as Rentell took a few moments to scan the room, he made eye contact with Florian. The fox nodded and grinned, and Florian just nodded politely in return to the young lord, not wanting to draw any undue attention or suspicion.

"Also, everyone, it looks like our very own Master Florian Innswick has come to join us," Rentell said, motioning over to the coyote, at which point all heads in the room turned in unison. *So much for keeping away from attention*, Florian thought to himself, feeling a swell of bashfulness.

Rentell paced around atop his table. "I know that Master Innswick has been a great help to all of you, as well," he said to the crowd, "and that, even if nobody can change or control the flow of seasons, it never hurts to have a magician on one's side, does it?"

The crowd started to laugh and clap, throwing their praise and appreciation at Florian. Rentell looked just tickled with himself, and the proud yet playful smile on his face made him ten times more handsome than he already was.

Rentell Centrène was the Count of Dunnis' third son; as such, his place in the political world of the realm was far from significant. Perhaps to make up for this, the young fox took it upon himself to at least involve himself in the lives of his father's subjects, and as far as Florian had seen, at least for the people of Honeybrush, he was a well-loved man indeed: he was always well-groomed and well-dressed, but he never flaunted his wealth; his nobility commanded respect, but he never abused his power; he was polite and well-spoken, but he wasn't above joining the townsfolk for a rowdy celebration down at the local tavern.

It wasn't Rentell's noble aspect that drew Florian's fondness, though. If anything, the fox's nobility was the one true impediment towards the coyote ever being able to indulge in or express that affection. As the two most noted and respected citizens in town, there could hardly be any discretion or secrecy—to think of two *men*, both in such positions of prestige, sharing a bed together? It would be beyond shameful; it would be an outright scandal!

Hopeless though it was, though, Florian couldn't shake himself free of his feelings. Even now, as Rentell happily congratulated the people of Honeybrush for their good fortune, as much as Florian should have been sharing the people's excitement, the coyote could think only of how beautiful the fox looked as he spoke, and of how much he wanted to wrap the younger vulpine up his arms, hold him, keep him safe, lay him down upon the ground and feel his body squirm underneath...

Rentell's assertive tone cut through the magician's daydreaming. "Now, good people, I do have one more bit of news that I feel I *do* have to share with you." Immediately, the crowd's murmuring shrunk, and the fox waited until he had everyone's full attention. "You are all aware, I am sure, that one of the matters His Grace the Grand Duke has been considering for this season's council has been the possibility of levying a new tariff on ale and beer from this region." All further whispering immediately came to a stop; not a soul in the tavern, Florian was sure, lacked direct personal interest in *that* particular matter.

"As I am sure you are also aware," Rentell continued, staying calm and reasonable in tone, "we are not due to receive word back from the Grand Duke's council until some time next week." The fox paused and took a heavy breath. "However, my father, the Count, tells me that word has come to him regarding what matters *have* been discussed. The official decree has not yet been made, but I do feel obliged to tell you this."

A heavy moment passed, and the feeling in the air was tangible as the people waited to hear Rentell's announcement. The fox bowed his head, and then announced, "The ducal council has decided *against* levying the tariff." At once, the tavern erupted into cheers, and Rentell raised his head back up, an enormous grin on his face. He swooped down with one hand, snatched his tankard up from off of the table, and called out, "Drink Up!" before taking a heavy swig. He then unfastened a pouch from his belt and tossed it to the tavernkeep, and the loud clinking it made when caught showed that it was full of coins.

With that, the crowd's eyes and ears were no longer on Rentell, and instead, the focus was on the tapping of kegs, the distribution of drinks, and the resurgence of merrymaking. Florian couldn't hold back a smile. The people really *did* love their Lord Rentell.

"Florian!" Rentell called out over the din of the now-distracted crowd. "Stop hiding back there! Come and join me!" With that, the fox then hopped off of the table, drink still in hand, and took his seat.

Florian sifted through the crowd, without anyone really taking any notice of him until he got to Rentell's table. The young lord's companions were all wealthy townspeople that Florian recognized, but he could only put names to a few of the faces. "Someone make room for Master Innswick," Rentell said, motioning to the others, who scooted around and let the coyote take a seat.

"So, you opted out of the festival, did you?" the fox asked Florian. "I should have guessed that much, I suppose." He gave the coyote a teasing look and shook his head in mock disappointment. "Always so, so serious."

"I couldn't right well steal the spotlight from you, could I?"

Florian replied with a smile, taking a tankard of ale from the scraggly bobcat on his left. "I've got my own reputation to maintain, after all."

Rentell laughed, and finished draining his cup. "Well, I'm glad you decided to put in an appearance here, at least," he said. "Otherwise, I'd have to drop by your place afterwards, and pound on your door in the black of night in some drunken stupor so that I could *force* my company upon you."

I might wish that you would do that, Florian thought to himself, but he bit his tongue. He hid for another moment behind the rim of his cup, and then said, "You know full well that I'd never dream of missing an evening like this. I don't think I'll ever be *that* busy."

"Oh, I'm not so sure," Rentell said, winking as another serving of ale came his way, as well. "I've known you to be pretty reclusive, from time to time."

"Only when it's been of sufficient importance," Florian said, beginning to feel self-conscious, since he knew that he had no chance of hiding the delight in his eyes as he and Rentell exchanged banter. "For now, though, nothing takes precedence over this."

"Hear, hear!" Rentell called out, raising his glass. The others at the table all joined in, and any awkwardness on Florian's part was soon forgotten as the focus on him and Rentell disappeared and gave way to more general conversation all around.

The entire tavern was abuzz, now, and the room just bristled with a wonderful sort of energy. For someone like Florian, who didn't leave his home nearly as often as one of the normal townspeople, the feeling was a different kind of special in its own right. Wizards weren't meant for carousing, as their general trends in personality went, but Florian appreciated the contrast with his typical day-to-day life.

One of the serving wenches, a wolf girl whose name escaped Florian, came by the table with a heavy tray loaded with food. "Lord Rentell," she said, ears flushed up as she began to unload dishes onto the table. "And Master Innswick," she said, turning to nod to Florian. "Truly, we are beyond lucky to have the both of you with us."

"I'm not sure how much you folks really need us," Rentell said, sliding one of the plates in front of himself. "You're the ones doing the hard work, day in and day out."

"Even so," the wolf girl said, laughing merrily as she passed more food around the table, "if it weren't for you taking such a stake in us, milord, or for Master Innswick's assistance and interventions, we'd hardly be here celebrating like this tonight."

Rentell bowed his head, then, accepting the girl's thanks. "Well, then here's to many more seasons like this one," he said, before taking a nice hearty bite from his plate. What better way to show respect to a place that serves food, really, Florian figured.

Yes, the people of Honeybrush really did love their Rentell. They might have *respected* Florian, sure, but however highly the townsfolk might have thought of him, it wasn't the same as what they all felt for Rentell. That much was obvious. The fox had charm and wit and the ability to win people over with his charisma.

One of those people, it would seem, was Florian himself, and he wished to the powers that he controlled that he could bespell himself out of his silly infatuation.

It was just after midnight by the time that Florian finally returned home. The evening spent with Rentell, their friends, and the other townsfolk had been certainly been enjoyable, but now that he was by himself again, the coyote felt somewhat bitter. He almost wished that he hadn't attended the festivities at all.

So many times, he'd come close to blurting out something to the fox that he would have regretted. As much as it was a trifling way to use his powers, Florian had used the aid of magic to ensure that he didn't ever get too drunk, but in retrospect, he wondered if that would have been such a bad thing. Would there still have been as much shame to bear, if he could just blame some offhand comment on an excess of alcohol?

No. It still would have been an awful embarrassment. Florian still would have lost face, his friendship with Rentell would likely have been ruined—it would have been a disaster, and so the coyote wagered that he'd made the right decision after all, leaning on the side of caution.

Sulking and sullen, Florian opened his front door and walked on inside. Standing there in the darkness, he snapped his fingers, and at once, the room was flooded with light, showing that the chamber was as clean and tidy as if it had never been touched, and there, standing in the corner, silent and unmoving, was Vico. The fox turned his head toward Florian, in case his master had a new command for him.

Florian removed his mantle and just dropped it on the floor. He trudged over to his workbench, sat down, and rested his face in his hands. Why did he have to put up with his silly infatuation? Surely, there were better things that a wizard should be occupying his mind with!

It was so frustrating to have a gift that most people could only dream of having, and yet still have it all be so useless when it really mattered. Florian was still just a reclusive, peculiar man who lived alone and spent his days absorbed in unfathomable arcane practices. No amount of fancy sorcery could win the eye and affections of a man like Rentell—unless, of course, one were to speak of sorcery specifically *for* that effect. Not only was that expressly forbidden by Magicians' Character, though, but also, Florian could never do such a thing. Besides being strictly unethical, it wouldn't fulfill that need that the coyote had: to have Rentell want him as much as he wanted Rentell.

"Why do I keep doing this to myself?" Florian mumbled, gripping at the fur between his ears, wanting to just start pulling it out. He growled to himself in frustration, and then let his forehead fall against the table with a thud.

In the ensuing silence, all Florian could hear was the sound of Vico's concealed clockwork heart working away as the fox just stood there. The coyote lifted his head up and looked back at his creation, who again merely stared back with empty eyes, awaiting whatever it was that the wizard had to say.

"Vico," Florian said, sitting upright again. "Come over here."

Vico responded without so much as a nod. He walked slowly,

with no sense of urgency, but the relaxedness of his gait made him seem more real as he approached the coyote. He came to a stop by the bench, and then looked down into Florian's eyes. His blank expression was almost like that of a hopeful pet, to Florian's imagination.

The coyote stood up from the bench. "Turn your head around," he said. "Let me look at you." Vico then leaned his head back and took his time, turning first one cheek to Florian, and then the other. It was a lazy motion that looked calculated because it wasn't rushed, and that made it seem almost sensual. If only Florian could someday be so lucky as to have Rentell respond to his tender words in the same way.

"My fox," Florian said, reattaining Vico's attention. "Let me kiss you." The coyote wasn't sure, at first, how the homunculus would respond to such a directive, but to his great surprise, the fox angled his muzzle forward ever so slightly, as if in anticipation. That cue was all it took for Florian to overcome whatever remnants of reluctance still clung to him.

The image of Rentell's face filled Florian's mind as the coyote pressed his lips to Vico's. It was that same handsome muzzle that the magician pictured as he reached up to stroke his creation's face, before he pressed the kiss deeper, feeling minimal resistance as he did so. Florian's heart was racing, overcoming his shame as he locked his muzzle with Vico's.

The mock fox's mouth was too cold to feel real, though. As much as Florian could only imagine what a *real* kiss with his *real* fox would be like, he could only suspend his disbelief so far. In the core of his mind, the coyote focused his thoughts and wiggled the fingers on his right hand; without being able to speak words, he would have to draw on some extra power in order for his spell to work, but he knew that if he broke the kiss, he'd never muster up the will to do it again. A tingling started in his hand, spiraled its way up his arm, climbed up through his throat, and spilled its way from his own mouth into Vico's, causing the homunculus' muzzle to flush up with warmth.

It wasn't a perfect balance, but it would do. Florian took both hands and grabbed Vico by the shoulders, hungrily working his tongue around in the fox's mouth, all the while attempting to imagine what Rentell's eager whimpering would sound like as he submitted to the older coyote's advances. Surely, the young nobleman would feel initial pangs of shame and uncertainty before he ultimately gave in to desire, confessing his mutual attraction to Florian by merely returning the heatedness of that passionate kiss.

But Vico, being the faultless servant that he was, could not fulfill that role, and with that all-too-quick realization, Florian's fantasy was broken. The coyote pulled away from the fox, wiping his paw at his damp muzzle. What had he been *thinking*? Was he really so desperate that he'd steal even fake affection from a fake fox? Had a wizard of the realm ever sunk so low?

"Hang my mantle up," Florian said without looking at Vico. As the homunculus walked off toward the front door, the coyote headed for his bed, canceling out the room's magical light with a dismissive wave of his paw. It was definitely past the time for sleep.

An Excerpt from "A Layperson's Guide to the Magicians' Legal Codex," by Simon Canopus Artyle

In accordance with the Magicians' Charter, any wizard of the realm who misuses his talents in such a way as to bring harm to his fellow man is to be first stripped of his powers, and then, sentenced further in a manner befitting the nature of the transgression committed.

The punishment itself is first proposed by the barrister handling the case, though it is ultimately the Ducal Wizard who assigns the final sentence. Accordingly, the nature of the punishment given can vary greatly from case to case, and also to an extent by the wizard presiding, and there are only a few cases that are so clear-cut as to carry a standard penalty: murder, for instance, carries an obvious penalty of death, but due to the nature of magical crimes in general (being both atypical and uncommon), most cases require careful deliberation in order to ensure that the resulting punishment is both fitting and fair.

"I'm very glad that you were able to make it, Florian. I realize that this is short notice."

Rentell sat across the table from Florian as the two took lunch in the fox's private chambers within the Count's manor. The trappings of the room were fancier than anything that Rentell ever allowed himself to wear in public when he was among the townsfolk, but he was still dressed subtly as he entertained his guest.

"Oh, not at all," Florian replied, waiting for Rentell to take a first bite before he dared to. "Nothing I was doing was anything that couldn't be put aside for the afternoon." He wanted to add something about being thankful for the invite rescuing him from his tedium, but in the aftermath of his shameful behavior after the celebration a few nights previous, he decided against it.

Rentell started munching away at his first course, and Florian took his cue to join in. "I'm also glad for the company," the fox said, mouth still partially full. "We haven't gotten to spend a lot of time together, lately."

"Well, you've been busy," Florian said, before pausing to take a sip of wine. "I heard that the festival itself went over extremely well. I'm sorry that I had to miss it."

The fox chuckled and shook his head. "I'm more just a figurehead, there, than anything else. It's the farmers and the shopkeepers and everyone else who do all the hard work." He, too, took a moment to wash his food down with a sip of wine. "It was a shame that you had to miss it, though."

"Perhaps next year," Florian said with a nod. He really didn't know what a man like him would *do* at a festival like that. In all likelihood, some of the more brash townsfolk would try to conscript him into showing off measly little cantrips like he were a clown and not a registered magician.

Rentell allowed them both to get a few more mouthfuls down

before he spoke again. "Speaking of company, though, I should probably get to the matter that I've called you here to discuss."

The coyote's ears pricked. Of course Rentell had wanted to talk about something specific, if he'd invited Florian to the manor, but in his excitement, the magician hadn't given that a whole lot of thought until just now. "Certainly," he replied, dabbing his mouth with his napkin. "Go right ahead."

"Mmm," Rentell murmured, draining the rest of his wine. "Well, what you were saying just now, about being able to set your work aside," he said, refilling his cup. "Is that going to remain true in the near future?"

"I... suppose that it might," Florian replied, confused. "Does the Count need me for some reason?"

Rentell chuckled. "Actually, I think *I* need you, Florian," he said. "I've got to go... go on a bit of a journey, and I'd rather not have to drag a contingent of soldiers along with me, if I can at all avoid it."

The coyote's ears, already on end, were burning with a blush that he hoped Rentell couldn't see. "A journey? Where to?" Best to seem as unsuspicious as possible.

"I'd rather not say that until I know whether you can commit to going on not," Rentell said, his manner quickly shifting into a more serious mode. "I know that I can trust you enough with secrets, Florian, but I also don't want to take unnecessary risks, you know?"

"Yes, of course," Florian responded. Did Rentell really place such trust in him? Were the two really that close? "I'll at least need to know when this journey would be," he said, keeping his voice disconnected from emotion, "and for how long we'd be gone."

Rentell took a sip from his fresh glass, and then nodded. "We would leave a week from today, and hopefully, we'd only be gone for five weeks, at the most." He paused for a moment, and then asked, "Is that something you'd be able to do?"

If Florian wanted to back out of the offer, it would have been beyond simple. Rentell wouldn't know nearly enough about sorcery or alchemy to be able to discern truth from lie if Florian were to invent a reason why he couldn't go. "I don't see why I wouldn't be able to go," was his reply, though, and he searched deep into the nobleman's eyes for any hints at what motive might lurk behind them.

"Excellent!" Rentell said. "Really, I hate to make such a big deal of it, because it's really nothing so dire." The fox got theatrically quiet for a moment. "More than anything, I just don't want to draw too much attention to my departure."

"You are planning on coming back, I hope!" Florian responded, voice peaking louder than he'd wanted it to.

Again, Rentell just laughed, looking so carefree as he did so. "That's what I need you for, Florian!" he said. "But perhaps I'd better explain more, before your fur turns complete gray on me."

The fox cleared his throat, drank down some more wine, and crossed his hands in front of him. "I need to go to Ephaia," he said. "Now, before you say anything, I want to point out that this is very much official business, and it's going down in the books as such."

Florian raised an eyebrow. "But we're on friendly terms with Ephaia," he said. "Why all the secrecy behind going?"

"It's not so much that my trip itself is a secret," Rentell explained. "I just don't want my *departure* to draw too much attention."

"I'm afraid I still don't quite understand," Florian said. It wasn't like Rentell to dance around a subject quite this much; he was playful—he'd remained a full-on whippersnapper until just a few years ago—but he tended to be more up front when it came to affairs like this.

"There are some mercantile contracts that need to be settled," Rentell said. "And again, this is an official matter, and I don't want anyone to be suspicious of that. However, my father had to... make certain promises to certain people in order to have certain matters properly affected at the ducal council, and let's just say that it's going to be necessary to have... a required amount of monies on hand before too long."

Aha. So, that was the catch. Rentell was a daring and cocksure young man, but he wasn't a fool, after all. "So, you need some extra escort for your way back, in case the wrong people catch wind of things," Florian said.

Rentell flashed his teeth in an apprehensive smile. "Actually, it's a bit more tricky than that, to tell the truth," he said, taking a few moments to readjust the cuffs of his shirt. "Given the, ah, *urgency* with which we need to get to Ephaia and back with said requisite monies, I'm afraid I'm going to have to take something of a shortcut."

"You mean—"

"Yes," Rentell said, nodding. "We're going to have to cut through Gundry." He held up a paw, warding off any shock or outburst that Florian might have. "Now, it should only be for about five days for each leg of the journey that we'll be crossing their territory, but we both know that my being found by the Gundrites would be… most unfortunate."

It wasn't the safest course of action, Florian had to admit, but cutting through Gundry *would* save a few weeks in Rentell's getting to Ephaia and back, and he had to assume that the fox had weighed the risks versus other options if he had come to this conclusion. "If you're certain that it's the only way…" the coyote said.

"Florian," Rentell said, leaning forward a ways. "I need you to keep me safe." The fox then reached out and touched the top of Florian's hand. "And I know that you can. I wouldn't ask if I thought that this would be too dangerous for you."

Florian stared down at Rentell's hand atop his own, too shocked at the touch to even pull away on fearful reflex. He looked back into the fox's eyes, clenched his jaw, and nodded. "No. I'm certain you're right," he said. "I'm honored to be of assistance to you and your family."

"Thank you, Florian," Rentell said, sitting back in his chair. "That puts my mind at so much ease." The fox then picked up his fork and his wine cup once more. "Now, enough with the grim talk," he said with another smile. "There's still plenty more food to get through."

The flask exploded in a burst of blue smoke, sending shards of glass around the room that Florian managed to avoid solely due to luck. Damn! That was the second time that evening that he'd managed to brutally botch his mineral transmutation! Over six hours—and a week's working wage worth of materials—all wasted!

All of it had gone to waste because Florian couldn't shed his distractions. He couldn't focus on the work he ought to have been doing, because he couldn't stop thinking about the honest and plaintive look in Rentell's eyes as the fox had asked him along on his mission.

The touching of hands that Florian had so desperately wanted to construe as something intimate was, he knew deep down, really nothing more than a sign of friendly request. But the sheer fact that Rentell was placing such trust and confidence in him! It was distracting beyond belief, and knowing that he'd be spending weeks alone with the fox wasn't helping him shake his hopes away.

He was so angry with himself. He huffed away from his workbench, knowing full well that any further attempts at experimenting that evening would result in just as much wastefulness as his first two. "Vico!" he snapped, distancing himself from the mess he'd made. "Clean this up for me!"

Vico, who had been cleaning some of the glassware that Florian had been using in his first failed experiment, set his work aside and went to answer his new call. The homunculus first surveyed the damage to the wizard's workspace, and then trundled over to the broom closet.

Florian sank into one of his chairs and sighed. Was he doomed to repeat his bumbling for the rest of the week until he and Rentell finally left together on their journey? He was liable to blow up his house before the day finally rolled around! The last thing that the town of Honeybrush needed was a magician who couldn't keep his focus on controlling the great powers at his command.

What if it *were* all true, though? What if Florian wasn't misinterpreting things and all, and Rentell really *did* return the wizard's interest? Could that be so farfetched? Certainly, even the third son of the Count of Dunnis could rationalize bringing elite guards along with him for a journey that was as crucial as Rentell had said it was. Was there any *real* reason that he'd need Florian along instead of someone else?

In the name of all decency, why did his mind have to keep going back to that? Why was he tormenting himself by clinging to those thin, unrealistic hopes? He could rationalize and rationalize to his heart's content, and it still wouldn't change the fact that, in the end, having something like that with Lord Rentell was impossible, regardless of how *either* of them felt.

Perhaps, though, while they were away, alone together, a tryst wouldn't be out of the question.

At once, Florian regretted even entertaining the thought. It was too late, though: he could feel his desire and arousal beginning to stir, and his mind had walked down that path so often by now that it was achingly familiar. No, Florian wasn't going to get anything done until he could rid himself of these accursed base urges of his, which went beyond simply attempting to sate himself in private.

The coyote's dutiful little house-fox went about his cleanup duties, oblivious to the thoughts in his master's mind. He was nothing more than a dumb creation, who could no sooner feel shame than he could feel love—in essence, he was a non-entity, conveniently shaped in the visage of a fox.

"Vico," Florian said, voice warbling as he got his words out. "You can stop cleaning, now. Please come here." He rarely ever affixed words like *please* to his commands when he spoke to Vico, lately, but here, in his desire to find some common ground with something at least nominally vulpine, the wizard felt compelled to add the touch of politeness.

Vico obeyed, setting aside his cleaning brush before walking up to Florian. The coyote stood to meet him, and looked over his body. Yes, so long as he could pretend, Vico would do just fine. His proportions weren't all that dissimilar from Rentell's, and whatever difference there was... well, it wasn't as if Florian were *that* intimately familiar with the curves of Rentell's body.

"Take off your clothes for me," the coyote said, stepping around the fox, who soon began to silently strip himself of his already meager garb. Florian had never seen Vico out of clothing since he'd activated the homunculus years back, cleaning and mending those clothes with magic as such became necessary. Now, watching the fox's clumsy motions as he disrobed, the magician did truly feel like he was bearing witness to something that he shouldn't— allowing him to more readily slip into the mindset of imagining his noble companion doing the same.

Florian had made his way behind Vico before the fox could get his trousers off, so that by not seeing the lack of anatomical correctness, he would not break the illusion. With the fox out of clothing, the coyote slipped in against his back and wrapped his arms around the narrow vulpine chest.

"*I need you to keep me safe.*" Rentell's words from the day's lunch echoed in Florian's mind as the coyote started to rub up and down the fur on Vico's torso. Yes, Florian could keep young Rentell safe. He could be the one to shelter the fox from the harsh realities of the world, protecting him with the virtues of age, experience, and mystical wisdom.

The coyote pressed his snout down at the back of Vico's ear, and took a breath in through his nose. The fur there was dry, though, with no real smell of its own. He tried to envision what Rentell's scent would be like, wrapped up like this in the older wizard's arms, but imagination failed him; having never been able to share such close moments with Rentell—or any other fox, for that matter—and so his mind couldn't conjure up anything to compensate.

Inspiration struck Florian in that moment. Of course! Why would his imagination need to conjure up anything at all, when *he* could do so all the better? He closed his eyes, and murmured an incomprehensible mantra to himself. Within moments, the scent of fox, simple and masculine, was filling his nostrils. The coyote let out a dull sigh, feeling his sheath stir as he pulled the fox in his arms back against his front. He let Vico's tail brush back and forth over his legs, and began to nibble at the rim of the ear he was pressed into.

Vico didn't resist. *Nor would Rentell, by this point.* Florian pressed himself firmly against the fox's backside, getting more worked up by the moment. He continued to stroke Vico's chest, ruffling through the fur there, feeling its bristly texture against his fingers. "Just hold still," he whispered, and of course, Vico obeyed, just as his fox should. The coyote's other hand went down to his belt, trying to unfasten it with as little fumbling as possible. After a few moments, though, he dismissed his attempt, instead focusing his mental energies on letting the magic work for him, allowing him to caress the fox with both paws as his breeches were pulled free of his legs by forces unseen.

With his full sheath now in direct contact with the fox's fur, Florian let out a growl of pleasure. Here, he would take his time, letting Rentell know, without question, that he intended to have his way with the fox, but he would goad him, just so, with firm presses near the base of his tail. Vico remained limp and still, moving as Florian's arms directed him to move, working with silent obedience. "Press back against me," he muttered into the fox's ear, and without any delay, he felt the fox's backside grinding against his crotch. "*I need you, Florian.*" Again, Rentell's words from earlier filled in where Vico himself couldn't, and everything was as it should be.

The coyote's member began to slip free, the damp tip brushing against the fur of the fox's rear end. As he went to maneuver it underneath that fluffy red tail, however, Florian remembered that Vico was ill-equipped in that regard. Here, unfortunately, the coyote's imaginary dalliance would have to come to an end. Were it truly Rentell, he would not have wasted another moment before shoving the fox down onto his hands and knees, moaning in delight as he sank himself into his lordship's willing rear. He closed his eyes and took another breath of the pervading essence of fox, letting himself hear Rentell cry and whine his name as he gave himself up.

Florian was fully erect now, his shaft nestled in between Vico's thighs, riding against the fuzzy cleft of his rump. Without having that all-important final bit to make his fantasy real, though, he knew that he risked losing whatever illusion he hoped to pull over his own eyes. He took a few moments to think, frantically, hearing nothing but the sound of his own ragged breath as his mind looked for answers, and it was within that sound that his answer came.

"Follow me," he told Vico, releasing his hold from around the fox's back. He headed for his bed, shedding the clothing from his upper body as he went, hearing soft footsteps behind him. Then, the coyote turned around, sat down on the edge of his bed, and looked up into the fox's face.

As he gazed into Vico's dim eyes, though, Florian knew that he couldn't bear to hear himself say the words he would need to in order to give the homunculus its next order. Instead, the coyote took his right hand and crossed his middle finger back behind his index finger, and then rotated his wrist in a clockwise circle three times. He looked Vico right in the eyes, and as he finished tracing the mystical sigil in the air with his fingers, he felt raw power rushing through himself, as if he'd opened some sort of magical sluice gate: he'd established a direct mental link with Vico, now, and while it would drain a bit of magical essence, it would be worth it.

Following with the suggestion in Florian's mind, Vico got onto his knees in front of the coyote's bed. Here, Florian would need no such crude words to deal with Rentell: the fox would know exactly what it was that the coyote wanted, and he'd be eager to give it. He'd lean forward—yes, *just as Vico was now leaning forward*—and nuzzle in against the inside of his thigh.

He'd lick, then, brushing his tongue just at the underside of Florian's tense, aching shaft. *Too cold!* Florian had forgotten to warm the fox's mouth, and so he quickly rectified that, giving no conscious thought to his muttering so that he could focus on keeping his link with the fox steady. Heat blossomed out from the fox's tongue, then, sending a shiver up along Florian's spine that ended in an airy gasp when it reached his throat.

Finally, he had Vico draw his snout up into position, and he looked down into the fox's face. There, he gazed into those eyes, and saw nothing but that shallow emptiness that was all the soulless creation had to offer. *No!* This was wrong! This would not do at all! His Rentell would be gazing up at him with adoration, a hint of questioning, and an eagerness that was masked behind hesitation. He would not look anything like this… this automaton!

Disgust gripped at the boundaries of Florian's mind, and he severed his link to the fake fox, feeling the channel of power slam shut like a door in the wind. Was he really doing this? Was he really allowing himself to manipulate his homunculus—an assistant he'd created for housecleaning and other chores—in order to satisfy the unwholesome, shameful urges that he should have been trying to exorcise from his mind completely?

The coyote flung himself face-first down into his pillows, choking on a rough sob. Why had he been reduced to this? Why was something so foolish proving to be so difficult for him to deal with?

He looked up from his pillows, then, and saw Vico kneeling beside the bed, right where he'd left him. The fox would stay there, too, forever waiting, until his master dismissed him, because that was simply what a homunculus would *do*. It wasn't a real, living creature. It was just a *thing*, a thing, and no matter how real it might look, it was never going to be Rentell.

It was, however, at least shaped like a fox, it looked like a fox, and with the assistance of magic, it at least smelled like a fox. "Vico," Florian said, shifting himself over as he drew his covers up. "Lie here next to me, and go to sleep."

The fox answered by dragging himself up into bed, and then, it rolled onto its side, facing away from Florian so that the coyote could drape his arm over it and nestle against its back as it went still for the night.

Florian spent as much time as possible out of the house, for the next few days. He made do with reading from his books in various quiet spots around town, and he told the people who asked that he was simply looking for a change in scenery. He could hardly bring himself to admit to anyone that he was too ashamed to even stay in the presence of his mindless clockwork vulpine servant.

It was still a few days before he was due to depart for Ephaia with Rentell, and in the meantime, he hadn't seen the fox at all. That wasn't unusual, though; especially with word from the ducal council on its way, any nobleman would be busy, even one of such a low station. Besides, it wasn't as if Rentell owed any special loyalty to Florian in particular.

Rather than brood, though, Florian was determined to at least put up the appearance of having a good time. That would bring fewer questions, for one. He had taken to eating his meals at the Grass and Moonlight, where he could be seen in public, but where few would be so bold as to actually take a seat with the esteemed Master Innswick without an invite.

It was precisely because of that fact that Florian was so surprised when the wolf wench from the night of the festival took a seat across from him as he was in the midst of eating his lunch.

"Oh, Master Innswick!" she said, obviously trying (but failing) to keep her excitement hushed. "Have you heard the latest news?"

"News?" Florian replied. "No, I don't think that I have." In truth, he hadn't heard anything, unless word of Rentell's upcoming journey had leaked somehow.

The young wolf looked like she was about to burst, brimming full of gossip as she was. "Oh, it's downright startling!" she said, giggling in a way that would have been considered inappropriate for a girl half her age. "I'm surprised no one's told you about it, of all people!"

Florian didn't know whether to be intrigued or frightened. Whatever manner of rumors the lass was intent on spreading, it must have been something strange indeed if she saw it "fit" to share it with Honeybrush's own Master Innswick. "I haven't heard a thing, honestly," the coyote responded, attempting to keep some semblance of propriety to conversation.

"It's about Lord Rentell!" the wolf blurted, clasping her paws over her face, as if it would somehow cancel out what she'd just said. Then, in more hushed tones (which did little good, now, since more than a few heads had turned), she said, "The tavern-keep caught him in bed last night with his *son*! Imagine it! Naked and all!"

But Florian was too dumbstruck by the words to imagine anything at all. His mind went as blank as his eyes went wide, and he dropped his fork onto the floor. He was dimly aware that the wolf girl was prattling on about further details of the torrid rumor, but he was no longer listening. Rentell and the tavern owner's son, caught in bed together? What sort of cruel twist of fate was that?

The coyote had stood up without realizing it, already making his way towards the door. "Master Innswick?" the wolf called after him. "Is something wrong? Master Innswick!" He just kept walking, though, stumbling out onto the street, even as he faintly registered the girl shouting, "You left your big, heavy book on your table!"

He didn't care, though? How *could* he care? Rentell Centrène, actually sharing another man's bed, and yet... with some plain, common lad? How had Florian's friendship with Rentell gone on for so long, and yet not so much as a single inkling of such desires had ever crossed the coyote's notice?

Moreover, what would drive someone as esteemed as Lord Rentell to choose a mere commoner as his lover? Even if it were simply a matter of sharing a bed for physical desire's sake, what was it that Florian lacked? He certainly wasn't too old—the infuriating urges of his own body would attest to that just fine!

Florian ambled about the streets with no real direction. His mind was slowly piecing things together, bit by bit. If Rentell had been in town last night, would he still be here, or would he have already returned to his manor? Perhaps he'd have holed himself up in the hostelry, waiting until cover over night before sneaking out of town, hoping to avoid whatever shame and accusations might come his way.

Perhaps, then, Florian could go and comfort him. He might be able to convince his brash, foolish, yet well-intentioned noble friend that the people of Honeybrush would always love him just the same, and that far worse things could happen to him. Surely, Florian could convince him that much. The two of them shared trust. They shared confidence.

The coyote dragged his slouching form toward the hostelry, then, stumbling from side to side as if he were dizzy. His blood felt like it was boiling, and yet all he could think of was finding Rentell so that he could talk things out and make things right.

From around the corner of the building came the ostler with a familiar-looking reptilian steed: that was Rentell's, all right! Florian broke into something of a jog, and he nearly bowled one of the patrons over as he approached the entrance. The coyote's eyes had to adjust, now that he was shielded from the midday sun by the building, and only once they'd refocused did he realize that he was practically standing on top of Rentell himself.

"Florian!" the fox yelped, once he, too, came to the delayed realization of who he was looking at. "What are you doing here?"

The poor fox sounded so nervous. Florian had arrived just in time. "I need you to come with me, Rentell," he said, laying both hands on his friend's shoulders. "There's something very important that you and I have to talk about."

Rentell quickly shook his head. "I'm sorry, Florian, I really am. It's a very bad time right now, though, and I've got to get back to my father's manor." He tried to duck away, but the coyote held on.

"No, Rentell," Florian said firmly. "I need you to come with me." As he said those words, he tried to look *through* Rentell's eyes, fixating on what might lie behind them. The fox went limp for a moment, temporarily hypnotized by the coyote's stare, giving the wizard just enough time to work the prestidigitation of his right hand.

With that, Rentell fell under Florian's control. "Come with me," the coyote repeated, turning on the spot and marching back towards his house. He heard Rentell falling into step behind him, and, satisfied in that knowledge, said nothing more as he led the fox along.

None of the townsfolk attempted to interrupt the pair as they walked. If Lord Rentell and Master Innswick had mutual business together, it had to be of great import, and it wasn't their place to stick their muzzles where they didn't belong. Florian was intent, now, and even if anyone had *tried* to stop him, he would have kept right on walking as if he'd heard nothing.

Finally, Florian made it back to his dwelling, and led Rentell on inside, closing the door behind him with a satisfying slam. He turned right back around and gripped the fox by the upper arms, pulling him into a deep, open-mouthed kiss.

Kiss me back. Crave me, Florian thought to Rentell. At once, the fox was spurred to action, sucking hungrily on the coyote's tongue, meeting the kiss with unbridled passion, like Florian had always known he could. That slender vulpine muzzle felt so delicate against Florian's own, and his lips and tongue were both so soft, only fitting for such a prime example of noble blood.

Florian then willed Rentell's paws into motion, making the fox caress his back and shoulders, working his dainty fingers against the coyote's more solid frame. The air was thick with mingling canid scents, and this time, it was not due to simple magical trickery on Florian's part, but rather, due to the two men clinging to one another, sharing in their heated moment of lust.

The coyote pulled his muzzle away from the fox's, keeping close to his face, and murmured, "Give yourself to me, Rentell. Love me as your one and only." With that, the fox's hands rubbed progressively lower, tracing over the muscles of Florian's body, until one of his paws grabbed over the coyote's crotch, eliciting a dull, throaty moan. That touch was so lovely, and his heavy sheath felt so good when caged between those slim, practiced fingers.

Once more, Florian locked his muzzle with Rentell's, mashing his own hand between the fox's legs, feeling a bit of swelling there, as well. He forced the fox to moan back into his mouth, by using his mind and his hand, steadily working the eager-to-please nobleman to erection within his fancy trousers. Finally, he knew what it was like to have the handsome young fox at his mercy, willing and excited and brimming with fervent lust.

With a hungry snarl, Florian tore away from the kiss, and gazed into Rentell's face. "Tell me that you love me, Rentell," he commanded, stroking the fox on the cheek with the rough tips of his fingers.

"I love you, Florian," Rentell gasped, but in that face, reflecting in those eyes, Florian saw nothing but the same clear, empty window into a soulless, hollow mind that he saw when he looked into the eyes of Vico.

Florian felt his will and resolve get pushed to the limits. This shouldn't be happening! Rentell should be gazing back at him with loving, happy eyes—happy to be surrendering his body and soul in such a complete, consummate act! The coyote tried to will Rentell's expression into something that would show that heartfelt desire, but try as he might, those eyes remained empty, looking back as if Florian weren't really there.

"Love me!" Florian cried, shaking the fox by the hips and shoulders. The fox tried to move in for another kiss, and continued to fondle the coyote's trapped erection, but nothing changed in his eyes. The coyote choked out tears of rage, anguish, and frustration, and shoved Rentell back against the door, but the fox didn't so much as flinch before he went after the coyote once more, intent on showing his love in whatever artificial way he could.

Florian didn't even register the second pair of footsteps, panicked as he was, and he was completely caught off guard as a fist caught him in the side of the face, claws raking across his cheek as he fell to the floor.

The magical buzz in the air died down, and the spell between Florian and Rentell was broken. The coyote looked up, clapping a paw over his bloody cheek, and saw Vico standing there, arm still outstretched from when he'd struck his master. His muzzle was pointed down toward the coyote, and while his lips were curled into something of a scowl, he still had those same haunting, emotionless eyes.

"Stop looking at me like that!" Florian shouted, but Vico did nothing—*could* do nothing—to obey. Rentell was slumped against the door, clutching his head, looking about ready to vomit, but Florian couldn't take his eyes off of the other fox that had just attacked him, without provocation, without reason, without a *direct order.*

"Stop looking at me like that!" Florian screamed, thrusting his hand out towards Vico, creating a shockwave of air that echoed throughout the house, knocking the homunculus onto its back. It didn't get up again.

Meanwhile, Rentell had fallen to the floor as well, collapsed against Florian's door. The fox coughed and sputtered, shaking his head as he tried to drag himself up into a sitting position, looking as if someone had just struck him over the head. His eyes finally found Florian, sitting there as he was in a heap, and this time, pain and confusion were the only things to be found on the fox's face. "Florian?" he gasped. "What... what did you do to me?"

Florian fell onto his side on the floor, burying his face into his palms as he burst into heavy, aching sobs.

The door creaked open, letting a stream of light into the dark dungeon cell. Florian didn't need to see the familiar silhouette against the doorway to know who it was.

"The Ducal Wizard has arrived," Rentell announced. "They'll be sending guardsmen down to fetch you in a few minutes, but... I thought I'd come to see you, first."

Florian looked up, his eyes slowly adjusting to the new lighting until he could make out the features on the fox's face. He looked older today than he'd ever looked before. What truly twisted at the coyote's insides, though, was that the fox didn't look angry. He just looked disappointed.

"Why, Florian?" Rentell asked, stepping up to the coyote, chained to the wall as he was. "Why did you do it?" Now, he didn't even look disappointed. He just looked blank, as if he honestly didn't know what kind of answer Florian would give him.

"I..." But that was all Florian could muster. Nothing he said to Rentell would matter. No answer could ever truly serve as a *reason.* "I just... wanted you," he admitted, too exhausted to even sigh in spite of himself.

Rentell brought a hand up to Florian's cheek for a tender little touch. "Did it ever occur to you to just… say so?" the fox asked. "That maybe… you wouldn't have needed to resort to spells or trickery?"

Hearing those words was a greater hurt to Florian than his upcoming punishment could ever hope to be.

"Before you go," Florian choked out, "could I… could I kiss you just once?" He locked his eyes with Rentell, silent there in the dark, and waited.

A few moments passed, but finally, Rentell said, "No, Florian. I've got to go, now. The Ducal Wizard will be ready for you, by now." With that, Rentell turned and left, leaving the coyote alone in his cell.

Minutes later, the guards did come, unshackling Florian from the wall in order to lead him up into the Count's audience chamber, where his sentence would be carried out.

In accordance with the Magicians' Charter, any wizard of the realm who had misused his talents in such a way that he had brought harm to his fellow man was to be first stripped of his powers and then sentenced further in a manner befitting the nature of the transgression committed; in Florian's case, for having unjustly and improperly forced his will upon the mind of another living, thinking creature, his old life would be forfeit and he would have his memories replaced such that his new life would find him someplace mundane, banal, and unremarkable, where he would live out the remainder of his days in blissful ignorance of the heights from which he had fallen.

In a very real way, it was more of a kindness than anything else. In this way, if nothing else, Florian Innswick could at least have the solace of knowing that, very soon, he would never be troubled by his unbecoming feelings for Rentell Centrène ever again.

An Excerpt from "On the History of Spellcraft, Volume II," by Simon Canopus Artyle

Though undoubtedly a useful tool in a magician's practice, the homunculus' place in the wizardly world eventually did come under question. While they had been a fixture of magicians' workshops for so long, they had mostly gone underscrutinized once the initial philosophical matters of necromancy and dark arts had been sorted out.

It was Madeline Thorndrake of Eulegarde who first postulated that homunculi were not, as originally put forth by the initial detailing thereof, merely automatons devoid of any true essence of their own. The real nature of the clockwork heart, as any wizard of the time would certainly have attested, was that it was a wellspring of magical energy, brought forth from the metaphysical core of the cosmos itself.

Thorndrake surmised that, with the nature of life and the nature of magic irrevocably intertwined as they are, that a homunculus must be—at least in some sense—"alive." The exact nature of that sort of consciousness was not at the core of the debate, but the open acknowledgement that a living thing could feel things suddenly cast the use of homunculi in a new light.

Furthermore, extended points were quickly brought forth by other scholars in the aftermath of this movement, a key point centering around the notion that, without a wizard actively dispelling a clockwork heart, a homunculus could, at least in theory, continue to function indefinitely. If that assumption were true, then by common thinking, a homunculus was something tied to the great chain of being like any other living thing, and it was no mortal's place to force something to exist without hope of an end to which to return.

The Magicians' Charter was summarily amended once more, and under the new regulations, the creation and use of homunculi were unilaterally forbidden.

When the Cat's Away...

Time for a lighter tune. Kyell Gold sent in a piece he'd written for the Erotic Furry Writing Group, which regularly issued challenges for short stories, which were to include specific settings, species and items, yielding wonderfully diverse results.

Kyell did thankfully give in to my urging, and removed the graph paper from this story—that was a requirement of the challenge, but in a fantasy fiction anthology, graph paper is a bit silly, don't you agree?

Magic and Mischief was one of the first submissions for FANG Volume 3, and to my mind the most playful, to the point of being downright cheeky!

Magic and Mischief

Kyell Gold

Sunlight crept in through the main windows of the small house, glinting through bottles of amber, green, red, blue and yellow, reflecting off of the clasps of several piles of small leather bags. The bottles, mostly upright, were scattered along tables and every other available surface, while the leather bags were piled on top of stacks of books. The books that were not serving as leather bag pile holders were either stuffed into a bookcase that looked dangerously close to tipping forward, or else scattered in a circle around a large wooden table in the center of the room.

Opposite the main windows, a doorway and a staircase led out of the room. When the sun had moved a third of the way up, shining through holes into the room beyond, the cloth that served as a door shifted slightly. A tawny paw pulled it to one side, and a golden muzzle poked cautiously through, sniffing the air.

The lion's nose was pink and his eyes were blue. He had a scraggly honey-colored mane just starting between his ears and down his shoulders. As he slid his muzzle further outside the cloth, looking around, he perked his ears forward to listen as well. Satisfied, he started to retreat into the room, then jerked his head around quickly and smacked it into the door frame.

"Yowch!" He turned more carefully to glare at the beaver who was lying inside the room, one paw up between his legs holding his balls and teasing his sheath. "Criminy, Daffyd, I didn't even know you were up."

Daffyd grinned a toothy grin. "Feels like you've been up for a while."

"Come on," the lion said, though he didn't move to escape the beaver's fingers, "we gotta start working."

"And that's how you were gonna go out there and work, huh? All naked like that?"

"No, I was going to put on my robe…" The lion closed his eyes and panted, shifting his hips slightly as the beaver's paw kept rubbing.

"Your robe's all the way over there. You had that cute tail waving in my face, and those yummy bits just hanging there, and you say you were gonna start working? Come on, Ali."

"I was…"

"Yeah, yeah." The beaver grinned, and shifted his position so he was up behind the lion. He kept stroking, and reached for a short, slender stick of white birch wood with his free paw. He touched it to the contents of a small bowl, then poked the tip against the small pink pucker under the lion's tail, murmuring *Lubridermis profundi.* A small glow spread from the wand onto, and apparently into, the lion.

"Ohhh," the lion moaned. "I love the Slickening Spell. So much cleaner than whiteseed oil."

"It sounds horrible." The beaver grinned. "Got all over your paws and had to be cleaned up after?" He tapped his quickly hardening member and murmured the words again. The small glow spread down his length, making him shiver.

"Yeah," the lion panted. "And smelled bad. And it would dry up fast."

"Mmm." The beaver rose up on his knees, balancing himself with his flat tail, and gave his length a few strokes, matching the rhythm his other paw was using on the lion.

His partner squirmed in delight. "You going to stick that in me, or what?"

"In a minute." Daffyd was starting to pant, too. He set his wand down and devoted his attention to the strokes of his paws, sliding up and down two now-very-hard shafts. "Don't worry, this won't dry up."

"I'm not worried about it drying up," the lion panted. "I'm worrying about me coming all over the floor before you get inside me."

The beaver chuckled. "I sure picked the right one," he said. "All right, all right, here we go."

"Oh, gawd, yes," Ali moaned, arching his back as the beaver's length slid easily under his tail. "That feels so good."

"Sure does," Daffyd murmured, bending over to rest on the lion's back. He kept stroking with his paw as his hips took up the work, sliding him back and forth inside the warm young lion under him.

Ali moaned again, a raspy sound that built in his throat and would become a roar in another few years. He liked the noise, and enjoyed making it, and he knew Daffyd liked it too, so he kept doing it so that Daffyd would keep doing the things that made him do it.

"Uhh... yeah," Daffyd panted, and then heard a flittering noise above him. He looked up and saw a mouse-sized creature circling in the air above them. Ali looked up at the same time. The creature fluttered on what looked like colorful butterfly wings, but its body was a ball of black fur. They could only tell which end was which because a thin tail hung from one end, and beady eyes glinted at them from the other.

"Blast it," Daffyd swore. "You woke up the Ko."

"I woke it up? Who grabbed my balls out of nowhere?"

"Never mind that." Daffyd reached for his wand without taking his eye off the hovering creature. It watched them impatiently, and when it started to get distracted, Daffyd gave Ali a couple of thrusts. The lion moaned again, and the Ko turned its attention back to him.

Daffyd grabbed his wand quickly and raised it, pointed it at the Ko, and said, "*Abati!*"

The beady eyes blinked, and the creature vanished.

Daffyd put down his wand and grinned. "Now," he murmured, leaning over to nuzzle the lion's shoulder. "Where were we?"

"I think you were right there, and your paw was there, and... oooh... yeah..." Ali reached up with one paw to hold the beaver's left paw to his chest, while the soft pads of Daffyd's right paw resumed their stroking. "Freaky li'l thing. Why does it like to watch us do it?"

"Dunno," Daffyd said softly. "Maybe because it can't."

"Isn't she going to make more of them?"

"Maybe. Dunno. Do you really want to worry about that now?" Daffyd pressed harder into Ali's rear, his magically lubricated shaft thrusting in and sliding out smoothly.

"No..." Ali breathed, rumbling. "Gawd, no..."

The two panted together, moans growing louder, though not so loud that they might float up the staircase. Daffyd chattered softly as he felt his body tense, and tried to hold back so that he and Ali could come together.

He didn't quite make it. "Unnh!" he moaned, pressed into the young lion's mane as he shuddered and came, thrusting into Ali's rear. A moment later, Ali gave a growling shudder himself, and Daffyd felt his member tense, spilling sticky fluid out onto his paw moments later.

"Mmm. That's a nice way to wake up." The beaver rubbed the lion's chest and nuzzled his mane, then sat back, sliding slowly out of him. He rubbed his paws over the tawny rump, and grinned as Ali turned around to kiss him.

"Clean me up?" Ali said, sitting back and spreading his legs.

"Sure," Daffyd said. He tapped the lion's dripping tip with his wand and said, "*Separi.*" The sticky fluid lifted away from the lion, the floor, and Daffyd's paw, and hung in the air until he said, "*Abani.*"

The white fluid vanished. Ali swatted at the air where it had been. "In another couple months I'll be able to do *abani*."

"If you keep practicing. And if you get old pruneface to give you a wand."

Ali flicked an ear. "I've been here two months...Oh." Both his ears perked straight up. "She's up."

"All right." Daffyd licked his muzzle. "Robes on, then."

They had only just cinched their robes when the cloth in their bedroom doorway rolled up. Standing on the threshold was a wizened old monkey wearing a purple robe. In one gnarled paw she held a steaming cup. In the other, she held a small bowl. She was glaring at Daffyd.

"One would think," she said in a creaking voice, "that an apprentice who learns enough to discover perhaps the only other creature in all the country who shares his age, magical aptitude, and recreational interests, would at least be able to fulfill his duties more often than once a month."

Daffyd made a noise of protest, but the monkey had already turned to Ali. "And one might imagine that a young lion rescued from a dull life of hunting and drudgery might show some interest in learning how to perform his new job. Or, failing that, at least a sense of duty to those who are housing and feeding him in this new job, which he shows no signs of wanting to leave."

"Daffyd's one of the ones feeding me," Ali said.

"Quiet." The monkey turned to Daffyd. "For three weeks my study has been in the same disarray it was in after the Magnate of Melanora needed that un-love potion for his daughter. As far as I can tell, all you have applied yourselves to in that time has been each other."

"I chopped some wood out back." Daffyd volunteered.

"I, uh, held the wood for him." Ali grinned.

"Tell me," she said, rounding on him, "in your pride, was it customary for young hunters to neglect their duties for pleasures of the flesh?"

"Actually," Ali said, "I did a lot of hunting because there weren't many other young males for me to play with. The other hunters all wanted to sleep with the lionesses."

"Thus making more cubs with less food to feed them. Perhaps we should return you to them," the monkey said drily, but Ali saw that she didn't mean it. "So, how did the Ko end up in the cream?" She held out the bowl, in which Daffyd and Ali could see a soft white substance and the black-furred body of the Ko, its beady eyes glaring up at them. It chirruped and resumed cleaning its fur off, which it was not having a lot of success doing, as every time it cleaned off a patch of fur, it sat back into the cream.

"It was spying on us!" Daffyd said.

"The Ko has the run of the house, so it was not spying. Spying implies that it is somewhere it is not supposed to be to observe something it was not meant to observe." She set the bowl down on the small table by the doorway, picked the little creature out, and left the bowl on the table. "You may keep the cream," she said.

"We started to organize everything," Daffyd said. "But it takes a long time."

"Yes, I know. So perhaps you would do better without the distraction of lessons."

"No!"

"I think, rather, yes." She sipped her tea. "I am going to visit my mother for a week. On the table is a diagram of how I want everything put away. I expect it done when I get back."

"Yes, Mistress Sollunia," the lion and beaver said together.

"The Ko is coming with me, so you needn't worry about it watching you." The black-furred creature chirruped again, very smugly, it seemed. "Now, come with me and make sure you understand what I want."

She led them out into the study, over to the large wooden table where she had laid out a sheet of parchment with several diagrams scratched into it. "Here, this represents the room. This is where the potions go, this is where the books should be organized, and I have listed each of the ingredients in all of the leather bags. It's time you learned them all anyway, Ali."

"Yes, ma'am."

"Daffyd, let him do the ingredients."

"Sure." Daffyd grinned.

"Good." She clambered over a pile of books and picked up a small flowered satchel by the door. Bending over it, she took a small gnarled piece of wood from it. "Oh, one more thing. Hold still, Ali." She pointed the wand at him and said, "*Abstinati.*"

The lion jumped. He stared at her and then rubbed his sheath. "What was *that?*"

"Chastity Charm." The monkey chuckled. "To make sure you stay focused while I'm gone. Have fun, boys."

She clambered onto her broomstick and was five minutes gone into the clouds before Daffyd and Ali managed to speak.

"Chastity Charm?" Ali said weakly.

"She does that all the time, for daughters of kings or earls or just nervous parents." Daffyd looked at Ali. "I didn't know it worked on males."

"How can it? Isn't that just supposed to keep guys from taking virginity? I mean…I didn't even have that when I got here. I sure don't have it now."

Daffyd grinned. "Well, only one way to find out." He knelt in front of Ali and drew his robe apart. He turned his head from one side to the other, examining the lion's sheath and dangling balls. "You look normal. Same as usual." Tentatively, he reached a paw up and brushed the lion's sac. "I can still touch you."

"Mmm." Ali shivered. "I can still feel it."

Daffyd ran a finger up Ali's sheath, and grinned. "Looks like you still get hard. And can come out of your sheath." He teased the pink tip, causing the lion to moan and push more of his shaft out.

"Not a very good charm, then."

"She is getting old. Maybe she's slipping." Daffyd gave the lion's shaft a long, confident lick.

"Uhrrr… speaking of slipping…"

"Yes?" Daffyd grinned and licked again, reaching around behind Ali to hold the lion's rump as he did. He wouldn't take the lion in his mouth, because his teeth got in the way, but he could still lick and pump with his paw.

"Oooh." Ali braced himself against the wall as Daffyd's paw slid along his slick shaft. "Finally, some privacy."

"Mmm-hmm." Daffyd kept his tongue and paw busy, until the lion was shuddering, but where he would normally be dripping and ready to spurt, his tip remained dry. Daffyd kept working, but began to worry. "You okay, Ali?"

"Yes, gawd, please don't stop…"

Daffyd licked and rubbed the hard pink length for another few minutes, until Ali's moans turned to whines. Still, the only fluid on his length was Daffyd's saliva. The beaver sat back and looked up at the lion.

"No, Daffyd, please, just a couple more minutes, I'm really close."

Daffyd shook his head. "No, you're not. That's what the charm does. You can't come."

"I can," Ali insisted. "I can feel it…I'm right on the edge…"

"Trust me," Daffyd said. "If I don't stop now, it'll just get worse. Chastity Charms… you're right, they're meant to protect the girls. But I bet some of those fathers don't mind tormenting the boys a bit too."

"Oh, no," Ali moaned, and then clutched his robe around him. "A *week?*"

"Don't worry," Daffyd said. "I can prepare a counter-charm. I'm pretty sure I can figure it out in a couple days."

"A couple *days?*"

"I'll abstain with you. Anyway, if I did anything for myself, it'd just torment you more."

Ali sighed and shook his head. "All right. That old witch. What do you need?"

Daffyd looked around the room. "First, I need the Romantical Remedies book…"

The lion looked around with him. "I'll get sorting."

It took them an hour to find the book. Ali started shelving the books and ordering them according to Sollunia's instructions. "What are you doing?" Daffyd asked.

"Sorting them."

"Just leave them out. We don't want her to win."

"I don't care if she wins. I just want to come. And if you can't find the counter-charm, I don't want her to be mad when she gets home."

When they found the book, Daffyd took another two hours to find the recipe he wanted and interpret the instructions. "Half of magic is just learning how to read the stupid wizards' handwriting," he grumbled, showing Ali a page of what looked to the lion like little more than random scribbles on the page. "There. Is that 'nightshade' or 'nightsbane'?"

"What's 'nightsbane'?" Ali asked.

"Bright white flower, opens up at night," Daffyd said.

"Isn't nightshade poisonous?"

"No. Nightshade's just a creeping vine. Night shades are poisonous, though. Don't go near one."

"What's a nightshade?"

Daffyd held his paws two feet apart. "Big, leathery wings, fly around at night. Don't worry, there aren't any around here. Sollunia killed them all to use in her potions." He considered the recipe again. "It must be nightsbane. We want an opening up, right?"

"Gawd, yes."

"All right. Go through the ingredient bags. We're looking for a bunch of small closed white flowers."

Ali put his paws on his hips. "Why me?"

"She said you were to do the ingredients, remember? I'm going to organize the bottles. I'll need some quickwater as well."

Ali considered the many piles of small leather pouches, and sighed. He picked up the first and looked inside. "Small yellow flowers," he said.

"Three petals, five, or seven?" Daffyd asked.

"Um...five."

"That's summerine."

Ali consulted the sheet and put the bag in its place. He picked up the next...

"I know she has nightbane. She has to have it!" Daffyd stared at the neatly arrayed cupboard and clicked his front teeth together.

Ali hugged the beaver from behind and buried his nose between the rodent's ears. "Come on, Daffyd, it's been three days already!"

"I know, I know." The beaver patted Ali's paw. "We can't do the counter-charm without nightsbane, though. Maybe there's another charm we can do. Let me check the book again."

He leafed through the book while the lion took a broom and started sweeping the floor. Daffyd looked up. "Ali, you've done that twice today already."

"I know. But if I don't do something I'm gonna go crazy."

"Go sweep out our room then."

"I've done that too."

"Go sweep upstairs."

"In *her* room?"

"Sure." Daffyd was paging through the book, scanning the spells. "It's going to take me an hour to decipher all this. And these are the simple spells. I can maybe tackle one of the complicated ones, but it'll take a day or two just to get the ingredient list together." He shook his head.

"All right." Ali disappeared up the stairs, muttering as he went. Daffyd wondered if the lion realized he was stroking the broom handle.

"Poor lion," he murmured, and absently brushed his own sheath, which had been half-swollen all day. "Poor me, too." He stroked himself a bit more and then jerked his paw away. He'd made a promise to Ali, and he intended to keep it. He turned his attention to the book.

"If only they used the shorthand names," he sighed. "*This spell will…can't* read that…*the disfigurement and…never mind.*" He turned the page.

Ali came down an hour later. "I emptied the dust into her tea leaves," he growled shortly.

Daffyd grinned. "I found a couple spells. Do you want to try the Easement Elixir or the Virility Enhancer?"

"Easement Elixir sounds like a laxative," Ali said. "We should put *that* in her tea."

"It is, kind of," Daffyd said. "But I think I can modify it."

Ali looked at him skeptically. "No offense, but I don't want to spend the rest of the week pent up *and* in the outhouse."

The beaver grinned. "If I didn't think I could do it, I wouldn't. I'm just worried that the Virility Enhancer might make you even more horny and frustrated."

"Yeah…" Ali said. "Save that for some other night."

"We never really need it," Daffyd said as he turned the page. "Okay, the Easement Elixir…get me some slippery honeysuckle, and a bottle of the extract of water glider."

Ali ran back and forth fetching ingredients, just as he'd seen Daffyd doing for Sollunia. Daffyd mixed the proportions careful-ly on the large table, now clear of all the scattered bottles and bags. After about forty-five minutes, he had a small vial of a cloudy blue liquid.

"I drink that?" Ali said.

"Hang on. I have to activate it." Daffyd concentrated, and touched the surface of the liquid with his wand. "*Laxari*," he said, and the liquid glowed brightly for a moment.

"*Laxari?*" Ali said, taking the vial from Daffyd. "We used to eat laxari plants when we got all clogged up."

"It's just the activation word," the beaver reassured him. "Honest."

"You're sure about this?"

"You want me to drink it too?"

The lion smiled. "No, it's okay. I just don't want to make it worse."

Daffyd grinned. "At least if something else happens, it'll take your mind off it."

"I guess. Well, here goes." Ali tipped the vial back.

For several tense seconds, they waited. The lion put the empty vial back on the table.

"How do you feel?" Daffyd asked finally.

"All right." Ali shrugged. "How long does it take to work?"

"Should be pretty quick." Daffyd stepped forward and rubbed the lion's sheath through his robe. "Feel all right?"

"Feels nice." Ali grinned. "Let's give it a try."

"Sounds good." But Daffyd's smile faded as he kept rubbing. "You're not getting hard."

Ali looked down and groaned. "That's what you did? You made me impotent?"

"No! I mean, well, maybe, yes, temporarily. But the Virility Enhancer will fix that right up..."

"No! No more spells. Gah!" The lion threw his paws in the air. "Let's just wait 'til she gets back. At least now I won't be walking around with an erection all the time."

"Yeah," Daffyd said, "but what about me?"

Ali's muzzle eased into a grin. "Well, I guess it won't torment me much to finish you, at least." Before Daffyd could say anything, the lion had dropped to his knees and stuck his muzzle inside the beaver's robes. Daffyd gasped as the soft tongue brushed his sheath and brought him quickly erect. Ali's paws circled him as his muzzle circled the beaver's hardness, slurping and sucking.

It had been three frustrating days, and Daffyd felt shivers up and down his spine and knew he wouldn't hold out long. He braced himself on the table and thrust back into the lion's muzzle, gasping and shuddering. It was only a few minutes later that he sucked in his breath and came in hot spurts onto the lion's waiting tongue, thrusting his shaft into the hungry muzzle eagerly.

"Mmm," Ali said, licking his lips as he stood. "You sure you didn't take a Virility Enhancer?"

"Ha," panted Daffyd. "Ha."

Ali grinned and hugged the beaver. "I think we can make it through the rest of the week."

"Yeah," Daffyd said, as his head slowly stopped spinning. "Sorry about the Easement thing."

"Sorry for snapping at you." Ali nuzzled him.

"It's okay. Hey...go find me some birchweed, can you?"

Ali pushed the beaver back to arm's length. "I said, no more spells."

"Not for you." Daffyd showed off his front teeth in a wide grin. "I'm going to make a Constipation Concoction to put in her tea."

Sollunia looked around the study and nodded her wrinkled head. "Much, much better." She looked at the two eager faces standing in front of the bedroom curtain. "You see what a little discipline can do?"

"Yes, Mistress Sollunia," they chorused.

"All right, then. I think I can remove the charm." She gestured at Ali with her wand, and the lion jumped again. Daffyd looked at him and got a wide answering grin. "And here," she said, removing a small leather pouch from inside her robe, "is the nightbane you were undoubtedly looking for to make the counter-charm."

"You took it with you?" Daffyd gaped at her.

"Of course. I have plenty of respect for your abilities when motivated. I just had to channel them in the right direction. Did you try the Virility Enhancer? That would just have made things worse."

"No," Daffyd said. "The Easement Elixir."

"Hmm. Modified, I presume." The beaver nodded. "It's a good thought, but not the right one. There are at least three things you could have done to get around it. If you're very good, I'll teach you one tomorrow."

"Yes, Mistress," Daffyd said.

"Right now, though, I suspect you have other things to occupy yourselves with." She waved a wrinkled paw. "Go, go, you're dismissed for the rest of the day. Lessons and duties tomorrow, sunrise!"

"Yes, Mistress," they chorused, and disappeared behind the cloth almost immediately. The tail end of Ali's robe fell just outside the curtain a second later, and remained there.

Sollunia shook her head. "Boys. Easier to manipulate than girls, anyway." She heard a small "chirrup" from inside her robe and reached in, bringing out the Ko. It rustled impatiently as she stroked its fur with a finger.

"Yes, all right, you can go watch," she said. "Come back upstairs after. I have a job for you. Some wolf duke thinks his bitch is cheating on him." She sighed, and watched the little black creature take flight and dart agilely around the curtain, then walked slowly up the stairs to make herself a nice, hot cup of tea.

Teacher and Student

*By Karai Crocuta's own account, this piece is the
'origin story' of a character whose tale is far, far from
finished.*

*It describes the sexual awakening of Kieran, a
young wolf, training under the wise tutelage of his
sensei, an ancient dragon.*

*In the wondrous stillness of the forest, the two
discover one another in a new light, and set their first
steps on a marvelous new path.*

DRAGON'S LOVE

Karai Crocuta

F ar from the streets and edifices of any town—indeed, deep in the wilderness of the world they called home, there were places of great power and serenity. For millennia, each of these sacred areas had helped to spread and control the power within the crust of the lush, moisture-rich biosphere, ensuring its fertility and growth. Though many of these ancient places of potence and reverence had been discovered and made into shrines, most remained hidden to all but those who wandered and sought shelter within their boundaries, sensing the invisible nodes of sentient energy which collectively held the entire planet together.

Deep in a forest, in one of the most tropical and densely-wooded areas of the planet, a pair of figures lay continuing to slumber regardless of the newly-rising sun's rays. From a distance, especially when looking down from above, one could easily mistake the two individuals for one due to their proximity and the fact that one fairly dwarfed the other.

One could also wonder why anyone would stray hundreds of leagues away from even the most isolated village where there was at least a semblance of technology and communication—not to mention convenience and quite to the point, company.

Of course, if one knew a bit about the figures in question, there would be little else to question about the isolation of the place where they chose to dwell. You see, one of them—specifically the

53

big, red one—was a dragon. The other, well... the other being was far more than he seemed, even to anyone who got to know him well.

Stormfire's Wing was the dragon's full name, though its translation into the common language of the world in question left quite a bit of meaning out of the title. It should suffice to say that the wyrm was named after one of the best-known heroes of the bygone times of his own home place (which was quite far from his current abode, and on the other side of a dimensional gateway).

Yes, he was indeed quite big and rather easy to notice against the greens, browns, and rocky grays of the landscape around him. Measured from nose to tail-tip, he was around twenty feet in length (most being the tail), and six feet tall at the shoulder. He was formidable in appearance and with his bright red scales, gold-plated underbelly, and giant claws and wings, there was no mistaking his power in a fight.

He stood upon four legs when not in flight, though he possessed the inherited ability to change his shape and size in a limited fashion. Like many of his compatriates, he had a pair of whiskers that protruded from the lower jaw of his angular snout, though the lips that lay above were scaleless and soft and had the tendency to stretch into a wide range of expressions when the dragon's emotions were properly stirred. White horns stuck out from the top of the dragon's head, and he had no ears, being somewhat more reptilian than some of his peers. Of course, the most striking features of the dragon's face were his eyes. Like twin pools of liquid gold, they burned with an intensity that could turn away the gaze of any mortal save one when the wyrm was riled.

Contrastingly, his companion was quite unassuming and even tiny by comparison. The wolf wasn't much more than a mere cub—hardly a teenager at that—and he was barely visible while curled up against the dragon's back. Kieran (loosely: 'little dark one') he was called, a name which supposedly told something about his nature, though it probably only referred to his deep brown fur. For his part, he was no ordinary cub, being an exceptional student possessing a sharp intellect and a hawk-like gaze. However, he was no match for the dragon in strength, despite his almost super-natural level of physical fitness. He was still a boy, after all.

The only weapons he possessed were his black claws (barely enough to scratch the larger being, even without scales) and a set of sharp little white teeth. However, the boy was quite far from being what he seemed. Though the softness of his rich, brown pelt and his youthful appearance marked him otherwise, he was a lad of great potential. If one looked into his active, piercing pair of amber eyes for long enough, there could be seen something unique. Something more powerful even than the dragon might suspect lay there in the confines of the youth's mind.

We shouldn't get ahead of ourselves, though. Young Kieran's story is quite a tale, of which what is here is but a small part. These were happy days, after the boy lost his family to the mysterious and bloodthirsty demon invaders, but before he began to battle against them with his unique powers and garnered new allies. During his adolescence, the cub and his sensei, Stormfire, shared a special and wonderful relationship that went beyond that of teacher and student. Indeed, their bond was of such a unique and powerful nature that it could bridge the gap between universes, penetrating even through the mysterious nothingness that sepa-rated one dimension from another.

So there they lay, great wyrm and wolfcub, oblivious to the world. You might have guessed by now that their current camp wasn't ordinary, and indeed it was a place of power, though a strange, one-of-a-kind one. Briefly put, it was an oasis in the mid-dle of a enormous, jungle-like forest. It resembled a tiny lagoon, really. A waterfall continuously poured into a large basin of rock, constantly deepening it over time only to spill over the edges and fall into another pool that in turn fed a stream. It was one of the more relaxing and idyllic places the two had visited in their trav-els, and it was surrounded by the lush beauty of nature.

The young wolf stirred, opening his eyes slowly. They beheld the bright light of morning, but found it a bit intense, so they flickered closed again. The boy took a moment to decide whether

or not he should rise. He could hear the dragon slumbering behind him, so he decided to wait after a brief contemplation. Sensei
always rose early, anyway. What was the point in getting up before
him? Actually, both dragon and cub usually rose before sunrise,
so it was currently a bit late even though the bright orb in the sky
was just now showing through the trees.

Kieran's wait was short. Soon, the wyrm himself began to wake
with a small rustle of scales. Stormfire inhaled sharply, savoring the clean, wonderful morning air. He rose rather quietly for
a being of his size, wasting no time with things like grogginess
or yawning. Though he was rumored to weigh at least six tons,
his movements were silent enough that anyone without especially
good hearing wouldn't even notice the sound of his footfalls as he
made his way carefully around the body of the young wolf. It was
time for his morning swim—something he quite enjoyed, and he
knew that it would be prudent not to wake the boy. The dragon
would have to do some explaining if he were caught.

Kieran slowly re-opened one eye. It wasn't often he woke up
before his mentor, and he was curious. He knew that the dragon
always tried to camp near a lake or pond, and that Sensei was
quite fond of swimming. He merely had never seen Stormfire
awake before the dragon's morning swim. So, he watched the
wyrm's huge front legs step around him, followed by the rest of
the gold and red-scaled body.

The cub always found himself admiring how those scales reflected sunlight. He also knew that the dragon's body was capable
of unleashing incredible power in a fight—something that the
young wolf could only look up to and admire until he met his own
potential. Kieran watched the heavy, muscular chest pass along
overhead. Then, he saw something completely unexpected.

There was a smooth, red pole jutting out from between the
powerful hind legs. It bobbed, glistening, and it was huge. Kieran
was used to occasionally seeing the dragon's large testes (and they
were still there, swaying below the shaft in their soft-scaled sac)
but this was a different thing entirely. Both of the young cub's eyes
opened; he was mystified. It was so big. He had never known that

his sensei had a 'thing' that large, let alone that his teacher actually had erections. Kieran had recently begun to have 'stiffies' once in a while. Actually, they had started almost a year ago. But the pole swaying between his master's legs was enormous!

Stormfire stopped at the edge of the water, stretching his wings for a moment or two. He let the exquisite feeling of anticipation wash over his body. The dragon always enjoyed a good swim followed by some underwater masturbation. It was a guilty pleasure of his—one that he didn't feel quite comfortable discussing with his young charge. After all, Kieran was probably still too young to...

Stormfire's eye-ridges furrowed as he realized that his cub had already reached thirteen seasons. That meant that unless the boy was a late bloomer, he was probably close to sexual maturation. The wyrm resolved to speak to Kieran about the cub's body later today, perhaps after lunch. He did not notice his young student lying there with wide eyes that followed every movement of his erect penis.

Kieran watched the organ bob as the dragon dove into the water. He hardly noticed the fact that his master hadn't made any sort of splash despite the dragon's enormous bulk. He realized that his mouth was open, so he closed it. Then, he couldn't help thinking about what he had just witnessed. He was suddenly filled with an urge to see it again.

Not thinking about what he was actually doing, he rose quickly and ran to the edge of the water. As he knelt down, he was conscious of how nervous he was. His paws were practically shaking with something. Was it excitement? He leaned over the edge of the shore, staring down into the surprisingly clear depths as he felt his entire body tense with anticipation. Why was Sensei so aroused? Why did the sight of the dragon's penis stir him so? These questions and more ran through Kieran's mind, mixing with a rush of adrenaline that was making his head swim.

He easily located his master's energy signature, though it was darting to and fro in the enormous pool. The dragon was an incredible swimmer. That fact was apparent in how fast he could change direction. He could move like a lightning bolt back and forth and around the circular pool with ease. After a few more laps the wyrm slowed, his eyes closing. Kieran noticed that the dragon's member was still every bit as erect as it was just a minute ago, and before the cub's eyes, the organ was slowly taken in a claw and stroked.

Kieran gasped softly as he watched the dragon-cock pulsate. What was sensei doing? Then, the wyrm's body began to curl up, his long neck arching down until his snout reached his erection. The boy watched, transfixed, as his master's thick tongue slid out, slowly wrapped around the bulbous cock head, and began stroking and winding up and down. Stormfire was lying on the pool's bottom, propped up by his wings as he took his huge dick into his mouth, lips wrapping around the flaring glans as he began sucking and bobbing his head on his own pulsating member.

Kieran couldn't stop his paw as it reached down to touch the bulge in his pants. The cub was too busy watching the dragon fellating himself to even realize what he was doing. He quickly freed his erection, sliding his pair of black trousers—his only article of clothing—down to his knees. He found his cock harder now than it had ever been, and began stroking the shaft in rhythm with the dragon's movements, gasping at how intense the sensation was turning out to be.

The huge dragon-dick was pulled from the snout, and a white, cloudy substance suddenly shot from its tip. Stormfire nuzzled his titanic shaft, then swallowed it again. The sight made Kieran stroke faster, the young wolf reaching down with his other paw to free his knot from his sheath with a grunt. The dragon was making the whole dick disappear into his mouth, and Kieran could see the bulge it made in the dragon's throat. Both teacher and pupil began thrusting and stroking faster and faster, their passions fueled by forces they could not understand.

Throwing his head back and stroking his huge maleness furiously with both claws, Stormfire let loose, his loud roar of pleasure sending powerful vibrations all the way to the surface of the deep pool. His cock jumped as first one, then many jets of hot semen shot through the water.

Kieran watched in wonder through his own climax as the fluid blasted out, causing ripples in the water to form and travel outward from the pearly strands. He hardly realized that he was also cumming until he collapsed, one paw instinctively gripping below his knot around that sensitive bundle of nerves, the other stroking and squeezing his shaft while one thumb pressed down on the tip, the rest of his creamy load exploding out of it.

He lay there, panting for what he imagined was way too long. His body was suddenly a little weary, and pleasure was slowly spreading to every corner of his nervous system. He remembered thinking to himself, so this is what that's like, before he came to his senses. He cleaned up quickly, hiding the evidence in the water below so that his master wouldn't find out about his actions. When he looked back down into the top pool, though, Stormfire was still there, relaxing with his eyes half-closed, the dragon's penis having receded back into its pouch-like sheath.

The cub sat down in the lotus position, deciding to see if he could get some brownie points before breakfast. Perhaps sensei would be especially glad to see the cub meditating, and would start cleaning up camp and let him be. The odd, relaxed feeling from jacking off helped, and the young wolf was still amazed at how it had felt. As he pretended to meditate, he found himself wondering, would it feel better if your cock were absolutely huge?

After a few minutes, the dragon finally emerged from the water, climbing onto dry land and stretching to his full length while spreading his magnificent wings out to dry. He smiled placidly when he saw that his charge had already started on the morning exercises. A perfect morning indeed, he thought. His session had been much better than usual, and now the boy was meditating on his own.

"...Kieran," the dragon said aloud after thinking for a moment, "you started to meditate without me having to order you to. This is your least favorite part of our daily routine. Is there something you should tell me, hmm?"

Kieran's ears flicked back. His sensei knew him too well. He did feel guilty about eavesdropping on what was obviously a private activity. Opening his eyes, and made himself look up at the dragon. Deep down, he loved sensei. It was the dragon who had saved him after the demon attack that had cost him the only family he had. It was the dragon who was teaching him the skills he needed to stop the attacks—to stop the pain and suffering of his whole world once and for all.

The lad sighed, and gazed up at the dragon's perfect features. He owed the wyrm his life. He may as well be honest to himself and to his master. So, he spoke. "Sensei... I woke up early today. I... saw you get up, and... I watched you underwater. I couldn't help it... you have such a big 'you know'..."

Stormfire blinked, visibly surprised for a rare second. He could see that his student was flushing with embarrassment. If dragons could blush, though, Stormfire would be turning redder as well. So, he thought, Kieran likes males. The cub likes to watch his master jerking off, in fact. Though Stormfire didn't know how to feel about these facts, he knew that the poor wolfcub felt bad for spying on his mentor so brazenly. So, he rested a claw gently on the boy's shoulder.

"I don't mind, Kieran. You're like family to me, and I shouldn't feel embarrassed in front of you no matter what... state I'm in. Don't worry about it. You are at the age where... well, your body is going through changes, and you may feel... certain urges... urges that even... I still feel."

The boy lifted his head. Stormfire would always remember that look of relief, with the morning sunlight shining on the deep brown muzzle, those amber eyes lighting up from their previous look of guilt. Kieran felt so much better. He even initiated a hug, knowing deep down how much his master had been missing them.

Their embrace seemed to last forever. Stormfire found himself closing his eyes. He loved the boy with all of his heart, and he knew how much it would hurt if he lost the trust of his young charge.

They parted finally, Kieran smiling because he felt better, but also because he had made sensei feel good. They continued with their daily routine after that, Kieran performing his physical and mental exercises.

The boy was still improving in leaps and bounds, his potential still so far from being realized. Stormfire had always marveled at the cub's progress, but now the dragon was downright amazed. They decided to stay another night at the waterfall, and both began gathering food for the evening meal. Kieran found himself thinking back to the events of the morning, and he knew that there were still questions to be asked, though he could not form them quite yet. He decided to wait until after the meal to speak to his mentor.

Dinner preparation was mostly for Kieran's sake. The dragon hunted independently and ate enormously, so he often had repast (which was always at least one entire animal) alone. He didn't want to boy to lose his appetite, after all. So, tonight Stormfire left Kieran after preparing the meal, to hunt.

Kieran ate slowly, smiling because he could just pick out the sounds of sensei bringing down prey. He thought about what questions he would ask the wyrm. However, no matter how much the wolfcub thought about what he didn't know, he could not keep the image of sensei standing at the edge of the pool earlier that morning, stretching his magnificent wings with his huge erection bobbing up and down. The cub wondered what caused the dragon's arousal. He wondered what if felt like when Stormfire put it into his mouth like that. Most of all, though, he wondered what it would be like to touch it with his own paws.

Such was the case that when the dragon returned from his 'humble' meal (several large-sized boar, and one small stag), he found Kieran sitting with arms folded, waiting for him. A crimson eye-ridge arched, the golden pupil gazing at the boy for a moment.

"Is there something the matter, Kieran?"

The dragon knew what was coming. He had been thinking about it on and off the whole day. He had no idea what thoughts the boy was thinking, or even what exactly had been seen that morning. So, not knowing what to expect, he sat down facing the cub and decided to chance a nuzzle since Kieran had been so free with hugs earlier.

The young wolf smiled as the dragon's snout nudged him, and he rubbed it, much to Stormfire's delight. "I'm sorry, Sensei. I know I haven't really been as cuddly as you like lately. It's been a long time I guess."

The dragon's eyes closed, his snout slowly rubbing against the fur of the boy's mid-section. Stormfire indeed missed the warm snuggly cub he used to know. This was a surprise—quite a pleasant one.

Kieran rubbed around his mentor's 'ears'—actually membranes that protected his aural sensory organs—and continued. "I've been trying to think about what I want to ask you. I know there are a lot of things I don't know about growing up, but... when I saw your penis earlier, I realized that mine can get... y'know, hard like that too."

Stormfire nestled against the boy a bit longer, then drew back reluctantly. These were issues he could deal with, at least so far. "I know what you mean, Kieran. It's called an erection. It happens when a male feels... desire for another. At your age it can occur without warning."

Kieran nodded slowly, absorbing the new terms. He thought for a moment longer before continuing. "Well... actually, I watched what you were doing in the water..."

Stormfire nodded. So far, he has having a simple enough time with explanation. "Just about every male does that as well. It's simple, it feels great, and it relieves tension. You shouldn't feel bad about doing it. I won't even mind if you feel the need while we are traveling. All you have to do is ask, and I'll wait."

Kieran bobbed his head again, his cheeks heating up. The next part was the most difficult, but he felt the need to tell it. He knew not what his words could lead to, if anything at all. In truth, he had no idea how the dragon would react, but he decided to say it quickly, lest he wimp out.

"Well... the truth is... seeing you underwater... made me get an 'erection'—like you said. Seeing you do that... playing with your penis... made me want to do it too." Kieran paused, watching Stormfire's expression. The dragon nodded, looking back down at him almost expectantly. "Err... what I mean to say is... I kind of like looking at it... you know, your penis," the wolf cub continued, then let out a breath. Nervous anticipation, coupled with an unfamiliar rush of what he would later recognize as desire, flowed through him after he finished speaking. He looked over at sensei, hoping desperately that he wasn't asking anything too difficult. He also realized that he desperately wished that the dragon would say yes.

Stormfire nodded again, more slowly this time. "You said that earlier, Kieran. I... don't mind... if you want to look at it."

Kieran's eyes lit up, showing the excitement he felt when he heard his sensei's words. After a moment of waiting, though, the boy's gaze dropped down to his foot-paws, which he was shuffling dejectedly. Disappointment crept into his voice as he mumbled, "It's ok if it's tired, you can always show me later..."

Stormfire, who seemed lost in thought, seemed to snap back to attention, remembering the boy's unspoken question. "Oh, you mean right now? ...all right." He said as he sat on his haunches, leaning back against a thick tree trunk to expose his underbelly. As Kieran stared, motionless, the dragon reached down with a fore-claw, and began massaging the pouch that lay just above his large testes. It wasn't long before the reddish tip emerged, and before the cub's eyes, the rest of the shaft gradually followed. As he brought himself slowly to full hardness, Stormfire caught himself sneaking looks at the boy. Kieran was obviously in awe of what was growing rapidly in size before his young eyes. Those eyes said 'wow' about as well as any look from any being could.

So, the boy is definitely attracted to males, Stormfire thought. Indeed, the wyrm felt a sensation that could have been pride as his member was stared at openly. This may be the first penis that Kieran has seen so far, but it would most certainly be the biggest he would ever lay eyes upon. Or, Stormfire could not help thinking, lay other things upon.

Kieran knew he was getting an erection the moment he saw sensei's huge dick emerging. He felt a strange euphoria as his pants tented, hormones raging through his body as his loins reacted and prepared for his first sexual encounter, though his conscious mind surely had no idea what was going on at this point.

It had finally stopped growing. Now the enormous dick was being held by the dragon's claw. Kieran examined the way it stood out straight, with a very slight curve upward. Unlike his own penis, it was a simple tube of flesh, tapering a bit from the base, with a very large, bulging vein running along the underside. Also unlike his, it had a fat tip with a mushroom-like ridge running around the top that parted at the underside. The slit from which the white stuff had shot before lay just above that place, and the whole head gave a plump appearance that Kieran somehow found very appealing. The whole organ was almost as long as the young wolf's body from ears to hips.

Stroking his penis slowly to keep it erect, Stormfire found himself smiling at the cub. "Well, it seems that you do like it, eh?"

Kieran's gaze flickered up to meet the dragon's, and he nodded. "Yeah... it's so big..." A movement below caught his attention, and once again he stared openly as the dragon grunted softly. The dick pulsated, a ripple traveling up the large vein and reaching the tip where to the surprise of the young cub, a drop of fluid emerged.

The young wolf gasped softly. He didn't notice his right paw moving downward as he watched the clear fluid dribble down the dragon's shaft, clinging to the big vein until it ran over the wyrm's claw and dripped to the ground. He reached into his pants, his paw wrapping around his own shaft and squeezing.

Stormfire grinned softly, watching the boy's reaction to what had happened. "That is the fluid released when a male is ready to receive a lover's touch, Kieran. What comes later is the male seed, which is released when one's pleasure culminates. That substance is part of what is needed to create offspring..."

Another nod, and a quiet gasp of surprise came from the boy as he realized what his paw was doing. Kieran just couldn't resist playing with himself now that the object of his desire was right in front of him. Despite his embarrassment, he found himself finally asking the question that had been in the back of his mind ever since he first saw the dragon-cock.

"...do you mind... if I touch it, sensei?"

Stormfire's claw never stopped its caresses. Gradually, the wyrm realized that the situation was turning him on a lot more than it should have. He couldn't deny his own desire to let it happen. Also, now that the cub had posed the question, Stormfire realized that it had been decades, if not centuries, since his penis had received any kind of attention from another being beside himself. The dragon found himself wanting the cub to play with his dick. The very thought made depraved fantasies appear in his mind's eye. He couldn't dislodge them; his own lust was so strong after all these years of loneliness. So, he nodded, his mouth clenched shut, his eyes glued to the cub's next move as feelings stirred deep inside that had laid dormant for decades.

Kieran stood up and took the few steps necessary to bridge the space between him and the dragon. He gazed at the dick admiringly for a few more seconds, then plaintively reached out a paw. The moment hung in time for much longer than the second or two it took to happen, the small paw descending toward the immense, throbbing muscle. They finally met, Kieran's soft palm-pad contacting the very tip of Stormfire's broad cock-head. It felt smooth, the skin soft and pliable. Also, it was hot—very hot in fact. Kieran's jaw dropped open slowly as he realized what he was doing. His palm softly rubbed just under the tip of Stormfire's glans, his fingers appearing so tiny as they splayed and pressed down on either side of the dragon's cock-slit.

Stormfire watched the young cub's palm stroking his dick through half-lidded eyes. It felt wonderful, even though the paw was small. In fact, a broad, stupid grin had already passed halfway across his snout after the first press of those tiny fingers. He caught it and managed to come to his senses enough to realize something.

Kieran smiled as his touch made the enormous dick bob and pulsate, just as it had done this morning when sensei played with it. Then, as an odd but familiar mist materialized around the dragon, it began to get smaller. He looked up, blinking before he realized what was happening. The cock, which had been almost at eye level, was shrinking along with the rest of the dragon's body.

Stormfire was changing into his smaller, anthropomorphic form. Kieran already knew that the dragon had inherited shape and size-changing abilities from his clan, though no one but the wyrm himself had any idea of their origin. Stormfire most often used his bipedal form for hugs and other interactions that required him to stand up straight on his back legs. The dragon was only about seven feet tall in this form, though that was still almost two feet taller than the young cub.

As he changed, Stormfire realized what he was inviting and even encouraging by doing this. In fact, the reason he did so was to make him small enough for the cub to handle his length—small enough for the cub to make him cum. A shudder ran through the body of the wyrm, his neck arching down as a wave of lust washed through him at the very thought. Was this really happening?

The boy frowned, watching the dragon's head dip. "What's wrong?"

Stormfire's head came back up with a smile, "Don't worry, Kieran. It's just been... a very long time since anyone made me feel as good as you are right now. Would you like to continue?"

The cub nodded enthusiastically, sitting down in front of sensei (who still stood chest, head, and shoulders taller) and taking the smaller version of Stormfire's cock back in paw. In its diminished state it was still huge—just over thirteen inches in length—and nearly three inches thick. The cub fondled it, not quite stroking it, but playing with it for the moment. The tip was now level to his eyes, that fat glans with its slit nestled just below the very end of the knob-like organ pointing straight at the cub's face. It kept throbbing with every one of the wyrm's heartbeats, and seemed to grow just a little bit firmer and broader with each passing moment.

The cub's innocent toying brought a soft groan from the dragon, who leaned back against the tree-trunk and watched with glowing eyes—twin pools of fiery golden liquid, smoldering with ancient, newly re-awakened desire that threatened to burn out of control at any moment.

Stormfire found himself staring openly at how innocently, how gently the boy was touching his penis. It was gripped here and there, the skin was rubbed back and forth a little, but most often the swollen glans was rubbed and played with. After a while, Stormfire realized that there were some things he needed to say before things got any further.

Before the dragon could speak, though, he gasped softly. Another large drop of pre-ejaculate came out of his dick, and ran down the large vein, slicking it. After a moment of watching the look of renewed wonder in the cub's eyes, he began: "Kieran... would you like to learn how to please your sensei? How to make me cum?"

Kieran's eyes opened wide as he heard his mentor's question. He smiled, his gaze still locked on the fascinating organ in his paw, and nodded. "Yes, sensei... you're my only family, and I owe you my life. I want to make you feel good... really good."

The dragon's eyes shone, illuminating the area in front of him where the cub sat. "Well then, let me show you a way. I want you to know something first, though. I will keep my word on the promise I made when you became my apprentice. I will never bring you to harm, or cause you to feel pain in any way without the direst of reasons. I love you, Kieran..."

Kieran managed only a small nod of acknowlegement before he was picked up gently, the wyrm's claws gripping him below the armpits. He was lifted rather easily into the warm embrace of the dragon, and soon returned the hug, overcome suddenly by the affection he felt for his teacher and mentor. "I love you too, Sensei," he said as he pressed snug against the smooth scales of the wyrm, feeling the powerful muscles and the heat of eternal dragon-flame that lay beneath.

Stormfire melted as the cub's arms squeezed him. He knew now that he wanted his student to be his lover, and the anticipation was going to be the death of him if he didn't continue soon. So, he balanced the cub on one arm and reached down with the opposite claw, taking the waistband of Kieran's pants and removing them deftly. He let the garment fall, then bore the lad's body back, looking down. "Well well, you are stiff aren't you?" He said with a soft smile. He gently lifted the appendage in question with his palm, making Kieran gasp in surprise. "And rather large besides."

The young wolf's cock was at least seven inches long, not including the knot that was gradually swelling up near the base. It was significantly larger than the norm for someone his age and species, though its veiny, red and white appearance was to be expected. Exploring below, the dragon lifted the cub's pair of plump, furry balls, nuzzling them and feeling the heat of the mammalian body. Stormfire instantly knew just how to pleasure the lupine dick. First, though, he needed to satisfy his own urges. By now, his own erection was threatening to explode with need.

Kieran's eyes closed halfway as sensei fondled him, pleasure and desire flooding through him. He felt another rush of anticipation and surprise as the dragon's claw cupped his firm rump, supporting his full weight. He noticed the dragon's other arm reaching down below, but could not figure out what it was doing. A moment later, he felt something blunt, hot, and rock-hard press right against the sensitive underside of his tail. His eyes opened wide in surprise and momentary panic.

"Uh... you're... going to..."

Stormfire nodded, smiling. "Don't worry, Kieran. Remember what I said."

The wyrm ran a claw from the base of the cub's thick tail down the cleft and over the tight little anus, causing a gasp and shudder from his young charge. Gently rubbing a knuckle around the boy's anal ring, he let a bit of magic do its work. A blue glow settled into the soft, virgin pucker. An odd cooling sensation spread into the cub's body from there as his inner walls were coated with something slick. *There*, Stormfire thought. Now, the boy was ready, and would feel no pain as a result of the stretching that was to follow.

"I desire your body, Kieran," the dragon whispered, looking back up into the boy's eyes, "I wish to give and take; to share pleasure with you."

The statement was almost like an invocation or spell of some sort. The wolfcub stared back into the metallic gaze of his sensei, spellbound for a moment. He smiled.

"So do I, sensei..."

The dragon responded by gripping the boy's hips with both claws, maneuvering him so that his body was aligned with the fat length of cock. Then, not wasting any more time, the wyrm pressed his broad cock-head against the heat of the wolf's entrance. Both males gasped as Stormfire's powerful arms pulled the cub down, the tiny anus suddenly opening wide and accepting the huge glans of the dragon. Half of the rest of the shaft slid in as the dragon groaned, and Kieran felt a sudden jolt of pleasure traveling up his spine as it nudged his prostate.

Stormfire's eyes closed halfway, his neck arching. He had never in all of his years put his dick into anything this hot, this tight, or this wonderful. He felt the cub's body straighten suddenly, the anus clenching around him with surprising strength. Looking down, he saw that the boy was dribbling pre-cum rather copiously. Stormfire smiled, and gently pushed the rest of his dick into the young wolf with a groan. The ceremony was over. Now, the real fun could begin.

He leaned forward, placing his snout close to his student's ear. "Now that it's all the way in you, we can start. If only you could know how good it feels to be inside you. Kieran. Get ready now..."

With that, the boy's body was lifted up, the huge organ sliding out until Stormfire felt the ridge of his glans tugging at the impossibly-stretched anus. Then, the dragon-cock was shoved back in, Kieran's rear coming flush against Stormfire once again. The boy shuddered, the huge dick forcing the breath from him as it reforged a passage deep into his belly. The dragon began repeating the deep thrusts, making the young wolf's head loll backward, his breath coming in gasps. Sensei's cock went so deep. He felt every part of the shaft acutely as it moved within, throbbing, and opening him even wider.

Stormfire was moving slowly so that Kieran could enjoy every moment of being fucked. As it was, the dragon was already having a lot of trouble holding himself back. In, then out the shaft went, making both males grunt, pant, and shudder.

The dragon watched the cub's expression closely, pleased that his dick was eliciting such pleasure from the boy. He slowly lifted the wolf off of his titan of a cock and flipped his young mount over, gently lowering the cub onto all fours for a different angle. His favorite.

Kieran gasped, the intense feeling of being filled by his master's cock leaving him. He wanted—no, needed—to feel it again. So, as the dragon's claws ran up and down his sides, caressing him lustfully, he raised himself, the cub wanting more than anything to feel the dragon's dick pushing into his body once more.

The perfectly round, incredibly tight ass was lifted up for Stormfire, the tail instantly raised and brought out of the way. The dragon growled with lust upon seeing how eager his student was to have the huge dick rammed in again. He wasted no time mounting the boy in earnest.

The forest echoed with the grunts of the rutting dragon as the huge dick plunged into the wonderful young hole again and again.

Kieran's body fairly rattled with the indescribable feeling of being fucked. His back arched, his gland being pounded as jolt after jolt of pleasure ran through his body. His cock was dripping and spurting clear fluid, his anus clenching around the maleness that was stretching it to an impossible degree. As he felt the dragon's hips crash into his rear again and again, shoving him forward with each lunge, the huge cock seeming to go deeper and deeper each time, it was all he could do to grip the ground with his claws and push back against the sensations that were going to send him over the edge.

Suddenly, Stormfire stopped again, the dragon panting heavily. After a moment, he bent down, wrapping his arms around Kieran as he lifted the boy up. "Good cub," he growled, running his claws all over the front of the young wolf's body, feeling the taut muscles below the cub's soft fur. Kieran's back was pressed against his chest, the wyrm's arms squeezing the boy lovingly as he holstered his fat organ inside his young student.

Then, losing the ability to restrain his urges, Stormfire resumed his hard, fast pounding, the dragon fucking the cub deeply and roughly and grunting loudly with unbridled lust. It was not long before Stormfire felt the unruly itch in his balls explode, and it was all he could do to keep from crushing the body of his new lover in his arms as his dick expanded, releasing an explosion of ecstasy through his own body and blasting a torrent of dragon-seed deep into the hot body of the wolf.

The dragon's roar could be heard for many miles. His body spasmed, his hips shuddering. Kieran's eyes and mouth opened wide as he felt the hot explosion from his sensei's dick filling his deepest insides with a pool of liquid warmth. Stormfire's claws gently squeezed the soft-furred body—so small compared to his own—his deep, loud, exultant grunts the only thing he could hear or feel aside from the raw pleasure of his climax for a long, long while.

Kieran, finally coming to rest against the shuddering body of his sensei, reached a paw up to stroke the dragon's quivering snout as it hung over him. He felt so warm inside now; he knew that the dragon's seed had filled him completely.

The dazzling gold eyes opened to look down at him, the wyrm finally catching his breath. "That... was, incredible, Kieran. You feel so wonderful," the dragon whispered, his expression showing a spark of amazement.

The brown wolfcub smiled, knowing that he had given his sensei something that had been missing for far too long. He was surprised, though, when the big shaft pulsated inside him, still erect. Stormfire's knowing smile made him grin back after he realized how hard that dick still was.

"It's not over, cub. This time let's see what happens if I concentrate on you as well..."

Kieran's body arched as he felt the shaft come out almost all the way. It was shoved in again, only this time it stopped right at

71

the point where it contacted his prostate. He gritted his teeth, throwing his head back as the now-familiar jolt of pleasure rushed through him harder than before. He felt the throbbing glans retreat, then slam past his prostate again amid the slick sounds that the dragon's first copious load was causing.

Stormfire grinned broadly, slowing his shallow thrusts until he found a rhythm. He concentrated, and before long could magically sense all of the pleasure he was giving to his wolfcub. At first, he couldn't believe it. His readings were much higher than he'd ever seen before. Then he simply grinned, and kept pounding, letting the cub stay right at the edge of orgasm, enjoying every moment. Before long he felt his own orgasm beginning to catch up—all too soon for the wyrm, but he was definitely going to make the best of it.

Kieran felt something smooth and warm stroke his muzzle, and he opened his mouth in surprise. Sensei's tongue entered promptly, and the dragon's lips pressed against his own. The two kissed passionately as the wyrm's thrusts gradually began to speed up. The moment was etched into the boy's memory as he shared his own lusts and passions with that of the dragon, transmitting them through the touch of their tongues and mouths, all the while feeling the unbelievable sensation of the huge, throbbing dick pistoning within him.

Then Stormfire's mouth left his, finding another organ to caress. The dragon's tongue stroked his painfully erect, throbbing wolfhood. It wound around the entire shaft, the forked tips encasing the knot and squeezing beneath it. Kieran lost control then, as the dragon frigged his shaft and pounded that colossal dick so deeply in him. A series of shudders ran through his body, hard spurts of cub-seed bursting from his cock to be guzzled down by the hungry dragon maw.

Kieran's whole world ignited with pleasure. All he saw and felt was his entire being exploding, again and again in a world of white light. His orgasmic cry was drowned out by the intensity of these pulsations, until finally, after a forever in his world of oceanic ecstacy, he gradually reawakened to the sound of his own grunts and the tremors that were still running through his young body.

Suddenly, he could feel the dragon-cock expanding and shooting powerful jets of cum deep inside of him again, and he was aware of his own orgasm, less overwhelming now, but still happening amidst the wyrm's own. The two bodies eventually relaxed after the dragon's own intense climax waned. Kieran watched with wonder as the long tongue coaxed the last of his semen from his tired cock. Finally, his body went limp, his dick following suit as it retreated back into the warmth of his sheath.

Stormfire laid the wolf down, caressing the cub's body with no small amount of wonder. He had never had a lover who lasted so long, or came so hard, or satisfied him with just two orgasms. At that moment, the dragon felt luckier than any of his peers. Though most of them were light-years away from pain and strife of any kind, they could never feel a love like this—not even if they had infinity to try. He took the cub in his arms, surrounding him with the warmth of his serpentine body.

Neither of them could stay awake for long, and it was Kieran who drifted off first. The dragon allowed himself to fall asleep only after setting up a temporary ward that would wake them if danger approached.

So began a relationship that had already been far more than that of teacher and student. Stormfire had become the wolfcub's only family, and Kieran in turn had given the dragon a mortal companion that understood and loved him more than his colleagues ever could have. Despite their isolation from the other inhabitants of the planet—a necessity because of the nature of Kieran's powers—they were happy, each finding something in the other that had seemed to have been missing in life before they had met. Kieran had found a mentor, and Stormfire had, at long last, found a true friend. As both lovers lay curled with one another, the energies of the glade nurtured their souls, strengthening their bond as they slumbered. Their dreams were sublime that night, but nothing came close to the reality of waking up entwined with the perfect body of one's student or mentor, lover, and friend rolled up into one.

Tooth and Nail

Whyte Yoté is a name as familiar to FANG readers as K. M. Hirosaki and Kyell Gold; his contributions are numerous—and long. 'Coming of Age' is no different.

As an editor, accepting a long story is always a hard thing to do as it requires far more work to polish, and it allows less room for other stories to fit in the anthology.

With Whyte, the decision is seldom difficult. His stories arrive in near-pristine condition and the necessity of their length is immediately clear. This story, perhaps, epitomizes those qualities.

Ario, a young member of a tribe of wolves, is cast out into the wilderness to prove himself, and learns that hunter and prey are more flexible roles than he believed.

Coming of Age

Whyte Yoté

It was the Magic Hour: the hour of unpredictability, when even the sharpest of eyes and ears were put to the test. All things under the sky remained a shade of blue before the light of the Great Circle painted them their proper colors, dissolving the cloying pre-dawn darkness.

Not only did the darkness cling stubbornly to everything it touched, it also refused to shake off the bitter cold that always came with it during the Cold Season. The air was calm, lending itself to a thick coating of frost that made the grasses crackle underfoot and fur stand on end, especially if its owner hadn't moved in quite a while. When hunting the most elusive game, and for such a high price, not even shifting position was allowed.

Ario's body hurt with each breath he took, and he tried to avoid shivering too much as he watched steam curl from his nostrils and float up into air that seemed to bite him down to the skin. Every time he moved just slightly the coating of white on his fur crackled minutely, and with every sound he could imagine his prey bounding farther away from him and his weapon.

His grey-green eyes scanned the open plain bordered by mountains on one side and forest on the other, looking for any movement at all. Seconds ticked by, each one another regret about deciding not to wear any heavy clothing to stay light, agile and quiet. It had sounded like a good idea last night when he had been curled up comfortably beside his fire, but sitting here exposed, even in his full winter pelt, was starting to make him regret his decision. It was beginning to look like an unsuccessful hunt, except this time the price of loss was worse than just his pride: it was rejection and banishment, and the possible death of his fledgling family.

There was no movement as far as he could see, and the sky was growing lighter with the rising of the Great Circle. Soon it would be too bright, and he would have to wait until the shadows grew long and disappeared before he dared hunt again. He had precious little energy remaining; his food had run out many days ago. The warrior wolf's body was rangy, his ribs and joints clearly visible even under his thick winter fur. He leaned forward, touching a pawpad to the ground so slowly he could feel the frost melting into the grass from his body heat. On trembling legs he balanced, his tail twitching this way and that to keep him steady.

Ario's ears swiveled to catch the sound of breaking wood underfoot within the forest. It happened again, and this time the wolf turned his head, squinting. He figured his prey was too far away to hear him, so he settled onto his knees, receiving many thanks from long-cramped muscles. Barely able to see above the cattails, his powerful lupine eyes scanned the darkness underneath the pine trees.

At first he couldn't tell if there was any movement, but after careful study of the shadows a figure dived between two thick trunks and ran off, not bothering to keep quiet. Either he knew he was being followed or he had become complacent. Ario hoped it was the latter, and that the element of surprise would make the killing that much more expedient. At least he was downwind.

The shadow moved toward the edge of the stand and retreated again, as if hesitant to come into the rising light. It did this repeatedly, over half an hour, each time coming closer to the edge and staying longer. Ario remained on his knees long after they had frozen to the ground and watched, gearing himself up for the time when he could finally see his quarry.

Morning had broken into its full splendor, casting the landscape in a neutral palette except for the trees, which stood proudly displaying their coats of dark green. It was a shock to see a moving patch of light brown after so much concentrating, but Ario tensed just the same when he saw it: the shadow stepped into the light, revealing a male whitetail deer.

The buck stood tall, just a little more so than Ario, and was clothed relatively lightly for a journey. He wore a beaded vest of a many-colored design, and a covering over his loins that extended down to just above his knees. The clothing was foreign to the wolf, who had seldom been on hunts, and those had all been in the Hot Season when such things were not required. At this distance he could tell little else, but he would see to that.

Cautiously, the cervine made his way across the snow, his hooves almost silent. One hand lay by his side, near a scabbard hooked to his waist. Ario crept low, maintaining a steady pace and keeping hidden behind the cattails. His mind was abuzz with calculations and ideas about how he would make the kill: there was only a short distance left before his shield would end, and hunter and hunted would be within spitting distance of each other. He knew he must act quickly or he would never catch the quick buck in this deep snow. He drew an obsidian dagger, self-made and his only weapon, from the scabbard hanging on a string over the back of his neck and turned it in his paw, waiting for the right moment to strike.

The deer moved more quickly now, nostrils flaring, head jerking back and forth. Something was telling him he was being followed, and he wanted to get across the field and up into the mountains in the shortest time possible. He tasted faint traces of droppings and wet fur on the air; the former was of no concern but the latter was cause to be jittery: it smelled faintly of wolf. The deer would have to keep an eye out.

And he cursed himself a moment later when he dropped his gaze and realized he stood exposed in the exact center of the clearing. Not only that, the origin of the wolf-fur smell was crouched not a stone's throw away, eyes dark as death.

The two looked at each other for a moment, as if to discuss the situation and come to a conclusion. There is a mutual understanding in the rules of life and death in the wild: when the time comes to fight, you must give everything of yourself without hesitation and without complaint. To do any less is a sign of a weak body and spirit, and there is no honor in backing down from what is expected of you. The wolf was the predator, and the buck became the prey. And when Ario bared his fangs and rumbled a warning from the grass, the cervine knew the game was on. Today he would fly.

Twin geysers of snow flew upwards as the buck launched himself from a standstill, turning back the way he had come and leaping over assorted small rocks. Ario dug his claws in and was up a split-second later, arms and legs pumping, propelling his meager body after the deer. His stiff, half-frozen legs would not cooperate; they felt misshapen and filled with liquid instead of muscle. The buck, who had claimed a generous head start, was gaining ground and soon disappeared behind a large boulder. Ario powered himself to the top of the hill and ran past the boulder, but a few paces more found the wolf coming to a bedraggled stop.

The pursuit had lasted only a few seconds and covered no more ground than one of his pack's fields, but Ario was winded and sore. He looked across the clearing back to the forest's edge and saw nothing. Absolutely nothing. With nowhere to hide, the deer had reached the trees and hidden himself again, well before the wolf could even follow him. He fell to his paws and knees, which were already bruised and painful from the cold.

He wanted to go back to his tribe and the warmth of its council fire, wanted to live his life without having to go through such torment just to be looked upon as an adult. But he knew to go back was to incur the wrath of the elders, not the least of them his mate's father. They would kill him and leave him to feed the spring regrowth, and his spirit would never rest. He couldn't stand that thought. And what of N'hela? What of the child?

He remembered the vision: how his mother had said it would be fulfilled during a great journey of life, what she had showed him, and how he couldn't make sense of the message.

It ran contrary to everything he felt, and had learned, but the

Great Spirits were rarely wrong. To not heed their advice was unholy bad luck.

The wind was picking up, ruffling his fur and numbing him from the outside in. No matter the failed hunt. No matter his mate, and no matter his visions. He would have to track the buck down again, following his weakening scent until the time was right for another chance to win his adulthood. The fact was, Ario simply didn't know if he would have the strength to last that long. The weakness of his traitorous body disgusted him. A pup of nineteen Hot Seasons had no right to feel this way. Perhaps it would be better to die in the snow instead of at the paws of his elders.

Ario wiped a sniffle from his snout. Another came, and he hit himself hard, yelping in pain. The sobs would not be stopped. With a broken heart, he raised his head to the clouds and howled the frustration of his life to whatever Spirits would give him audience.

Once upon a time, long before Ario was born, the packs thrived upon the Earth and its lush bounty. At this time they had been little more than walking beasts, at that awkward stage of evolution between quadruped and biped. They used little more than sticks and rocks to hunt; the skills of carving and sharpening were yet to be discovered.

Ario's ancestors of tens of thousands of years past lived in much the same area as Ario's tribe occupied in the present day, but at this time the wild wolves could walk upon a large hill to the north and look upon a vast continental lake, which was the source of all rivers and their drinking water. Prey was plentiful and never wasted; life was relatively calm and there was no reason for rival packs to fight.

In these early awkward years, language was a new and ever-changing thing. The growls and barks and low grunts used in the past were slowly becoming replaced by organized sentences and the old-fashioned ways of pointing and waving now seemed excessive by comparison. It was in these times that the pack started giving names to their pups that described something of their birth and character instead of just relying upon olfactory identification. Usually the names had something to do with the position of the Great Circle or the Silver God which ruled over the night, the time of year, or a relationship with another family member. But there were rare times when a tragedy overshadowed the birth of a pup, and the pup itself was considered an omen and bad luck.

For thousands of years, pups such as those were sacrificed to the Spirits so that the misfortune within them would never get the chance to manifest itself in the pup's adult years. It was for the good of the pack, but many a mother wept over the loss of her newly-forsaken child. Eventually, as the wolves evolved, rituals and beliefs changed and so did the barbaric practice of sacrifice. Instead, the pups were cared for and looked after very carefully, but when it came time to step into adulthood their tests were much more difficult than those of their "normal" peers. This was done both so they could prove themselves worthy despite the omen on their heads, and be accepted once and for all into the pack. Those who did not succeed were exiled to live in solitude or find a place with another pack. Some killed themselves before they would face such dishonor.

So it came that one winter, not too long ago, a wolf named Feravel (it meant "leaf of grass" in the ancient tongues) gave herself to her mate Yumelo ("one-eye"). Two months went by quickly, and the snow gave way to fresh grasses and bright days, which gave way to a hot and dry season that set the forests aflame and made the rivers recede to almost nothing. By the time Feravel went into labor, many hunting parties had been sent out and never heard from again. Water was at a premium, and the tribe would not move. A shaman and midwife came to her side, and brought her into the council's tent.

The labor was long, painful, and difficult. Yumelo was not allowed to see his mate, and he paced about outside, cursing loudly every time he heard a scream. The pup came feet first, a sign of bad luck in itself. When he stopped breathing and moving, the midwife had to pull him the rest of the way; Feravel simply did not have strength enough to push anymore. The little wolf had come roughly into the world, followed by a river of blood which could not be stemmed. Minutes after the delivery, the pup was breathing on his own and his mother lay dead in the shady dust of the tent.

He was cursed from the very start: Yumelo had disowned him outright and assigned the midwife to raise him, he had numerous ailments which required rare herbs and elaborate ceremonies, and he was considered tainted goods. After much deliberation, he was given the name Ario, taken from the ancient tongues to mean "born of spilled blood." It described him very well.

To say the least, he was a troublemaker. Teased by his peers as a pup, he was labeled as weak and stupid and useless. Never invited to games and never allowed to play with the others, Ario became of the mind that he would never be good enough to do much of anything. On the other paw, his time alone allowed him to use his imagination to keep busy. Most of the adults left him alone as long as he didn't cause trouble, which forced him to mature much slower than the other youths in the tribe. Unfortunately, there were some aspects of life in which he never got the chance to mature.

One day, in his eighteenth Hot Season, Ario was walking along the riverbank, skipping stones and lost in one of his many daydreams, when a scent came to his still-undeveloped nose. He followed it around a bend and saw a female bathing herself across from him on a shallow island.

Her name was N'hela, and she was a quiet female who also kept to herself. Ario watched her bend down to scoop water in her paws and rub it into her bluish-gray fur, watched it drip off her nipples and run down into the cleft between her legs. He had never seen a female unclothed before, and N'hela's exposure excited him in a way he had never been. The scent reminded him of wildflowers just blooming in the Planting Season, sweet and tangy and stirring something deep within his brain. He sat there, watching from behind a large tree, finally looking down and discovering his maleness hardening like when he went off in secret to pleasure himself.

N'hela turned away from him, and Ario stalked up behind her, the scent coming from her estrus stronger with each step. She turned when he was right behind her, making her yell out and cover herself, albeit with little success. Without a word, Ario bent down, rooting around for the source of the heavenly scent, unmindful that he had taken his loincloth off and let his member continue hardening outside of his sheath. The female protested, but Ario's cold, curious nose on her forbidden flesh froze her to the spot; the male could kill her if he wanted, and she would not provoke him.

Without warning, Ario licked her labia, and when she tried to push him away he responded by growling and shoving her back into the flowing water. He wanted to taste more of that lovely pinkness; even though he didn't know what it was or what it was for, he knew he wanted to lick it and his hips wanted to thrust of their own accord. Ario moved up to the female's breasts, and when he felt himself accidentally penetrating her as he lay there the instinct was born a fiery birth within him. He thrust like mad, not even feeling the resistance as her maidenhead gave way to his lupine shaft.

Like an inexperienced cub, Ario flopped around on N'hela, who cried for him to stop, but knew he could not help himself. All the male knew was the pleasure coming from his wolfhood, and that he must get to the end as quickly as possible. It was clumsy and unseemly; when he came inside her he jerked and fell still, feeling his knot swelling and tying them together. When he finally looked at the female, seeing the fear and shame in her eyes, he knew he had done something very serious and very wrong. Ario tried to pull out, but they both cried in pain. As soon as his shrinking penis was free of her, he plucked his loincloth from the riverbank and ran as fast as his young legs would carry him away from the place of their mating.

For a day and most of a second, Ario did not come home until hunger drove him to desperation. It was then he discovered that N'hela had told her father of the rape, and the council had been alerted. An emergency meeting was called as soon as Ario's arrival had been communicated to the elders, and the tribe gathered to decide the fate of the whelp who had never grown up. He was questioned, and admitted that he didn't know what he was doing when he was mating with N'hela. He did, however, know he had done wrong. He was put into quarantine until N'hela's condition could be determined.

It was one week later that a midwife had announced the pregnancy, and the council convened again.

"My foolish boy," decreed the tribe's chief, "do you know the full ramifications of your actions?"

The wolf looked at the ground and said in a small voice, "I do. That I have planted a child in the loins of a female, and it will be mine forever to raise and take care of." As much as he tried to act grown up, he thought he sounded like a chastised, indignant puppy.

"You will see nothing of your child!" roared the chief, his fur fluffed out in anger and an almost palpable hatred. "You have been a burden on this tribe for too long. Do you think we would allow a bad omen like you to raise a pup? What makes you think you can do anything?"

There was no answer.

"I expected nothing better. I would banish you now had I the power, but..." The chief rolled his eyes. "Tradition requires that you be given a chance to prove yourself worthy of fatherhood and acceptance into this tribe once and for all. If you can complete the task set before you, the Great Spirits will look down upon you with favor. But I do not expect you to succeed. No one does with a runt like you."

Ario flushed visibly and wanted nothing more than to be invisible at that moment. The chief's words stung him because they made him realize all that he had done wrong in his life. The wolf knew not everything was his fault, but that didn't make the scathing commentary any less painful.

The elders were silent. The chief spoke: "In order to become an adult, those deemed ready for the change are sent far away into

the forests and hills on a journey of self-discovery. Some go together, but most stay alone. During this journey they take no food
or water. They must go on a vision quest to connect with their
guiding spirit in the beyond, and be told the ultimate purpose of
their lives so that they may shape themselves accordingly. You will
be required to do the same. But—"

Ario's ears perked up.

"But," the chief continued, "you must do much more to prove
yourself in the eyes of this tribe. Tell me, pup: what is the strongest symbol of power?"

There was silence for a while, but Ario couldn't think of anything. He had never been invited to council meetings where such
things were discussed.

The chief scowled, his dark gray brow wrinkling. "Blood. Blood
is a sign of lineage, of life and death, and of power over others. It is
what we feast upon for our life, and it is a sign of a successful hunt.
You must prove yourself not only as an adult, but a hunter as well,
if you are to raise a family and take care of it. You will come back
and present me with blood from a kill. A large kill. I will be able to
tell otherwise, in case you are thinking of trying to fool me." Some
of the elders chuckled, already having given up on Ario's chances
of ever becoming an adult.

"Silence!" shouted the chief, raising his paws high. "Do this, you
who have been born of spilled blood, and you will have a place in
this tribe, in our pack. Should you fail, and return to plead for
your life, we will have no mercy."

"I'll rip your heart out myself and feed it to you before you die,
you lascivious whelp!" came a cry from deep within the crowd, and
Ario realized it was N'hela's father who had spoken. If he did try
to come back without success, he would not live a day beyond.

"You will go now," said the chief to the shaking wolf, his face
stony and unmoving. "Good luck." The statement was empty of
goodwill.

They had sent him away in the middle of the cold night not
empty-pawed. Since the trials of adulthood usually took place in
the Planting Season when it was warmer, blankets were not nor-

mally needed. But it was getting close to the middle of the Cold Season, when the Great Circle stayed only a short time in the sky and the darkness brought unimaginable cold even to thick-furred wolves. He had been given pelts and nothing more than the loincloth he wore.

A few hours after leaving the camp, he spied a cave to crawl into. His feet stung from the snow and his muscles twitched from miles of unaccustomed walking. He discovered a few black, shiny stones that were sharp to the touch and, with nothing better to do, started carving them as best he could into sharp points. One of them would become a serrated dagger.

After his paws were aching and bloody, he finally stopped. Laying down on the blankets which did little to alleviate the hardness of the cave's floor, Ario tried not to think of the tasks ahead, and cried himself to sleep.

Ario awoke nearly frozen to the ground on which he slept. Reeds and grass were pulled out by the roots and stuck to his fur, which had taken on a white sheen from heavy frost. He coughed so hard he doubled over, and for a moment he was sure he would vomit... And then he remembered there wouldn't be anything in his stomach to make it worth the effort.

The two days since losing the buck had passed quickly. Ario had howled his heart out on top of that hill by the boulder, but finally he had come to his senses. Following the scent of the buck, the wolf had used his keen nose to track his quarry for countless miles in nearly every direction. It was clear that the cervine was trying to fool him, but somehow some clue would reveal itself each time he seemed lost. Ario thanked the Spirits for their help.

He had left all his possessions behind, with the exception of the dagger, in favor of the speed of traveling unhindered. Adrenaline drove a renewed spirit within him that the cold couldn't extinguish. Ario was glad for such a strength again; it helped to know he still had tenacity in his heart after such heartbreak. But he knew that, strength or weakness, the situation had not changed or gotten any easier. The scent was there, and it was closer.

Sleeping in a drift of deep snow last night had effectively rendered his own lupine scent undetectable; if he spied the deer and snuck up on him, there would be no warning. One quick swipe of his dagger would kill without trouble and leave plenty of blood. Even better was the fact that he would still be able to track the buck while carrying a temporarily neutral scent.

So often had he thought of killing a squirrel or rabbit, or even cutting himself to get what his chief required of him, but there would be no chance for deception. Besides, Ario wouldn't allow himself to stoop to such whelpish tactics.

He ran in tight circles to warm up and get the kinks out of his back, wandering to a nearby still-unfrozen stream for a drink. Ario's body told him every day now it desperately needed something to eat, but until he could find sustenance water would have to do.

The buck's scent was strong, smelling of earth, elderberries, and wood. Just a small distance away, the forest in which the wolf stood gave onto a sloping hill that descended into a small valley before topping another ridge. He walked carefully, nose at the ready, and when he crested the first ridge he found a pile of deer droppings. Fresh, less than two hours old. The nagging hunger that had plagued him for so long took a back seat to knowing he had stayed on the trail so long.

Over rocks, through streams, leaping from tree to tree like a cub again, Ario kept the scent strong in his muzzle while making up as much distance as his legs could offer him. Scenes of surprising the buck, of taking him down and goring his throat in one swift maneuver, filled his head, but the feeling was short-lived when the wolf realized just how much energy it might take. If this failed, he simply would not have the strength for a third.

Ario's heart felt about to burst from nervousness at the thought of being so close to his prey. Without looking over the edge of the cliff he could tell the deer was just beyond it, and had been there for some time. There was something else, something irresistible: food. His stomach growled loudly, scaring him into thinking he would be found out just from that alone. For a moment he thought that even if he wasn't able to kill the deer, he could at least take his food. Kill or no kill, his belly would be filled either way.

He sprawled out and plastered his stomach to the ground. The edge of the cliff grew nearer little by little. Ears perked, he slowly drew his eyes over the precipice and saw the buck once again, closer than he had ever come. The wolf was practically on top of him. Below the cliff about twenty feet was a field of berry bushes that had not had a chance to shed their harvest before the first frost. The Cold Season had come so quickly, and so extremely, that many trees and bushes hadn't had a chance to drop. Ario could see that the berries had been frozen and well-preserved.

Walking among the bushes, the buck seemed at ease, picking berries by the dozen and putting them into a satchel he carried aside his waist. He was well-clothed for the day, and probably had left his bedding nearby while he gathered food. His beaded vest and odd loincloth were accompanied by the satchel, a water pouch and a sheath on one hip. He hummed an unknown tune, eating the plump red berries as he picked them.

The wolf almost couldn't contain himself. The sight of the deer made him want to complete his task right away; the sight of the berries got him salivating like a common dog. Not only did he see all that wonderful sweetness down there in the clearing, he could smell something else he thought he would never smell again: bread. There must be some in that satchel, he thought, and it would feel very good lining his belly.

He quickly began formulating a plan. The element of surprise would be best, of course. There was no way he could get down to the buck without backtracking quite a distance and making all sorts of noise, so he determined the only viable way—and the quickest—would be to simply jump down upon the unsuspecting creature.

Ario spent a few minutes praying to the Spirits, asking for their help and guidance in this most difficult of tasks. The sun broke through the thin clouds and warmed his bare body, permeating the thick gray and black fur of his back and giving him strength to move better than he had in days. Today would finally be the day, he thought, and then he could go home and claim his adulthood, his mate and his unborn child.

He stood, confident and calm. Crouching on strong legs, he leaped high into the air and away from the cliff, judging the correct angle to land, ready to pounce. The ground rushed up to meet him, but he was ready. He hit evenly and without the slightest trace of sound; his springy legs sank almost to the ground. Ario was just preparing to spring forward when he heard the sound like a whip slashing through the air.

There was no time to react; he registered the sound just before his head exploded in pain. Stars danced in his vision but he did not fall. As soon as he could see, the branch was swinging toward him again. Sidestepping it this time, he recovered quickly and darted behind a nearby tree, using its thin trunk as a pivot to speed him around in a circle.

The buck stood prone, with the branch at the ready, gripping it tightly, an expression of deadly intent on his face. Ario rushed him, ducking when the branch came swinging again and turned his shoulder to broadside the buck in the chest. He didn't expect that the deer would swivel his body away, so he ran full bore into nothing; then delivered an arcing kick to the back of his neck. The wolf stumbled and fell into a nearby bush, berries raining down onto him. Already his malnourished body was losing energy.

By the time he turned to look up and prepare for another attack, the cervine was on top of him and shoved the sharpened end of the branch into the center of his neck, rendering him helpless. The wolf lay prone, throat bared in supplication, gagging a bit at the sharp point on his larynx. The buck stood tall over him and gave the wolf's near-naked, weak body a once-over. Ario thought he saw a smile prick the corners of the other male's lips, probably in expectation of the bloodshed to follow.

He tried to kick upward, hoping to catch the deer where it counted, but his footpaw only found a hard knee. His toes popped and he whimpered—a small, adolescent sound.

The buck pressed the branch even harder, kneeling and snarling, their noses touching. Suddenly the branch was gone and a rough-edged blade replaced it, a dark flash in the light. Ario shuddered at the wet coldness.

"Oh no, my puppy... You will not have me so easily," he murmured in a smooth voice. "I am afraid your hunt has ended in failure. My name is Dande, and I am going to kill you."

The first night away from home had been the worst by far. There were dreams that caused him to sweat and cry out and wake many times, and when the Great Circle finally lit the sky he gave up trying to sleep and continued working on the obsidian dagger, stopping only when the morning shadows had dwindled to dark puddles at his feet.

He staggered out of the cave feeling dirty and worthless. There were leaves in his fur, dark circles under his bloodshot eyes. He was scared and ashamed, but most of all he was worried about N'hela and his still-unborn child. The elders thought him nothing more than a whelp who was too immature to care for a family, but he couldn't help but feel as though he had already failed them all. Unsure of how to proceed, the confusion only heightened his hunger and weakness.

On shaky legs Ario slowly set about the only thing he could think of at the moment: gathering fuel for a fire. He would need food and water eventually; he could spend only a night without nourishment, assuming he kept warm enough to stay alive. It took some hours to obtain what he thought was a decent amount of wood for a few days. The wolf found himself humming a disjointed version of a traditional tribal tune, and he stopped abruptly after realizing it was a cub's lullaby. It was true: Ario had not grown up at all.

Well, said a voice inside his head, if you're so much of a cub, how come you can gather firewood by yourself? Or carve a dagger out of hard black rock? Somehow he knew it was the voice of his mother, although the only thing she had ever said to him was a string of curses as he slowly, mortally, left her womb so long ago. Had she forgiven him for taking her life? It was a good sign, and despite his dire situation the wolf was heartened to think so.

Ario wandered through the middle of the day, following a depression in the land to a small stream of fresh, if leafy and half-frozen, water. He made a game of chasing rabbits and what few squirrels remained outside for the Cold Season, but his heart was not yet in the hunt. When the dagger was finished he could use that to his advantage; his supple wrist was better at aiming than his paws alone.

For the rest of the day and into twilight the warrior thought long on how he should best go about finding a suitable kill for the rite of adulthood. The hard part would be finding a group of deer or elk, or even moose. This late in the year most tribes or herds would be to the south of his present camp, where a deep valley protected them from the harsh winds and temperatures of the Cold Season. Ario's pack, because they took up less space, camped uphill from this valley to take advantage of the view for tracking purposes. Where Ario was camped now, however, there would be little to no chance of finding a herd, or even a stray. Taking on the whole group would be suicide; maybe he could find food and wait... There were so many options, it would take much patience and scent-tracking to locate prey. But he would watch, and wait, for as long as it took to earn his place as an adult.

The point of the blade poked into his skin with every beat of his heart. The buck had it placed so that if he moved an inch, the blade would have no trouble slicing directly into an artery. Death would come swiftly and silently.

Dande, as the deer had called himself, sat rigid, ready to strike, his arms and legs quivering ever so slightly. Ario was on his back, panting and trying not to split open any more flesh than was necessary.

The wolf had no idea how prepared the cervine had been for his attack. The only way he could have countered so quickly was if he had known of Ario's presence beforehand. Somehow, his scent had preceded him despite his downwind position.

"Do it then," he muttered, baring his teeth but trying to keep the quaver of fear from his voice. "If it makes you a male to kill a father, then finish me now." His eyes met the buck's, a deep brown that, had he known of it, he would have called coffee-colored. They burned with malice and unbridled hatred, and an intelligence borne of intense living.

Keeping the blade close to Ario's neck, the deer lifted up slightly to ease the tension in his legs. Then he spit in the wolf's face, something he apparently had been saving up for awhile. He did not smile. "You foul wretch," he spoke purposefully. "You lie with every word that comes from that bloodstained maw of yours. You are no more a father than I."

"If you wish to doubt me, I do not blame you. I only ask you to believe what I tell you, hard as that may be. I am not here of my own choice."

The cervine snickered. "Oh, really? And who, dare I ask, sent you here to kill me, one who has done you no harm?"

Ario ignored the snide sarcasm, but was relieved that the deer was relaxing bit by bit. He no longer considered the wolf a direct threat. "As soon as your blade moves, my packmates will make sure you never leave this place." He allowed a little confidence to sneak into his lie. "I'm sure you will make a decent enough dinner for—"

In a flash the deer was on his hooves, the dagger gone. He whirled around in a tawny blur before something struck out and connected with Ario's ribs, the sound of breaking bone and cartilage breaking the cold, still air. The wolf uttered a wet cry and curled up in the thin snow until the blade forced his head back onto the ground. His lungs felt as if they had been set aflame and he fought the urge to cough up what would surely be blood.

Dande was smiling coldly. "I am offended, pup. Do you honestly think I would fall for such a weak ploy? You may think you've been tracking me, but I have been doing the same to you. I know you discovered my trail no more than a week ago. I knew exactly how far behind you were, but despite my best attempts to throw you off my scent you stayed on me. I will give you that much. You have no packmates, and you have been alone for days and days now. Your nose may be keen, but so is mine."

"They'll come looking for me."

"And what then? By the looks of you, they won't want you any-way. What good is an injured puppy such as you?" Dande nudged Ario's broken ribs, gaining a gasping half-scream from the lupine.

"Others depend on me. My life is theirs." The wolf reached a paw up to the deer's ankle, but it was warned away by the dag-ger. "You would not understand." His ability to speak was almost gone, as was his spirit. What had before been a brilliant plan had utterly failed, his own tactics turned against him. As much as he hated it, Ario would have to either reason with the cervine or beg for his life. And the latter was, in his opinion, akin to death. But he would be no good to his family dead.

"I do understand," Dande uttered, his face set. "All I have to do is take one good look at you to know you do not belong to your pack anymore. You've been out here for more than it takes half the Night Circle to wane . I know about hard journeys. You have had no food and little water. You would easily have enough strength to kill me outright were you well-nourished, but from what I can see neither your elders nor the Great Spirits think you're worth anything."

Ario remained silent. The words were too true and hurt too much.

"In all my years I've never seen such a sorry excuse for a wolf. I have no pity for you. I'm surprised you were able to sneak up on me like you did." The buck stood now and circled the prone wolf, always keeping the dagger aimed at his neck or his groin. Either wound would bleed most painfully if inflicted. "No matter, you won't get the chance to tell your pack, or anyone else, of your har-rowing encounter and victory over the helpless little deer. Would you like to offer a prayer or apology to your invisible gods before I skin you alive and take home your fur as a trophy? I would love to sleep on something soft for a change."

There was something in Dande's voice... Maybe it was his haughty confidence, maybe the calm way he talked about killing him. But a seed of fury sprouted in the lupine's mind. There was no reason for murder of this caliber; the buck could clearly see he posed no threat at all. Ario had a reason—no, a noble purpose—for hunting Dande, but prey was not supposed to kill the predator. He would not be subject to such atrocious dishonor.

He had to wait only a few seconds until the cervine stepped behind his head and he rolled forward in a flash, almost with enough effort to send him into a somersault. He used the extra momentum to launch into an all-out run out of the berry patch, brambles catching and ripping lines into his thighs. A shout of anger came from the stunned deer, but Ario did not look back. If he had, he would probably have been able to avoid the dagger as it tumbled end over end through the air, covering the distance to the wolf much faster than he was running.

Its aim was true, and it sunk into his left shoulder with such force the lupine was thrown to the ground, further hurting his aching ribs. A hot, dull throb spread throughout his shoulder quickly, rendering it useless; a strong burst of iron in his mouth told of a split tongue. He had only one chance to pick himself up, but his upper body had gone almost totally rigid. Then a hard hoof slammed into the small of his back to pin him to the snowpack; a high-pitched growling yip of frustration signaled Ario's physical defeat.

There was rustling from above, and the wolf's paws were forced roughly behind his back and bound with a thin but painful rope. Without so much as a warning, Dande pulled his feet up to meet the captive wrists, and soon he was rendered completely immobile. His back screamed from the unnatural position; each movement only served to force more blood from his open shoulder wound. He moaned weakly.

Dande knelt down close to the wolf's head, which was half-buried in snow, his flaring nostrils sending out ragged clouds of steam. "I must admit," he panted lightly, "I didn't expect such quick action from you. Appearances can truly deceive; I shall not make that mistake again. You have made your execution that much longer and more painful. Would you like to see your entrails before I cut your throat, or would you like to watch your own body convulse as your head tumbles to the ground?" The deer was grinning mercilessly, his eyes pools of emptiness.

"You monster," Ario replied through gritted teeth, trying not to get a muzzleful of snow. "Nothing... nothing but a coward hiding behind your awful words." He waited for another hoof to the side, but when none came he continued. "Have you no honor? I am willing to die for my cause, but what will it prove if you dismember me, or slice me open, or skin me? Honor is about fighting for your side, and what you believe in. Tying me up and torturing me will not gain you respect from the Spirits—"

"How do you know that?" asked the cervine, impatience creeping into his voice. "I do not worship the same gods as you. Yours would smile on the killing of innocents, and the plundering of villages. You are not hunters; you're opportunists who will do anything to make the lives of others miserable whether it benefits them or not. Not even the most gracious god would allow your survival in this world. A curse on your kind, now and for always."

Now Ario was perplexed, and angrier still at the buck and his apparent death-warrant on lupines as a whole. He could not do much tied up on the ground, but he had to try to talk his way out of his ropes. He would not beg, no matter how bad it became—he must retain his honor above all else. Maybe there was something he could offer Dande that would soothe his hate and alleviate his unfounded fear of wolves.

He tried to steer to a new subject, speaking in even, measured tones. "The circle of life should be maintained. It is the job of the predators to keep others in check. We prey on the weak and sick, only those who—"

Dande was on him fast, his hoof a mere blur as it connected squarely with the top of the wolf's muzzle. Ario's words ended in a wet grunt punctuated by a loud snapping sound that seemed to fill the forest around them. The wolf's neck stretched forward so far and with so much sudden pain that he was sure the numbness he felt would be permanent. But his body regained feeling again, and as his vision cleared he could see the new dent in the top of his muzzle. He dared not move his ruined nose.

"My sister and niece were not weak!" cried the buck, drawing the poor lupine off the ground and holding him face-to-face. He shook Ario as he spoke, fairly spitting out the words, thick fingernails digging bruises into his shoulders. "They were not sick! They did not lag behind. They were murdered." Ario had time to see the beginnings of tears brimming in his eyes before Dande let him drop hard on his side. The lupine stared up at his captor with fear-filled eyes: he had stumbled on something much more serious than he knew.

Clouds had started to build and cover the Great Circle. The clearing was cast in dull gray shadows that seemed to drain color from even the berries. Ario lay on his side, breathing laboredly and wheezing. Dande was now pacing back and forth, his fists balled and shaking, staring intensely into space. White plumes jetted from his nostrils. Suddenly he pointed a stiff finger at the wolf.

"How dare you say you are innocent of murder! It matters not who killed them. You all think alike and act alike. It is nothing if you lose one of your pack, but for us... for us it is more than that. We lose family, friends, parents! All the time, it seems, we are surrounded by death. Separation is the ultimate torture. Keep us away from our kin, kill one of us... you can't possibly see the anxiety that causes. We're not weak creatures, but unlike you we feel emotions, and they control us."

"That's not true. We feel—"

"Shut up, wretch," muttered the cervine, tapping the side of Ario's ribcage. "It was three months ago that I lost my sister and niece to a pack of bloodthirsty bastards like you. We were foraging for the last harvest before the cold winds swept in. Suddenly we were surrounded on all sides, but we fought them off bravely and easily with our number. They stood watch in the hills above us until we were almost gone, then..." Dande's voice took on a more emotional tone. That baritone quaver didn't fit his character. "My niece coughed. She coughed, damn you! The wolves thought she was sick, an easy kill, and swarmed around her and my sister. They were too fast to stop; I saw them taken down and their throats... ripped out right in front of me."

Ario winced. He knew what Dande spoke of; a neighboring pack had boasted of the easy kill that yielded such young, sweet venison. Thinking back on that night, the wolf's stomach rolled as he watched the buck pace before him, tears of rage and pent-up mourning streaming down his cheeks and staining his tawny fur dark. He could do little more, he was in so much pain.

"Please listen to me," the wolf said, cringing when Dande turned to him, his muscles so taut his whole body shook like a nocked arrow. The buck stayed silent, waiting for him to continue, and Ario sighed gently. His voice was ragged and wet-sounding. "I had nothing to do with that. But I know those who committed the act. They violated natural law by preying on the healthy, and even more so by taking a female and child. I don't condone it. My pack doesn't condone it. But I am afraid that nothing can convince you to spare my life."

Dande looked away briefly, and when he turned back his face was normal again. In fact, he was smiling slightly. The wolf took no comfort in this. "Do yourself a favor and stop begging. It does not do you justice. Now, tell me—if you can—exactly why I should let you go instead of murdering you like my family was murdered?"

"If I die," said Ario slowly, conviction behind every word. "You will be responsible for three lives, not just one."

The buck scoffed. "And I'm supposed to believe that. You'll scamper home to your pack, and tell them where I am, and bring the lot of them back to kill me for bloodying your pretty fur. A curse on you, I say."

The lupine never missed a beat. "I don't ask you to believe me at all. If you let me go, what good would it do to tell my pack about you? You would be long gone by the time we traveled back here. I wouldn't be able to return to my pack anyway. My wife and child will die without me."

"How—" started the cervine, but instead he thought as he paced. His face worked; Ario could see him struggling with a difficult decision. Silently he prayed that the buck would decide not to kill him. All he could see were two faces, one female and one very small with big, still-blind eyes. He hoped they were safe and alive. He wondered what color his pup's fur was.

At length Dande stood facing him at the edge of the clearing. "Someone must pay. Their blood is on your paws."

"So will the blood of my wife and child be on you!" the wolf yelled at the top of his lungs, enraged. "They'll die without me, you murderous scum!" He writhed on the ground, the bonds cutting into his wrists and ankles. His shattered muzzle burst into an agony-filled grimace.

"Then why did you leave them and come on a pointless quest for me?" Dande shot back.

"Pointless?" sneered Ario, no longer caring how much he angered his captor. "I will tell you how pointless my hunting you was. I have a bastard child, conceived out of a lust I could not control. My pack already sees me as a burden, and now I try to bring into the world another mouth to feed without consulting the elders or the spirits. Nothing could have prepared me for these new responsibilities! I'm still considered a child in their eyes!" The wolf felt his spirit rapidly diminishing, and the first tears of regret began to form.

"I must prove myself worthy of adulthood by bringing back blood as evidence of a hunt. I tried my best for as long as I could and it still wasn't good enough. I tried, damn it, I tried." He sniffed back the oncoming rush of sobs, but only temporarily. His embarrassment was already too great without having to cry in front of the buck. To his surprise, and utter relief, Dande sat upon a short stump and sheathed his blade.

"I'm sure your wife and child will be well provided for." Dande was still trying to maintain his vengeance, but the conviction in his voice was markedly diminished. When the bound wolf rolled his head back to meet his gaze, two thick, shining tears rolled backwards up his forehead and into his dirty headfur. Even upside-down, the buck could see the fear: a pup forced into the real world before he was ready, unadulterated love and a commitment to that love, and the heart of a great warrior that seemed too big for its host.

Almost a whisper, Ario said, "They will be killed. N'hela... my wife... er, partner... we haven't gone through the marriage ceremony yet. Without me she is illegitimate, as is my pup. They will be sacrificed to the great Spirits as a fertility offering for the rest of the pack. Without me they are tainted. You see, now, why I can't die? This is not for me. But all you want is revenge for something with which I had nothing to do. Will it really make you feel better?"

"Did."

"What?"

"Did," the deer said. "I did want revenge for my sister and niece. I was determined to make someone pay as long as it was a wolf who got punished. Yes, it probably would have made me feel better, but only for a short time, and it wouldn't have brought them back to life. Anger makes us blind, don't you agree?" The wolf allowed it did and nodded, his spirits lifting a bit as he began to see a side of Dande completely hidden from him until now.

"What are you suggesting?" asked Ario.

"A truce," said the cervine, standing and approaching the curled-up wolf. "Not between our species, of course, but between us two. You have a family to protect and I have better things to do than look for a fight. I admire you, actually. You may think you're still a pup, and you are in many ways... But you have heart full of love in you, and I respect that. You'll make a great husband and father." There was sincerity, but also some contempt in his voice.

"But I can't go back. Not without proof of a hunt."

"You hunted me, but you did not succeed. You can't very well bring me back alive, can you? I'm sure you can find some other small creature to chase down and kill to please your pack."

"They'll know!" the wolf cried desperately. "Don't you think they can tell the difference between a squirrel and a moose? Blood is our life!" He recalled the words of his great leader.

"That is not my problem." Dande began to walk from the clearing. "You should be able to find your way out of those ropes before nightfall. Wouldn't want you following me, would I?"

"You can't leave me here like this!" Ario shouted, his voice cracking. "There must be something I can do! I will die without your blood!"

"I will not wound myself for you, pup. I wear only battle scars."

"No! Come back! I..." The lupine hesitated before finishing his sentence, afraid to say the next few words. It was against his nature and every instinct, but he was truly out of options. "...I beg of you, Dande. I will do anything you ask. The only thing that matters now is my family."

The cervine was out of the clearing and walking down a path away from the raucous wolf when he stopped, just his antlers visible above the bushes. Slowly they turned, and when Dande came into view again, walking toward him, there was a smile across his muzzle. It was genuine, but immediately Ario could see an ulterior motive behind the expression. He swallowed hard.

"Anything?" he cooed as he approached, kneeling down by the wolf's legs. Those dark brown eyes traveled to and fro, a long tongue licked his lips. "Were you serious when you said that?"

"Do you think I will leave here without what I came for?" Ario's heart seemed to be gaining weight with every beat.

"No, I don't suppose so."

"What do I need to do to get your blood?" The wolf's neck was cramping from being held up while he was tied, so he let it drop back down. The sky was deceptively blue again, with a few silver clouds traversing its space but none of them daring to block the Great Circle's light.

His legs were lifted a bit, and the wolf thought Dande was going to undo the knot holding them together, but instead he felt a rustling of his loincloth and a sudden heat as an appendage pressed over his genitals. The touch made him jerk and sent a shiver of momentary pleasure bolting up his spine. It contracted and moved up to his sheath, cupping its length and stroking a few times until he could feel his cocktip emerging against the leather loincloth. Then down, over his testicles and into the cleft of his buttocks, deep down to the base of his tail, which curled up and tried to cover him as best it could. It was moved out of the way as a finger traced circles around his exposed hole, pressing in a few times and eliciting gasps from the lupine... But from pain or pleasure he couldn't tell.

The finger moved back up to the tip of his cock, and then there was no more heat. Dande's face appeared above him, blocking out the sky. The buck smiled like a youth at play, his eyes shining, and when he brought it to his mouth it was glistening wet. Finally the cervine's intent registered to the confused wolf, and his heart felt about to explode.

Dande licked his lips, savoring Ario's taste. Finally answering the wolf's question, he said, "I can think of one thing."

One of the first lessons Ario learned out on his own was that hunger has a way of ruling the body and tricking the mind. Berries sufficed to keep his stomach quiet for the first week or so, but soon his muscles ached and protested the lack of meat in his diet. How he would down a full-grown deer was currently beyond the grasp of his thoughts. Thankfully, the Great Circle gave him energy with its bright, heatless warmth. His bushy winter coat kept him comfortable as he trekked, keeping close to streams to slake his ever-present thirst. In the back of his mind, the wolf couldn't keep from sensing something building up slowly, like a drift of snow in a driving wind. Little did he know the accuracy of that analogy.

It didn't seem so long ago that he was in his shelter-cave on his first night out, curled up within his own fur and a few pelts for heat. He could almost feel the flames as they danced along the stone walls, caressing him into dreams...

Ario blinked away the image. To wish he was back there would only serve to make him feel worse and increase his hunger. Until he looked up he didn't realize that before him lay the peak of a particularly steep hill, and it looked like a plateau where he could get some well-deserved rest before moving on. A few more minutes and his footpaws hit bare stone, lifting him up to the flat, snowless surface.

A groan escaped his muzzle as he took in his surroundings and the ground that lay before him. So caught up was he in daydreams that he had never looked up to the rocky peaks spearing the sky. Two massive mountains wrestled for dominance of the horizon like beasts with arched backs and patches of splotchy white fur. Directly in front and below the lupine, the hill angled downward toward a waterfall at the bottom before angling steeply up again. The brown grassy hills gave way to outcroppings of rock that eventually overtook the flora and the only good place to rest for the night would be right where...

Ario trained his eyes on a patch of tall brown grass that covered the only flat place near the top of the cliff face. Something was moving, and the only reason he had spotted it at all was because it had been the only large living creature he had seen that day. Standing tall on his footpaws, he squinted, trying to shorten the distance. The Great Circle appeared from behind a cloud and the wolf almost jumped in excitement, drooling instinctively just at the sight.

Though very far away and much higher than Ario, the deer was still visible, male by the chest-covering he was wearing. The wolf saw movement and little else, but the coloring and antlers were a dead giveaway. Regaining his aplomb, Ario immediately sank to his knees and raised his paws to the sky, talking hurriedly: "Oh Great Spirits, I thank you for listening to my song and granting me the sight of this creature so that I may fulfill my duty to you and to my pack." He sang the song once again, just for good measure, making sure to keep his upwind voice low. After a brief sit, all the time watching the deer across the gorge, he started off with renewed vigor.

He fairly bounded down the hill, sidestepping small stones and just plain jumping over others in his way. Sweat emerged from his head and groin in small beads, then rivulets, making his fur shine and cooling his journey. It was a long journey, though, longer than Ario had thought, and by the time he reached the waterfall's edge and plunged into its cooling depths with gratitude he realized the Great Circle was nearing the horizon, almost below the hills he had left behind. All smiles, he wolf-paddled around, not mind-ing the freezing water one bit, drinking his fill of the crisp, clear runoff.

At length, and reluctantly, the lupine emerged on the opposite shore, shook vigorously, and sat on a rock to sun-dry. There was a patch of berry bushes on this side, but they were a bright red, and mottled with white. The wolf's stomach was louder and much more persuasive than his brain, and he stuffed his gullet until he could barely breathe. With a long belch of satisfaction, Ario caught a scent on the gentle breeze wafting down from above. It was fresh, a white kind of smell, the scent of snow.

The wolf looked up.

What little blue remained in the sky was quickly covered up by dark, heavy-looking clouds. A storm was coming... A big one, and with dread Ario knew he should have been aware of that earlier in the day. He should have stayed where he was, but the need to climb up to that ledge and get the job done, the need to eat some fresh meat, was nearly overpowering. One more look at the threatening sky and he was off, sprinting up the hill toward rocks and slick cliffs. He never looked back.

The first third was easy going, the sheltered ground bare in many places. Ario panted, literally feeling the berries in his stomach burning away, fueling his muscles for adrenaline. When the first rock approached, he leaped, hearing a feral growl emerge from deep within his throat, and landed, bounding onto the next in line. This was short-lived, however, as each boulder was bigger and harder to cross than the last.

He was scaling up a section of loose rock when his footpaw suddenly sank into the side of the hill, triggering a miniature avalanche all around him. The wolf scampered and sidestepped out of the way just in time as a torrent of water burst where he had been. Sinking all eighteen claws into the pliable ground, Ario stopped, his body heaving, heart pounding as he realized how close he had come to being swept to a bone-crushing death.

As he rested, the lupine could take in, for the first time, his precarious position. His fingers and toes were chilled, wet from more freezing water lurking just beneath the rocky soil to which he clung. The refreshing breeze down near the waterfall had turned into a gale, whipping his tail to one side and biting its way through his fur. Bad things were happening far above him: snow and freezing rain, falling so fast the runoff had no time to soak in. The sky was menacingly dark, with the first traces of flurries making frantic circles around the rocks.

Ario steeled himself and raised his head. There were precious few spaces between boulders through which he could squeeze even his lithe body, so he would have to crawl to the base of the cliff. The cliff itself, foreboding in the gray light of the dying day, was covered in lichens and would be slippery unless he could find pawholds. The wolf's head felt light, his muscles oddly liquid and warm. His mind seemed on edge, honed to a point, but there was also a thin sheet of opacity, the kind that clouded his judgment just slightly. But he couldn't stay here.

Thoughts of the past occupied him as he climbed from the scattered boulders to bumpy outcroppings to the nearly-vertical slab of rock. He thought of N'hela, the young sweet beauty that had first attracted him on such a primal level as it started to snow and flakes flew into his eyes. Of his child, not yet named or brought into the world, who would undoubtedly be kicking N'hela's belly by now, when his footpaw slipped on a patch of moss and he yelled out. Of his mother, that great faceless matron whose strength somehow kept him going when the world started to spin.

It hit him without warning: a great swirling in his stomach that turned to a heat radiating out through his veins, numbing them. His head pounded; the wind roared in his sensitive ears. The sky was dark but a brightness formed in front of his eyes, a kaleidoscopic rotation of prismatic colors.

"Ohhh..." moaned the trapped lupine. "Those damned berries. Why didn't I wait?" Even as he cursed his overzealous appetite he knew the energy, tainted or not, was needed to get up this cliff. Ario elected to look at the wall in front of him and go one step at a time; looking anywhere else would surely get him killed. Cold and wind pinned him close. He was beginning to lose feeling.

The visions of his family and what had conspired to bring him to this precipice grew more colorful and intense with each passing moment. He was in a field, yellow with ready-to-harvest wheat, rolling, happily tied to his love in the throes of passion as it should be, not a mating but two beings enjoying their bodies. He watched his son (he was hoping for a male, at least) growing up too fast before his eyes, passing into adulthood and hunting on his own, strong with his father's courage and tenacity. His heart swelled with pride, despite his numb body. But then...

The vision changed. Colors became darker and dire, and all he could see was the tribal council circled around a funeral pyre, flames orange and smelling of death and charred fur. Somehow the wolf knew what it was, and he did not wish to see it, but his legs carried him unwillingly closer. He shut his eyes but he could still see.

"No... why are you showing me this?" he screamed above the wind, claws dug in so tight his fingers and toes bled without pain. "What do you want from me?" There was no answer, just more whistling in his ears and the clearing image of two corpses engulfed in flames. The smell hit his snout and Ario almost retched. He knew burning flesh well. And he was looking at his wife and child, now just masses of black tissue peeling away from bone. Tears flowed and froze on his muzzle, in his whiskers.

"What do you want from me?!" he pleaded to Mother Nature, to the Great Spirits, to any god or demon who would listen. His voice rose, cracked and fell in a failed howl of desperation. The dagger came to his mind then; strapped right to his waist, it would yield a deep wound that could kill him long before he hit the jagged rocks far below. Just one good swipe across the throat...

"No! Ungh... Not for you... Not for anyone... But me," Ario whispered. And then his right paw left its hold and lunged upward, searched blindly, found another place to hoist him up. His legs, heavy as if turned to stone, followed and pushed, shaking hard. There was nothing in his vision now but a mass of colors... At least he thought they were colors. There could be no sane explanation for what his brain was telling him to see at that moment.

Time passed agonizingly slowly; the lupine did not count his steps for fear that he would give up after a certain point. When his left paw reached up, ragged and raw, and found nothing but a clump of grass on a flat surface, a deep exhalation left him and he stopped. A great brightness stabbed at Ario's closed eyelids, and finally he gathered enough courage to open them.

The sky still boiled blackly with cold fury, still pounded his body against the cliff-side, but there was a streak of light seeming to form right in the middle of the maelstrom. It parted the clouds and Ario found himself preparing to be taken up to the Great Spirits after all. Oddly, he didn't feel regret for failing his family, but what he saw next brought him back to reality. One last push tumbled him limply onto the dry grasses on the ledge, and while he lay on his back, wheezing and stiff, his mother came to visit.

How he knew the wolfess in the sky was his mother he could not discern, but Ario could smell, hear and taste her somehow. Perhaps the few moments after his birth he had memorized all of these, but most of all he just knew. The lupine reached out one dirty paw to her, and nearly bawled like a cub when she smiled dotingly down at him. Suddenly he was very, very warm.

"My son," came a voice so smooth and creamy it could never have been terrestrial. "I am very proud of you. I will let you know that the hardest physical challenge of your journey is complete."

"Mother... Mother, it's you? How do you know me like this? Is this a vision?" There were so many things he wanted to say, so many unanswered questions to ask, but he could manage little more than these.

The regal female laughed gently. "Yes, I suppose this is a vision. But do not be troubled by these things, child. There is one, more difficult, task you must complete before you can become an adult male. It has not to do with physicality, but mentality and pride. You must set aside your own self-thought to save your family. I tell you this now so you are prepared when you are faced with the decision."

Ario was a bit dismayed, but seeing his mother overrode any feelings of disappointment. Right now, he would do anything she said. "What? What is it I must do to finish this wretched quest?

Please, just tell me and I will obey you!"

"I am sorry, Ario. It is not me you will have to obey, but one other. The opposite and the same, child. You will know when the time has come. I am sorry, my time is short here and I must go now." She turned her head, almost too slowly to be real, and started to fade, and Ario thought he heard the words 'such a beautiful boy' barely audible above everything else.

The wolf reached out as far as he could to the sky. "Mother! No, wait! I must understand! I must—"

As quickly as the wolfess disappeared, another figure took her place. Its form was nothing more than a blur, but a pair of intense dark brown eyes stared at him from the shadows. It approached, dropping like the prairie-funnels that could destroy an entire pack in the Planting Season. It snorted, a definitively cervine noise, and covered his body. Immense heat wrapped around him, melted the snow from the ledge, and there was pressure between his legs. His tailhole was caressed by a feather-light something; his sheath squeezed and stroked. Something snuck inside him and drew him out, already fully engorged. Sensitivity seemed to drain from the rest of him and directly to his member. The air swirled around his cock, rapidly bringing him to a climax so hard the backs of his eyes hurt. As he emptied himself to the ghostly apparition and screamed, high and airy, a foreign muzzle clamped down on his; a tongue explored his throat, making him choke. As the invisible lover snorted again, Ario inhaled the strong scent of male...

He opened his eyes and nothing was there, except for a calm, clear night and his own exhausted, trembling body. The wolf's tortured brain finally gave out and he welcomed the embrace of unconsciousness.

Dawn broke coldly and drearily. A thick ground fog clung to the ledge, and when Ario finally woke he believed he had actually died after all. He looked up into grayness, waved an invisible paw in front of his muzzle and clipped his snout for his trouble. Groaning, the lupine turned over onto all fours, stretching each limb in turn before standing. He had slept deeply, but his mind again raced with images from the previous night.

Night? he thought. Was it night, or was I just dreaming that? Did I dream the whole thing? There was only one way to find out: he looked down. Sure enough, he was nude, except this time (the thought struck him as both silly and relieving) his penis was safely flaccid and hidden away. He patted it reassuringly, making a mental note to relieve some tension later on. But as he touched himself, he felt the crusted fur around the opening and followed the trail up to his navel. Similar drops were on his shoulder, neck and right ear. So he had come last night... Or whenever. But how, and who had done it? Already the memories were vague.

The Great Circle had begun to break through the fog, and Ario judged the time to be later than he had thought when he first woke up. A few moments of crawling yielded his loincloth, with the dagger still attached. He donned the cloth and fastened it just as shadows burst forth, made by the surrounding trees. The mist lifted from the clearing, which was somehow devoid of snow, and something hit his nose... hard. The wolf sneezed three times in rapid succession, breathing in the strange scent. It was so strong, in fact, that he couldn't tell what it was until most of it had evaporated with the fog.

It was deer. This was the spot where he had seen his quarry yesterday; it fairly reeked of fur, urine, droppings... and semen? Was that the unfamiliar woody odor underneath everything else? Maybe it was his own seed, but either way it didn't matter. It was evident the buck had made this his bed for the night not too long ago and moved on before Ario finished his climb.

The wolf could now see the valley before him, waterfall and berry patch included. The berries could have caused his odd vision, but maybe some of that was all in his head. Either way, he had the buck's scent, and it was only a matter of time before they would meet muzzle-to-muzzle, predator-to-prey, and Ario would claim his prize and go home... finally.

His stomach, now empty, told him he should move on and find something to eat. Ario thought he should also find a stream in which to wash his bloody paws. After one last stretch and another bout of sneezing, the lupine set out, his nose keeping the trail.

Helpless claustrophobia wrenched the poor wolf's gut as his body fought between the pleasure from Dande's touch and the disgust at being fondled by another male. He kicked out fast, but the footpaw was caught and twisted at an unnatural angle. Every other wound on Ario's body seemed to ache along with the sprain.

The buck removed his touch and scooted a few feet away, the superior smirk on his face replaced with a lustful grin. It was that same grin the wolf had seen when he was first immobilized. Now those eyes roved up and down and across his bound form, heaving chest, and half-hard wolfhood. Dande went to his own groin as he appraised his captive, rolling the cervine cock around until it was noticeably visible underneath the leather shorts he wore. Then they met the wolf's, and it all came back to him: the shadow-figure swooping down and ripping an orgasm from his body, the heady scent of its breath... The scent which, he now knew, had dominated the grassy ledge.

"The opposite and the same," he mumbled. "The opposite and the same. Oh, great Gods no..." His voice trembled with the realization of what he must do to return to his pack victorious. It wasn't about physical exertion, it was about mental strength. He didn't know if he could do it. Just the thought...

"You seem to be ill, puppy. Why is that? You looked as if you liked what I was doing just then," Dande said innocently. "Didn't you?"

Tears of frustration, anger and fearful resentment left Ario's eyes, flowed down the sides of his head to pool in his ears. He was blushing, grateful his winter coat hid the redness. "You... can't do this to me," he growled. "It's unnatural."

"The only unnatural things," said the buck matter-of-factly, "Are those which cannot be done. And I'm pretty sure that what I have planned for you is very doable." He sat cross-legged, haughty and sure of himself. He had the lupine by the balls, literally and figuratively.

Wishing he could at least get up to look more directly at the deer, Ario asked, "Don't you have a family of your own? What do you find wrong with females?"

"The thought of mating with a female disgusts me. But I don't expect you to understand. I am simply just not like you in some ways... Ill-adapted to mating and raising children. In fact, I've probably done more to help Mother Nature than to hinder Her. No young to raise and forage for, no extra mouths to feed."

"I thought your family were killed by wolves."

"You didn't listen," Dande insisted. "My sister and niece were killed. I have no 'family,' as you call it."

"How can you be attracted to other males?"

"How can you be attracted to females?"

There was no quick and easy response to Dande. Any answer Ario thought of could be true and undeniable for both parties. Still, he would never give his consent...

"Am I supposed to feel sorry for you?"

The deer scoffed, stifling a small laugh. "I expect pity from no one; I live for myself and only for myself. No, you shouldn't feel sorry for me. Not that it would help any. Your lack of cooperation will be painfully reciprocated." At the look of abject shock on the wolf's face, Dande continued. "Speaking of which—" the wolf's crotch was cupped again, his sheath slid up and down delicately "-if you value your life, and those of your family, you'll sit there like a nice obedient wuff and do as you're told."

Ario snarled as menacingly as he could, but his penis continued to get harder.

"Oh wait... You don't have much of a choice now, do you?" The cervine squeezed Ario's balls together tightly, eliciting a yelp that made him smile. "Good boy. Now let's get you situated."

Ario couldn't believe what was happening. He was rolled over, wincing at the pain of his open wounds, until he sat on all fours. Dande pulled him through the snow to a tree stump about two feet high, still tied.

"Hold still or your balls are mush," he heard the buck sneer from behind him. The wolf wanted to curse Dande, to turn around and smash his face in somehow. He could kick him in the groin, he could turn and bite... But despite his brain's refusal to let him be raped, he knew there was no choice, not if he wanted N'hela and his cub to live. And struggling futilely would only injure him further, possibly rendering him incapable of returning home. He could not suppress a rather loud whimper of defeat.

Dande stroked the lupine's back from neck to tail slowly, placating the visibly terrified creature. "Good boy," he said condescendingly. "It won't hurt too much. Who knows? You may even like being mated by another male. Maybe it's something you've been wondering your entire life." It seemed the buck was reveling in his superiority over the carnivore.

In a flash the wolf strained against his bonds and the stump, clipping Dande's thigh with his claws and snarling ferally. He was beyond words.

Dande looked down to see a deep cut beginning to bleed to his knee, staining the snow an odd pink color. "Okay, then," he snapped right back. "You just lost your chance for pity, puppy." He took the wolf's arms and stretched them forward over the opposite end of the stump so escape was impossible. Ario's knees butted right against the roots and did a good job of spreading his legs automatically. Of course, a tail was tucked securely between them in a useless attempt at chastity.

"Raise it." The words, cold as frost, in his ear. Ario refused to be exposed, resolutely keeping himself covered each time his tail was pulled. "Raise. It." The tip of the serrated blade was on his throat, pricking just into the surface but not far from his jugular vein. He finally released, and grimaced in shame as his tailhole was exposed to the air. The dagger was removed, shortly followed by two soft snaps as his loincloth slipped away. The wolf could feel his semi-hard sheath swaying below his belly with his ragged, panicked breaths.

"Thank you," said the deer, stroking his sides in a soothing manner that didn't soothe Ario at all. He stared straight ahead; just a few feet away was the edge of the clearing, and he spotted a few birds and small mammals watching the morbidly erotic show with dumb interest. The lupine thought he heard derisive laughter.

There were rustling sounds from behind him: Dande's loin-cloth being removed, the cervine's increasingly deep breathing, the soft swish-swish of flesh on flesh. Then hands were on his sheath again, appraising, patiently and progressively moving the fur back from the member underneath as it filled with blood. Ario knew the touch well, knew it was pleasure, but could not under-stand how he was being aroused by another male. When his knot slid through into the open, steaming and purple, Ario felt aroused in mind as well as body. Suddenly there was an end to be met, an inevitable end, and the only person around was Dande, who was preparing to mount him like a weak bitch in heat. Confusion reigned within him.

"My my, puppy," said the buck, smiling at the wolf's reaction to the usage of the word. "I'd say you very much like the attention I am paying to you. You look like you need something. Can you tell me what it is?"

"What?" stammered the wolf, unbelieving. "I... I don't need anything, you monster."

"Oh? Then the little wolfcub will have to do without, won't he? It feels a lot better if you paw at yourself when being taken. Takes the edge off the pain. I guess you don't need my help then..."

"No!" A desperate cry.

"Then what, puppy?"

"I don't know, I d-don't know, please just do it and get it over with, please..."

"Do what?" asked Dande, slipping a slender fingertip into Ario's tight, twitching passage. The lupine screamed unintelligibly, suck-ing in muzzlefuls of air.

Ario blabbered, trying to make words amid the sharp pain un-der his tail. "Touch me just stroke me do anything I don't care just do whatever you want just make the pain go away!" He strug-gled forward as far as he could, but the finger only followed. He jerked as his cock was enclosed and squeezed; a copious string of precum shot onto the ground. The wolf sighed; Dande had been right. There was almost no pain when his cock was being stroked. In fact, the pleasure almost seemed to increase. Nevertheless, when he thought again of what was to come, his stomach turned circles.

Dande spoke low now, in even tones, mumbling baby-words of encouragement. The wolf felt the buck settle onto his knees, inside his straddled thighs, and the finger twirled a bit inside him, making him squirm. All the while he was fondled and touched; part of him was glad for the distraction, another part called him a traitor for giving in. The finger was removed, but was shortly replaced by something else, something with a more sinister agenda. It poked restlessly at him, forcing his tail to try and move but he found no success.

"You had better relax, my friend. I only tell you this for your own good. I take no pity on stupid little puppies like you who can't even obey simple orders." The buck's thin head prodded at his entrance, each time going just a little deeper before meeting Ario's resistance. He intended to put up as much of a fight as possible.

"How dare you call me a fr-aaugh!" His words were interrupted as his tailhole relaxed and all the pressure from Dande's pushing abruptly shoved half his length into the wolf. There was a painful stretching, as if a fire-hot stick were being inserted into his rear, followed by an intense burning as the deercock passed his inner ring and slid, without lubrication. The buck leaned forward and over his back, grasping the fur below his ribs and clenching it as his pleasurable moan overrode the lupine's scream. Ario's muzzle remained open, mouthing silent words and wheezing, then before he even knew what was happening his body convulsed and there was more pain and burning as his stomach rejected its meager contents. Dande smiled, watching the lupine retch until he lay dry-heaving on the stump, trying to avoid his own fluids.

The wolf felt completely open now, and violated. The pain and heat were unbearable, true, but even worse was the shameful helplessness of his position: unable to move or retaliate, nothing was left but to count the minutes until he was marked forever with Dande's seed. The odor of vomit was right in his face, but at least his stomach had finally stopped cramping. Unable to clench his tailhole any longer, he relaxed and felt the buck inch forward until testicles nestled on top of testicles. He was vaguely aware of his cocktip rubbing against the bark of the stump.

Already sweat dripped from Dande's armpits and head onto Ario's back, steam rising from them both. "I bet that was quite painful," said the cervine huskily. "To incite such a reaction takes a lot of nervousness, intolerance to pain, and fear. Mostly fear, but I think it was a combination of all three. Don't you, puppy?"

"Yes," came the whispered, ragged reply. Dande reached around and fondled his cock for a few moments and, to the wolf's disdain, the pain was almost gone again. How could his own body, weak though it may be, give in so easily? His back already ached from the buck's weight.

Dande flexed some muscle, flaring his member and putting more pressure on Ario's already torn hole. The wolf gritted his teeth, trying in vain to suppress his pathetic whimpering. His entire lower torso was aflame with feelings coursing from cock to anus in a mixture of ecstatic shocks and dull, heavy throbs. He was sure he had never been as erect as he was now, and all he wanted was the sweet release of climax, but Dande knew how helpless he was and would not satisfy the urges. Instead he withdrew slowly, making the lupine cringe and think he was about to void his bowels, then reentered. This time, however, the only thing Ario felt was a smooth and tactile bolt of pleasure somehow connecting those two very different places on his body. Another long, thin shot of pre fell into the snow.

"I knew you would grow to like it very quickly," said Dande, apparently able to read the lupine's body with no trouble. "You see," he continued, making a second, slightly faster thrust, "there is a point within all us males, some place that sets the senses afire when touched. The only way to reach this place is by giving yourself to the whims of the same sex. Now aren't you glad to be taken by such a special creature as myself?"

There was no answer, save for a few puffs of steam.

"Aren't you glad," repeated the cervine, burying his hips into straining, lupine buttocks and circling Ario's knot with two fingers, "that you were spared the pain and torture of rape by having someone as patient as me show you the ropes? You should be grateful, you little whelp, that I haven't killed you yet."

"Yes..."

"What you are experiencing now, puppy, is the broad extent of my mercy. You can go back to your pack, like I promised, but you will bear the scars of my vengeance. You will be a walking, talking reminder not to toy with the laws of the cycles of life. You will have your life"—thrust—"You will have your family"—thrust—"But not without certain sacrifices." Dande lengthened this last word as he drew his circled fingers to the tip of Ario's cock, so oversensitized from the beating on his prostate (he would never know it as more than 'that special place') that he nearly drove himself into the rough bark of the stump. Noises, unmistakable feral desire, crept eagerly from his throat.

Ario forced his eyes open to a bright world of severe colors. Creatures small and large looked on dumbly from the depths of the forest at the fervent mating taking place. Everything had taken on a tint the color of dried blood, of the Harvest Season twilight; the lupine's tailhole was no longer a violated orifice as much as a source of great polarizing, conflicting feelings. The wolf's member swelled with anticipation of an involuntary climax, and the means to gaining that climax faded from import.

Dande plunged himself deeper into the now-docile lupine below, shifting forward to cover Ario's back and show him the true meaning of being mated. The wolf knew this was not just about sex; it was about revenge for the buck's sister and niece, for all the opportunists in the world who preyed on the truly innocent. Anger drove him onward, unmindful of the wolf he was tearing open.

"Aaghh, stop it!" came the desperate cry from a muzzle gritted shut. Ario's loins were beginning to boil too quickly for his system to keep up. Those fingers squeezing behind his knot were relentless, somehow bypassing the normal plateaus of masturbation and instead allowing a near-constant stream of fluid to drip out of him. As Dande's thrusts increased and he found a better angle, the special place deep inside him was pounded repeatedly, pushing him to a height of sensual awareness that had somehow not overloaded him yet. Pain and pride forgotten, the bound wolf actually found himself moving backwards to deepen his penetration... Anything to get him closer to release.

"Oh no, puppy," breathed the buck into one ear as Dande went faster, feeling the wolf's broken body respond with sudden and amazing vigor. Ario tried to hunch forward onto his fingers more, but they would not budge and the lupine settled for as much travel over his flesh as the cervine would allow. The wolf would pop much sooner than he had thought, but that only meant he would have to sit and wait until the cervine finished himself. It would not take long, in any case.

Something very odd was happening to Ario. His loins bathed in a building orgasmic inferno, his wolfhood started to pulse without the accompanying peak of climax. Hips thrusting against Dande's fingers, trying for any friction at all, he felt trapped just short of some final destination, as if he were being kept inches away from his goal. He bore down lewdly onto the buck's cock, going for that one special place again, that one final push that would end it all.

A few humps later he found that push, quite surprisingly, and dug his claws into the ground to keep the world from falling away. Without moving or touching his cock at all, climax crashed through his already weak body, canceling out the pain from his shoulder, ribs, muzzle and paws. The lupine lifted his head and tried to howl, but what ended up emerging from him was a choked, savage, grating noise of a creature given up to outside control. Dande continued to work himself inside the wolf, pounding through his clenching hole and helping to send uncountable ropes of thick white seed into the already melted snow beneath Ario's belly. It seemed as if he would never stop coming.

But he did, and the taken wolf's mind cleared abruptly, as did his afterglow. Reality came crashing down; he was spent, weak, and the pleasure coming from his abused rear end was rapidly turning to burning pain again. Ario suddenly wished he hadn't shot off so easily.

"Now what are you going to do?" said the buck evilly between pants.

"Gods... It hurts! Now can't you stop?" These were weak questions, of course, not even deserving of an answer, and Dande didn't bother to.

"You can't... possibly expect me... to stop now, when I haven't... claimed my prize," Dande huffed, speeding up slightly and causing Ario to try and pull away, strings of cum still dangling from his cockhead. Somehow the buck had pressed even deeper now, beyond that pleasure center and was hitting a bend, sending shivers of pain rifling up his back. His yelps of helpless restraint went unheeded. The forest was conveniently blind and deaf.

Dande stopped just long enough to get to his feet, holding himself inside of Ario so as not to give him the impression he was getting off easily. Bent at the knees, he resumed mating the lupine in long, agonizing movements that gained an uninterrupted groan from below. He gripped Ario's shoulders and lowered himself onto his back, perspiration matting their combined fur. This position was much easier and gave the buck more pleasure and an easier path to the finish.

"Won't be long now, puppy," he grinned into one laid-back ear, "until you become mine." Ario tried to form a reply but only succeeded in gasping aborted curses in his ancestors' tongue. The buck's regulated thrusts became steadily ragged and marked with sudden jerks and airy breaths. "You really should have held off." With that, he started to nibble on the lupine's right ear erotically, making Ario wince and try to shake him off, which only resulted in a blinding pain in his head.

Ario's cock ached, as did his throbbing wounds. No longer did he try to resist, or even try to cancel out, the burning in his rectum. Now, he just waited, emotionless tears flowing down the sides of his muzzle and pooling on the age-rings of the stump. He knew it would all be over soon, and then he could claim his prize and go home to his family, but it did little to ease the pain of humiliation.

The nibbling on the lupine's ear increased, and Dande's thrusts became longer and more delayed. Every inch going in and out of him seemed to scrape like a dry piece of kindling now that Ario had lost all sexual interest in the matter. His tail hurt from being pinned to his back for so long (how long? he thought, but couldn't tell in his position).

Suddenly the buck grunted loudly, irreverently, in the clearing, and a flock of birds took flight from the barren trees. His hips moved like lightning, fingers clenching furrows in the lupine's shoulders, and Ario screamed in agony as he felt Dande's teeth meet through his ear, and the flow of blood down his head. Then a great sigh of relief escaped them both as Dande powered through his long-sought after climax and flooded the wolf's tailhole with spunk. Through the searing pain of his ear, Ario noticed the deer-cock floating away from his passage and the almost cooling effect the seed had on his now-throttled tailhole. A wave of total shame descended on his mind, and he just waited until his marking was completed.

After a short eternity, the cervine finally pulled out with a dull pop and a flood of white and red from Ario's loosened bowels. The wolf heard crackling snow and then Dande appeared in front of his prostrated form. He somehow mustered the strength to raise his throbbing head just in time to see the buck spit something into the snow. He realized with diluted horror that he was looking at the top half of his right ear.

"Oh... Oh great Heavens that was good," Dande commented after clearing his mouth. "Had you been taken willingly you would have made a great lover." He idly scratched his drained testicles. "Oh well, sometimes it's better when they fight," he said as casually as if he were merely discussing the weather. Bending to retrieve his dagger, he quickly undid the ropes binding the defeated wolf's paws. However, Ario did not move. His body was simply too weak. He looked at the chunk of ear on the ground, the ragged bottom edge already crusted over.

"You bastard," he managed in a gravelly whisper.

"Me?" Dande chuckled. "You owe me your life. You should be praising me right now."

"For what? For forcing me to be your lover? Raping me for revenge? I might as well be dead, you merciless devil."

"Devil indeed. I believe we've already had this discussion." The buck took Ario by the scruff and rolled him roughly onto his back. "And we agreed to respect our respective opinions and call it a truce. You wanted a convincing show for your pack, and you got it. I wouldn't be surprised if they elected you to the council, or whatever it is you have." He looked down at the wolf, whose eyes were bloodshot and barely open.

"Speaking of convincing, I have my end of the bargain to fulfill." Dande knelt next to Ario and began to inhale and exhale deeply. The lupine could only watch as the buck sank into some sort of trance, quiet punctuated by sharp intakes of air. After hyperventilating and filling his lungs to capacity, he held his breath and brought the dagger around his body and to his forehead. Closing his eyes, he dragged the black blade across and into the skin, parting it deeply. There was a momentary glimpse of inner tissue before blood rushed to the surface and down into the buck's eyes.

"Get up," Dande said, bending his head and letting the first drops stain the snow. When Ario didn't obey, the deer uttered a curse under his breath and moved over the wolf's body, taking his useless paws and running them over the wound. They were soaked almost immediately, and Dande rubbed them over his body wherever they would go, paying special attention to his muzzle and neck. When he was satisfied with the coverage, he let go and wrapped his shorts around his head to stem the bleeding.

Ario stared after him in awestruck wonder. He wished he could just take pain like that. Then again, a voice inside mused, you've probably taken more abuse than a whole pack of wolves could stand. He smiled inwardly at that. Maybe. With groaning, shaking difficulty he rose to his footpaws and gathered what was left of himself: a penetrated, broken, bloody mess.

"I suppose I should thank you," the wolf said cynically.

"No need. There are no thanks in order here." Dande was already headed out of the clearing, opposite the path Ario would take to get home. "We are pretty even. But I will tell you this: take care of yourself, and your family. You have earned my respect, a difficult task in itself. Be humble."

Ario just nodded, silently.

The buck nodded back once, snorted into the cooling air, and was gone over the edge of the clearing. Faint crunches died away to nothing, and Ario found himself feeling like no time had passed at all since he had jumped Dande for the first time. The failing light told a different story.

The lupine tied his loincloth in a rudimentary knot around his waist, checked for his own dagger and limped crookedly out of the clearing. Night would fall soon, and he was glad, because he doubted there would be much time before both his mind and body gave out completely. He figured that if he could survive what he had just been through, sleeping where he fell would be a mere trifle.

Ario traveled much farther than he would have thought, walking until long after darkness overtook the forest. His night vision was still as good as ever, and he moved relatively pain-free, most likely due to the excess adrenaline in his system. When that was gone, however, he gave in willingly and sprawled under a rocky overhang to sleep.

And sleep he did, for over a day. When he finally came to, he could hardly move. He swore he could still feel a slick substance in his tailhole. The pain was mostly gone though, and his experience with Dande had already begun to fade as a distant memory. He was grateful for that.

His spirits lifted, the wolf made quick work of the journey home. It was much easier to track his own scent back the way he had come, and he even found a shortcut around the sheer cliff he climbed before. He stopped at the bottom to drink his fill at the waterfall, but he cautiously avoided the berries; there were plenty of things he could find elsewhere. His wounds were sore and coagulated, but he dared not wash himself for fear of losing Dande's evidence slathered all over his upper body.

One day, roughly half a week after he'd started back, Ario was crossing a long, sloping barren hillside when he realized his mind was wandering. It seemed like it had taken forever to cross a short distance, but he was not fatigued. The lupine sat down to think and rest his legs, and suddenly he found that his mind was unusually clear. It was as clear, he thought, as it had been before he had taken N'hela and impregnated her. It was the clear mind of someone whose life is on track, with direction and purpose. And for the first time in countless weeks, he was happy and unburdened.

Inevitably his thoughts turned to Dande, and what the buck had accomplished despite raping him. Had it all been pure reaction? He was dedicated to his mate, of course, but he couldn't help but wonder if there were members of his own pack with affinities like the buck's.

It scared him to ponder such deep questions, and he feared he knew the answers to them. He could not talk to anyone about this, especially his elders. No one would be able to understand, and of course his faux pas would be unveiled. Ario wished he could have stayed just a little longer to discuss things with the buck, but he had been too worn out and afraid. Still, when he came out of his reverie he was welcomed with three inches of pink cock staring needfully up at him.

"Just for a little while," he said aloud to no one in particular, and stretched out on the dead grasses, careful of his still-fresh wounds. It felt so good to have his cock in his own paw again; the familiar feelings calmed him. Pulling his sheath the rest of the way down, he began a slow stroking and found that he wouldn't need much time. Eventually his eyes closed and he was left to his imagination. He envisioned N'hela, legs spread and waiting for him. In his fantasy he covered her with ease, sliding through her tight labia and making her moan, smiling, with each slow thrust.

This was a typical fantasy for Ario, but he let his mind wander a bit. He pounded into her with regularity, each time forcing more of his knot through into her depths. This time, however, he felt a pressure on his tailhole as he moved, and he looked up to see his wife's grinning muzzle just before she shoved a claw-tipped finger up and into him. The wolf tensed and pushed hard, tying N'hela with enough force to make her scream. She crooked the finger and hit that special spot dead-on, and Ario literally felt the seed forced from his testicles and out into her.

The vision dissolved as the lupine felt warm splatters on his face. He opened his eyes to watch his member spurt and cover his chest with yet another layer of fluid, adding to what already sullied his winter fur. Licking cum from his muzzle as the last bits ran over his paw, he moved his left arm and was surprised to feel a finger slipping from his hole that he never realized had been inserted. He sniffed it out of curiosity, and found the mingled scent of wolf and buck pungent but interesting. Ario sat under the passing clouds for a long time, watching himself resheathe and just thinking.

It was only a few days later, when crossing the last low mountains before descending to his pack's camping grounds, that a sudden snowstorm took him by surprise. A cruel leeward downdraft drove at his back, threatening to push him that extra bit to make him lose his footing and fall to even more injuries. It was not nearly as bad as his climb up the cliff, but by the time dawn broke through the driving white his body was mostly numb. He couldn't remember the last time he had eaten.

Unbelievably, through the whipping wind and snow Ario could still track his own, weeks-old scent. Humming to himself to maintain his wits, he kept his nostrils flared and tried to crawl as low to the ground as possible.

It was like a wall of granite.

The odor hit him as a solid mass of assorted scents; numerous colors and shadows erupted in his mind, forming into familiar faces. The wolf tilted his nose up, inhaling deeply. Even more scents, some new ones he couldn't recognize, but after some concentration he found what he was looking for: a semi-sweet flowery smell, combined with birchbark and traces of clean, crisp water.

"N'hela..." Sweet heavens, she was still alive! The reaction from his brain and body told him all he needed to know. Ario strained hard to find the scent of a pup among the others, but his search was fruitless. Even though the cub had weeks yet to be born when he left, there was a small hope that he would be able to find some recognizable trace. Ario picked up the pace, now on a clear and direct course home.

Darkness fell, and the wolf was forced to bed down when he kept stumbling over roots and rocky ground. He slept little and lightly, waking numerous times. When morning had just started to give depth to the failing night, he continued on, noting that the snow had decreased to the point where he could see a few feet in front of him. His pace quickened.

As Ario moved, more scents came to his nose: the heady scent of a recent kill, probably two or three days old, sharp wood smoke and fire, medicines and salves commonly used to treat Cold Season illnesses. The snow had softened into mere flurries when he came down through the trees of a hillside and entered open ground, almost on top of a shelter-hut.

The sight of it, familiar and alien at the same time, was a welcome one. He was finally home, although that thought had not sunk in yet. The lupine, beaten and cold and limping, made his way through the maze of huts, noting that there were more than when he had left. Still early in the morning, the camp was barren of life; sounds of rustling and snoring emitted from closed flaps of leather.

Ario smelled meat. His mouth, devoid of saliva for lack of water, started to drool uncontrollably, dripping onto his footpaws as he came into view of the central campfire and its lone attendant. The dark brown wolf was roasting a rabbit on a spit, turning it this way and that, poking with a claw every now and again to test for doneness. He started when he caught Ario out of the corner of his vision.

The two stared at one another for a moment, then the other wolf's lips lifted up in a snarl of warning. Ario held out his paw in greeting, his face weary and soft.

"Belrahi," he said, startling the lupine at the recognizance of his name. "Ne kones pa amitri, Belrahi?" The darker wolf crept forward warily at the use of the ancient tongue, sniffed at the proffered paw, recoiled but did not attack. He knew.

"Ario? Is that you... really you?" Ario nodded. "They told us you were dead long ago."

"They didn't bother to ask me. Now, Belrahi..."

"Yes?"

"Could you spare some of that delicious-looking meat? I haven't had a thing to eat in days."

Belrahi backed away from the spit, almost in disgust for looking so selfish. "Please, please! Eat your fill! I'm going to wake everyone up and tell them that Ario's back from the dead!" Ario thought about stopping him, but figured he could use a little attention after all he'd been through. He ripped into the rabbit with abandon, literally wolfing it down. His stomach quickly rejected the first two bites, after which Ario slowed down to give his body time to adjust to solid food again.

He was so busy eating, in fact, that he didn't notice the gathering crowd until there were nearly fifteen wolves surrounding him, some with menacing half-snarls on their muzzles at the filthy newcomer. Belrahi tried to explain who he was, but they all would have to see it for themselves. Ario stood in the center of them, still a bit shaky but better then he had felt for a long time. He turned and found who he was looking for.

The chief stood a good four inches taller than Ario, his traditionally-patterned fur lightened with his old age. He regarded the skeletal wolf with little more than disdain, and when utterances of "Kill him!" and "Sacrifice the foreigner!" circulated throughout the crowd he put up his paws to silence them. His deep blue eyes narrowed, studying...

"Your paw. Give it to me." Ario raised his right paw and it was taken by the chief. All at once he felt like the same old, immature Ario who couldn't keep his cock sheathed around a female. On the other paw, he sure felt older than his years at the moment. The larger wolf examined it, sniffed it, his nose wrinkled in repugnance.

"Down," came the command, and the younger lupine dropped to all fours in a presentation stance like he had seen other males-in-training do. The chief did the same, walking around him and appraising every inch of his soiled body. Paws roamed over his half-ear and bent muzzle; traced along his sore ribs and the still-swelled gash in his shoulder. A cold nose sniffed under his raised tail carefully and at length, and even his sheath was inspected. At last the chief stood up and instructed Ario to do the same. When they were eye-to-eye, the larger wolf put a paw on his shoulder. Everyone around them went silent. Ario thought he saw the beginnings of a smile twitch his leader's muzzle.

"I believe you have a visitor," he said, glancing to the left. The wolf's head turned and for a moment his brain could not process what he was seeing. Pushing the crowd aside gently, N'hela stepped dreamily into the inner circle, rubbing sleep from her eyes. Ario let go an emotion-choked bark and she came to attention, staring down at him in shocked recognition.

"You came back." The words were unbelieving, faltering. Ario stood up, his broad smile turning quickly to a groveling rictus. He took two steps toward her and fell to the ground, screeching in incoherent sobs loud enough to wake the rest of the camp. N'hela came to him. His love... The wolfess who, despite the opinions of everyone around her, had refused others' advances and appeals for marriage and who had raised her son alone and waited every day for Ario's safe return, held him and petted him as he wept like a newborn in her arms.

Today was supposed to have been a day of rest for the pack, but the return of Ario after nearly two full cycles of the Silver God made for a special occasion. First, though, Ario's body was tended by three thorough females who took him to a nearby stream and spent much of the morning washing the collective fluids from his fur and treating his wounds, none of which were infected, miraculously. After shaking himself and lying on a rock to dry, the wolf felt light as a feather. It helped that he only weighed ninety pounds anyway.

Ario was led to N'hela's hut, where he beheld his young son for the first time, now covered in a fine coat of fur with bright, intelligent eyes and an ornery spirit that made him laugh as he held the squirming cub. After a short talk, N'hela suggested that they perform the marriage ceremony that night, with the permission of the pack council, now that he was an adult. The quicker that happened, the quicker they could settle into a proper life among the pack as a family. Ario agreed enthusiastically and went to the chief to ask his blessing.

The wolf never asked why there had been no rite of adulthood ceremony performed for him; there seemed to be an all-around consensus that none was needed. The tasks he had completed far outweighed any menial competition cubs went through to get their ceremonies. It wasn't celebrity Ario sought, or to be any kind of hero. He just wanted his family back.

"Welcome, my boy," waved the chief in a tone completely different from the one he had heard send him away to almost-certain death so long ago. "What is it you require of me?"

"I came to ask you, sir, if you will give your blessing for my marriage to N'hela, and if we could have the ceremony this evening."

The chief looked flustered. "Well, I see no problem in giving my blessing, but it's much too short notice for the ceremony to be tonight. Decorations will have to be arranged, garments made and pigments mixed. And those are just a few—"

Ario silenced him with a paw. "We won't need any of these things. We just want a small ceremony to make it official. It's been long enough in coming already."

"But, it's tradition..."

"I know, but won't you make an exception? N'hela wants the same, and I am sure her father will be pleased to know I followed through on my promise to him."

The large, foreboding wolf pondered heavily on his ground-blanket for a minute, then nodded. "Granted. Gather yourself a party and we will have the ceremony with our evening meal, by the light of the fire."

Smiling and looking every bit the groom-to-be, Ario thanked him and turned to leave.

"Just one more thing, ch—I mean, Ario."

The wolf turned back. "Yes, my leader?"

"How did you do it?"

"Do what?"

"How did you manage to down a full-grown buck on your own? When I inspected you I smelled traces of... Seed. What did you do with this buck?"

Ario began to sweat underneath his fur, but the chief could not see the moisture on his skin. "He was a fighter. Tracked him for days, until I was nearly starved. He pulled a dagger on me, kicked me around with those hooves of his. I eventually had to chase him until he tripped and broke a leg. After that, it was only a matter of getting to his neck and severing the arteries." He lied well through his teeth; he had seen the same tactics hundreds of times as his friends earned their rites of passage.

"And what of the seed?" The question was dubious, as if the chief had given a show to the pack in public but still didn't believe Ario in private.

Without pause: "I admit I was a messy eater, but I ate everything. Afterwards, I desecrated the carcass with my fluids to prevent other predators from interfering with my kill." He said this with mock assurance, the coup-de-grace.

"What about the buck semen I smelled, hmm? How do you explain that?" The chief was confident, but not the kind of confident that indicated the truth would set Ario free.

"Like I said," Ario smiled, "I. Ate. Everything."

"You know more about hunting than I thought, boy. Or should I say male? I commend you on your particularly... thorough tactics. You've earned your place in this tribe. Have your wedding, and leave me to my business." The chief shooed him out with a wave of his paw. Ario had to stifle a giggle as he left.

The rest of the day was spent preparing for a modest but happy wedding. Ario and N'hela donned humbly decorated garments and stood before the pack as the Great Circle fell beneath the horizon, casting golden bars of light onto all present. N'hela's father took a moment to pat the wolf on the back in a show of hearty congratulation, boasting to anyone who would listen that his daughter was marrying the most capable predator since the dire wolves of the past. The chief presided, promises were made, and the pack sang the song of bonding, followed by a group howl of celebration. Even Ario's son joined in his own, squeaking voice.

Afterwards there was much revelry and dancing. A veritable feast was set out, including two fresh kills from that afternoon. The entire pack was able to fill their bellies, and after the meal some retired for the night while others stayed to join in the fertility dance.

Ario and N'hela were placed in the middle of a circle of dancers, and as they gyrated and sang for procreation, Ario took his wife again as a lover, in a more proper and traditional way. They mated furiously within the circle, both secure in the knowledge that since they already had a child, and N'hela was nowhere near estrus, this was just for pure pleasure. The male howled as he climaxed, wrapped around his wife who followed soon after, and the song ended with the couple sweating and tied together. Afterwards, Ario watched with proud interest as some of the males, still a few years away from adulthood themselves, quietly exited the firelight to the surrounding shadows to quell the obvious arousal beneath their loincloths.

Perhaps with each other, the wolf's mind thought idly as he continued to pump seed into his mate. He quickly shook his thoughts off. They were adolescents, after all, and prone to experimenting.

Finally Ario pulled out and they cleaned up a bit before heading back to their hut, repeatedly refusing requests to stay at their own party. The truth was, they were both exhausted and wanted to get back to their son. N'hela went to a neighboring hut and brought him back just as Ario was adjusting the bedding for three. She closed the flaps just enough so there was light to see by.

"Hand him to me," said Ario, and took the cub with gentle paws and the enormous grin of a new father. In fact, that definition was almost the truth. He held the energetic little lupine and watched his short muzzle coo and babble.

"You know, you never got the chance to tell me what happened out there. How you came back with all that blood on you," said N'hela softly.

Ario shook his head. He wouldn't be able to tell her now... Maybe never. But he wished that someday he could at least tell her the truth and make her understand. "I'll tell you later," he said curtly, and as if on cue a thought popped into his head. "N'hela, what is our son's name?"

N'hela smiled. "He does not yet have a name. I wanted to wait until you returned, so we could name him together."

"What if I never returned?"

"I doubt we would have survived long enough for it to matter." Ario shivered at the honesty of her voice, but he had to agree.

There was silence as Ario thought long and hard about a name for his son, his legacy to the future. What could be a fitting name for all the circumstances that had conspired to make a life for this child? Finally he set the cub down and put his paw on the scruffy little head, tousling the fur there.

"Doneki."

N'hela closed her eyes, mouthing the word until she smiled around it. "I like it; it's very pretty. What does it mean?"

"In the tongues of the past, it means 'second chance.'"

"It's beautiful," N'hela said, hugging her husband and letting Doneki crawl over them both to nibble on Ario's good ear. "I couldn't have come up with a better fitting name if I tried for years and years."

Ario pulled Doneki from his ear and put him on his chest, where he led the cub's eyes around with a finger, watching him grab for it with his own stubby, claw-free digits. "Neither could I," he replied as he played with his son.

College Days

Whether you're in an English, American or French university, in the twentieth or the twelfth century—or even in an academy for all trades and magics, as in this story... college romance is still college romance.

I loved this story the moment at first sight. It's quirky, fun, tender and when it was submitted, it immediately represented everything I was looking for in stories for this volume.

Slender, graceful mage-in-training Jared has an eye on his roommate, of a squirrel-like race called the Tiki.

Will he have the courage to make a move?

BLACK & WHITE

Veritas

Candles were lit all around Merkan College of Trades, illuminating rooms and corridors. Outdoors, or in other draughty places, torches thrust out of wall sconces, burning, like the candles, with pure, clean flames that neither smoked nor sputtered. In places where open flames might be a danger, shielded lanterns instead cast their warm glow.

One such place was over the desk of Jared Corlin, up late as he often was, poring over tomes and measuring reagents. He brushed an errant snow-white forelock out of his eyes and reached over to fan the brazier. With a satisfied nod, he tipped a spoonful of fine white powder into a tube sticking out of the glass flask. He put a stopper on that tube and pulled a knob, dumping the powder into the clear solution. It dissolved immediately.

Presently, a pale blue fluid started appearing in the condenser and dripping down into the receiving vial. He smiled a tight smile and leaned back to watch it collect.

Three measured taps came from the door, and the latch clicked, then paused. Jared smirked, tossing a few lumps of incense into the brazier and turning just in time for the door to swing open.

It was his room-mate, of course—tall, as Jared was himself, but there the resemblance ended. Irel was lithe and agile, dressed in forest colors, with a small quiver strapped to his thigh and a larger one slung over his shoulder. His pelt was unspoiled black, showing now only in his squirrel-like face and such of his bushy tail as emerged from under his cloak.

"By the Tree, Jared," the Tiki archer sighed. "Do you have to do your alchemy in here? We just got rid of the stink from your last effort."

"A little tolerance, please," the skinny Human replied, tugging at his azure tunic to settle it. "Everything's airtight this time, and I've put the brazier to use you'd approve of."

"All right, all right. I suppose the heat's welcome, too, with winter coming." Irel hung up his quivers, stuffed his gloves into his pocket, and tossed the cloak over a chair. "So what's cooking this time?"

"My Alchemy final," Jared replied. "Drake is allowing us to substitute a practical with a report in place of a written exam." He leaned back in his chair, letting his hair sweep the smooth stone floor. "May his roots grow deep and his seed spread wide."

"Assuming it finds fertile soil. He scares people, you know. Is this," Irel waved a hand at the glassware, "related to that time half the floor couldn't stop laughing?"

"Only the most remote of connections." Jared's dusky cheeks flushed. The laughing gas incident had not been good for his pride. He'd been trying for something that would encourage talk, and instead come home giggling like a jackal, so much of the vapour clinging to him that it had worked on his floor mates. Or maybe they'd just been laughing at him for botching his project.

"Whatever. I'm going to the baths. Try not to blow up the room." Irel paused with his hand on the door to look over his shoulder, locking eyes with Jared, a smirk on his face that went far deeper than the light teasing of his words. Deep enough to make Jared's blood sing.

Then he was gone, a towel over his shoulder, his chuckle fading in Jared's ears. Jared stared at the closed door for a few moments, as though that would let him see the one who'd just passed through it. "Damn you, Irel Morhana," he breathed. "What did that mean?"

There wasn't much point in trying to figure it out; he never could. He stood up to stretch, peeling off his tunic for mobility while he did so. With night fully advanced outside, not even the moon over the bay to break the darkness, and no torches beneath the window, the glass was as good as a mirror, and after a few minutes he paused to consider his reflection in it.

He wasn't quite so thin that his ribs obviously showed, but if one looked close, there they were. He'd never eaten much, even as a child, and a mage's sedentary life hadn't given him the need to put on muscle. His build had come so naturally that he wasn't all that proud of his body, and he sometimes wondered if others, sensing that, stayed clear. But he liked to think he had a good face, clean-shaven, with hazel eyes and aquiline features. A good face for a mage, anyway.

Then, of course, there was his hair.

He leaped into a pirouette, and just as abruptly stopped, facing the window again, to watch it swirl and fall around him, to feel its weight shifting. It had gone white long before he had started growing to manhood. How he'd been teased for it! People had said his seriousness had already made him old. But he had made it into his emblem, resolved not to cut it save to make it even until it reached down to his feet, and then only to keep from stepping on it. Snowlocks, his village had called him, around when his hair had first reached his shoulder blades. Now it was down to his knees.

Then the spark of magic had flared in him. Then he had come to Merkan, and his hair was like a symbol of office, acquired just so much earlier than most of those in his trade. He smiled at his reflection. With recent advances in life-extending magic, he might be able to keep an ageless image—a young man in the prime of his virility, but with pure white hair and a wealth of arcane knowl-edge—for a long, long time.

Reaching over, he closed his fingers around the condenser and muttered a few different words for cold. The words were not themselves important, but they focused his mind on their mean-ing, the very essence of chill, and his focus subtly warped the ener-gies that flowed all around. The web of cooling magic around the condenser was reinforced.

Bunching his hair together and tossing it around himself, he sat down on the edge of the bed. People like Irel had come by their bodies more honestly than had he, who had his handed to him, and he found them all the more attractive for it. Not the scarred, muscle-bound types, perhaps, but those who took what fruit the Worldtree offered them and made the best of it, honing their natural strength—Well.

At least Jared himself had no major need to be ashamed of himself when visiting the baths. He made a point, however, of not being in the same bath chamber as his room-mate. That would give him something to be embarrassed about, right enough.

Speaking of the baths, though, he could use one himself, once his solution was done distilling. He might as well take advantage of the waiting time to see who was there at this time of night.

Scrying the baths—or, indeed, scrying people's actions at all—was considered low taste, but none in his class was better than Jared at making a full projection. He sat up straight, closed his eyes, and shifted his thoughts into his shadow.

Then he cast it elsewhere.

A moment of vertigo, the world seeming to melt and mix before his eyes, and then he was there.

Compared to the solid but plain stonework in the rest of the school, the baths looked downright palatial. This particular chamber seemed to be made of polished black marble, right down to the paler variegation, save for the bathing pools themselves which were lined with sapphire-blue tiles. The blue dome overhead cast a cool radiance over everything, and thick rugs with fanciful designs lined the pathways, both to keep people from slipping and to entertain the eye while they bathed.

A burly, dark-skinned man with a frizz of short black hair nodded at him. "Snowy," he said casually, as though translucent images of people often appeared from nowhere. Then again, in Merkan, it wasn't that rare. "Thinking of paying a visit here? Did a speck of dust land on you or something?"

Throwing his voice was, strangely enough, even harder than

making the projection, but Jared managed. "Very funny. Yes, I'm getting the feeling I could use a soak, but I've got a project on the brazier right now."

Dannel, a would-be blacksmith, nodded. "Irel mentioned. Said you didn't volunteer much and he thought it'd be pointless to ask." Against his dark face, the white of his grin was striking.

"How highly he thinks of me," Jared drawled. "I don't want my project copied from his head—or yours—by someone with more mind-mage talent than good sense."

Dannel's expression abruptly sobered. "Right. That one girl, Shayndra was it, was expelled, at least."

"Shayndra," Jared growled. For a moment his surroundings started to waver, but he forced himself to concentrate, to put his anger aside for now, and the baths came back into focus. "That harlot almost cost me my whole career, and she didn't even want one herself. She just wanted Professor Drake to think she had a good reason for taking dream-spice from his cupboard—not just to share with her harem."

"I know, I know. That girl could have gone so far if she'd tried, though," Dannel mused. "Mind-magic does odd things to a lot of people, doesn't it?"

Jared grimaced. "At least some people confine themselves to just becoming eccentric. Madame Ptarmigan may be excessively fond of her bell collection, but at least she's harmless."

"And you've never given me any reason to see you as lacking in integrity," Dannel observed. "But there's thirty other people in that class with you, right?"

Jared sighed. "Exactly. They wouldn't be able to get it out of my head, and they'd have trouble with any mage, but an alchemist, or some other trade that doesn't involve a personal store of magic..."

"Right," the larger youth said. "Or even simpler." He glanced around, then leaned a little closer to Jared's shadow. "There's something not right about that Vessla—Vardrasven, I think was his name? I heard he was Ptarmigan's favorite until you came along, and he's got a lot of friends. Friends he wouldn't need to dominate to get them to do something unpleasant—just give them a little suggestion. Watch yourself around him." He sat up a little straighter. "Scared to death of Tiki, though. Speaking of eccentric. You're probably safe enough, having the room-mate you do."

Vardrasven was easier to deal with than he was to spell; he didn't worry Jared, though if he wasn't beyond moulding his cronies into a lynch mob, that could be... unpleasant, however it turned out. But things had come back to Irel again. Jared glanced around, but didn't see any sign of pitch-black fur. "You said he'd mentioned my project. He's here, is he?"

"Met him in the change-room. Well, there's plenty of room tonight, so feel free to drop in. In person."

Room there certainly was; weakening the projection a little, Jared looked around to see that the vast chamber was sparsely populated.

While surveying the throng, he withdrew some of his consciousness, seeing his room as well as the baths in a strange double vision. A careful motion tipped some more incense into the brazier and a gentle spell fanned it with a light breath of air.

He returned his full attention to the baths just in time to see him come out of the changing area. Yes, him—Jared's own room-mate, dressed only in the white towel he'd brought and his own black pelt, the latter already damp from the steam and sticking to his body. Jared let his projection get a little more vague as he watched Irel—introverted, withdrawn, even stand-offish Irel—saunter over to one group of young women of varied species, exchange words with them which echoes kept Jared from hearing, and then—yes, he was unwrapping the towel.

Tiki weren't all that different from Human, despite their cursory resemblance to squirrels. With his fur plastered down, every smooth line of Irel's body was deliciously visible, and barring the head and tail, Jared could have found his way about it with any treatise on the Human form for reference. If there were differences, they were too small for the eye to see, and his fingers would have to feel all over to find them. Not an unpleasant prospect, that...

Then Irel bent down, murmured something to one black-haired

lady that made the whole group laugh, and slid into the water beside them with a grin on his face.

"Must go," Jared blurted, and recalled his shadow and his perception so fast, the perceived movement made the room spin around him for a few minutes.

"Damn you, Irel," he sighed.

The Tiki simply defied all his attempts to understand. Sometimes Jared thought there was some mutual attraction there, that Irel, for all his jests, enjoyed his company, even thought him nice to be around. Perhaps even nice to look at? But then he would do something like this, and Jared would wonder if it was all part of the joke.

Was it just his presence that made Irel seem so socially awkward? Was Jared too obvious with his attraction, and did Irel find this uncomfortable, even offensive?

Sighing, Jared moved back to his desk, dipping a quill in ink and carefully taking some notes. The receiving vial was as full as it was going to get. Jared closed a valve at the top of the condenser, counted for a few heartbeats, and muttered a charm to move the brazier out from under the whole set-up. Carefully, he separated the condenser from the vial and put a stopper in place, all in one smooth motion. He held his breath, just in case, and opened the window to let any vapors air out.

After leaning there for a few minutes, the cool evening air caressing his skin, he shut the window and sat cross-legged on his bed, sitting upright in a posture of meditation, inhaling the smell of incense. His back was straight, each foot on the opposite knee, hands held palm-up over his knees as he emptied his mind.

Try though he might, he couldn't get the black Tiki out of it. Even if he tried to distract himself first, contemplating what Dannel had said about Vardrasven—the Vessla was indeed vindictive, and had a strong hold over his friends even without giving them a mental nudge—brought him right back to what the blacksmith had said about Vardrasven being unreasonably terrified of Tiki. Somehow, even the threat of bodily harm—or possible expulsion if he used magic to fight back, and went too far—couldn't get Irel out of his head for more than a second or two.

Meditation wasn't working. He went back to the desk and tried writing his report, but after wasting three vellum scrolls he gave up and just tossed himself onto the bed. He needed to get out, to experience something different, something other than classes and homework, interspersed with sleep and the occasional so-called meal. Hells, he could probably find a tolerable paramour if he put his mind to it for a while, someone he could actually rely on for conversation once they were done, and bedding someone might help to stop him from obsessing over his room-mate.

As if on cue—three taps, click, pause, and the door swung open. The smell of wet fur assailed Jared's senses, mingling with the incense in ways that would have been quite interesting, if Irel weren't so frustrating... He stayed face-down on the bed.

"You," Irel declared as he shut the door, "look like you need to find a bed to share, Jared."

Jared gave him a pained look over his shoulder. His clothes were in hand, and he was once again wearing just that towel. *Are you offering, Tiki?* Jared carefully didn't say. *And am I that transparent?* What he did say was, "Not all of us are blessed with your good looks, Irel, that we could find a willing partner anywhere we please." He did his best to say it lightly, and succeeded, he thought, rather well.

Perhaps not. Irel snorted. "Is your branch a little bent, Jared? Nine in ten of the school population is Human, and nine people in ten wouldn't do anything with someone outside their own race. Look, maybe, but it sometimes seems like they're sure they'd wither away—or at least their delicates would—if they ever touched. Heard a number of people wishing you'd been the one to wander on down, tonight. Everyone knows you've got talent, Jared, and some people think you're rather comely as well. That, and you give people the feeling you won't just take your own pleasure and fall asleep. You've got a reputation for being very thorough, after all." He grinned.

"Never thought that'd work in my favour," Jared admitted, sitting up. "Not in a social setting, at least."

"Depends on the people, I guess. Doesn't change the fact you've got a whole bunch of people asking me to set them up with you, damn near draping themselves all over you when they can, and you don't even seem to notice. First I thought maybe you were more into males, but even they don't have any luck. You waiting for someone special?"

There was an unusual pained tone to Irel's voice. This didn't seem to be the usual jesting. Jared brushed a forelock out of his eyes and tried to decipher his room-mate's expression. "One might almost think you jealous, Irel."

"So what if I am? Who wouldn't be? All you'd have to do is snap your fingers and you wouldn't be able to move for all the people wanting to take turns or even share, people shameless enough to ask me—me!—to put in a word or two for them—and they won't so much as look at me beyond seeing that I'm your room-mate." After a moment of sullen silence, Irel, hanging his towel up and leaving himself clad, alas, in a loincloth, took a peek at Jared's desk. "All done?"

"For now," the mage replied, all too willing to change the subject. No wonder Irel was so hard to read, if he'd been bottling up that bitterness. Not that Jared blamed him in the least for being bitter, if things were even half so bad as the Tiki was suggesting. "I've still got to analyse the stuff, do a controlled test, and make sure I can make it again following my notes, but that batch is finished."

"I see. So much to do yet, I guess there's no chance you'd be willing to say what's so important you have to do it here?"

"Once it's safely turned in, Irel. Then nobody else can steal it out of your head, use it as a thesis, and try to hand it in first."

"Somehow I thought you'd say that." He picked up the vial, looking through it at the lamp. "It's pretty. Sparkles."

"Be careful with that," Jared hissed, then bit his lip. "Sorry. But I'm not sure how stable the stuff is. I really should have it in a dark place as it is."

Irel turned to face him, cupping the vial in both hands. "How—stable? Are you saying this could blow up or something?" He suddenly looked very apprehensive.

"No, no," Jared assured him. "Not that. But it might break down, lose its effect. I don't know whether it would or not."

"Ah. Sorry." Irel put the vial back down, and tapped a mortar with his finger. "This clean?"

"Yes. Good idea." Jared relaxed a little as Irel put the mortar over the vial, shielding it from light, heat, and rough handling.

The Tiki leaned over to sniff the incense. "Good blend," he said. "Where'd you get it?"

"From Madame Ptarmigan. She keeps a stock of good stuff, says it's better for students to meditate with. The pouch cost me ten silver, but I think it was worth it."

"So do I. Would she sell to someone in another faculty?"

"She might. She might also tell you how meditation benefits everyone, not just those who work with the arcane. Helps with tension, and even the good incense is still cheaper than a masseuse. Though I'm sure there are some people who'd do it just for the chance to get their hands all over you, regardless of what you said earlier." Jared swung out of bed. "Excuse me," he said, slipping into his chair and working some more on his report. He was not generally a gregarious person, but talking often helped to clear his head. Tonight was no exception; his thoughts were flowing well enough that he already knew more of what to write than ten minutes of thought had given him earlier.

Irel politely looked the other way, though he did lean on Jared's chair. "Well, if you find one with more in their head than a nutshell after Harvest, feel free to say where I live. I'd rather feel like I'm not only getting it because that person will give it to anyone, you know?"

"Yes, I'm familiar with that caution myself." He dipped his quill and wrote a bit, then winced as Irel's twitching tail passed all too close to the upturned mortar. "Irel, your tail..."

"What?" Irel turned—the wrong way. His tail caught the mortar quite neatly and yanked it off the desk. "Thorns!" he cursed, diving down, even as Jared scrambled to catch the mortar. He succeeded in that, but not the main intent—the vial tumbled out, knocking against the desk. Irel darted a hand under it, and ended up lofting it back into the air, but the stopper had been knocked loose against the desk, and brilliant sky-blue liquid was spraying all over.

Jared caught the vial, but the damage had been done. There was only a little bit of the solution left. His arm was damp, and Irel's face was freshly wet.

They looked at each other for a few moments, breathing hard. Then Irel said, "This... this smells pretty nice, actually."

"It's not a perfume," Jared sighed, finding the stopper, putting it back on, and unlocking his desk drawer to put the thing there. He wondered if contact and fumes would have the full effect, and bit his lip, determined to keep his mouth shut, as he dug for a cloth in the wardrobe to get the stuff off him.

When he finished with that, he caught Irel looking at him, appearing decidedly unsettled. "I feel strange," he said softly.

That was one question answered. Or was it? The effect might be different. "Strange how?" He leaned in, watching Irel's eyes for any abnormal change.

"Well—" Abruptly he grabbed Jared and hauled him in close, his mouth covering the Human's in a fierce kiss.

Triumph! Jared had never been so elated. The stuff worked—it worked perfectly! Jared could feel his mind relaxing even as his heart raced, and for it to have this effect on Irel could only mean one thing.

It lasted a few seconds, then Irel tore free, gasping. "About like that," he breathed.

"You're rather good at that," Jared replied matter-of-factly. Tilting his head, he trailed a few kisses of his own along Irel's neck, making Irel whimper and lift his chin. Jared's hand brushed over the black-furred belly and down, feeling through the thin material of the loincloth. Yes, even through that, Irel felt as good as he looked—and he was already stiffening by the time Jared's fingers made contact. Yes!

"Leaf and bough, Jared," Irel moaned, strong fingers sliding down Jared's spine. "What is this stuff, some kind of—of love potion?"

"Hardly that, gorgeous," Jared breathed, nipping at Irel's collarbone. Part of his mind was screaming at him, but that part, that control, was succumbing to a soft mental lassitude, leaving only the urges of the moment. His fingers slipped beneath the loincloth and stroked bare flesh, making Irel whine and shiver against him. "There's nothing more strictly controlled than philtres, and beautiful though you are, I wouldn't get myself expelled using one to get you."

"Then," Irel's hand slid over Jared's rear, giving it a firm squeeze that made the Human gasp. "Mm, Jared—then what is it?"

"I've been calling it an emotional filter, with an F," Jared replied, leaning into those strong arms with a sigh. "Though I really should think of a less troublesome term before I turn it in. Instead of heightening emotions, it relaxes them. In this blend, it relaxes inhibitions, lets the real thoughts and desires show through. I've been wondering about you for weeks now, Irel. Wondering and hoping."

"H-how do you know that's what's going on? Oh—" The Tiki's lips brushed over Jared's earlobe. "Maybe you wound up making a philtre after all."

"Can you really make that claim?" Jared slid his hand a little lower, cupping under the archer's fuzz-covered pouch. "Believe me, I wouldn't normally be giving this many details, either. But since you got the strongest dose you deserve an explanation, unscrupulous mind-mages be rotted. That laughing gas didn't simply make people laugh—it made them more likely to react to what they already thought was humorous. Even thoughts running unvoiced through their heads."

"Root and vine, Jared, you mean to say that—that you've wanted this too?" A gentle hand started sliding down Jared's hair, caressing his back as it did. "You've got so many people wanting you, I never thought you'd settle for someone like me."

"Boreworms, Irel, you're not some consolation prize. Maybe other people won't let themselves see, but you're stunning, you're perfect, and nothing could salvage my night half so well as you bedding me now."

Irel pulled back a little, staring into Jared's eyes. In the Tiki's own golden eyes, Jared could see doubt giving way to wonder, fear and worry crumbling under the onslaught of lust. Oh yes, he'd done his work well, and this accident might speed things up between them by months, if neither of them had been willing to make a move under normal conditions. The irony was that Jared had, after that earlier tirade, been about to try.

Irel did move now, though, drawing Jared's face toward his for a longer, gentler, and more thorough kiss, tugging with his free hand at the mage's belt, even as Jared's fingers fumbled at the knot securing his room-mate's loincloth.

Irel was left naked by the time he worked Jared's belt free, a respectable erection jutting out from his fur, black against black, still swelling a bit. Jared reached down and slid his fingers over Irel's sac, trailing them up over his shaft as Irel, churrling, sank down to his knees, his cool, damp nose-pad sliding along Jared's neck and down over his chest. Sharp teeth grazed Jared's nipple, sending an electric shiver through his body. The firm suckling which followed drew out a longer groan. Still those strong, able fingers did their work, rendering him just as naked—perhaps more so, given his lack of a pelt.

Irel looked down, curling his fingers around Jared's manhood and licking his lips. Then he looked back up, anxiety all over his face, ears folded down. "From here on all is theory," he admitted. "Be gentle, cha'kar?"

Jared blinked. The weight of that particular revelation briefly drove other concerns out of his mind. Cha'kar? First lover? "I... I can't believe it," he breathed. "Not one person?" Suddenly he felt guilty about all the things he'd thought Irel to be doing in the past, while Jared himself was studying, or working, or simply in the room reading, and especially for those few occasions when Jared had, in fact, managed to find a willing pair of arms.

Irel shook his head, pressing his cheek against Jared's shaft.

The soft fur felt so delightful. Jared smiled, reaching down to stroke Irel's ears. "Well, you're doing just fine, handsome. Take your time."

Irel bit his lip, then tentatively flicked his tongue across Jared's length. He followed with a longer lick, then, eagerness building in his eyes, started kissing his way upward. Moaning with delight, he took Jared into his muzzle, slipping down, down, almost all the way until he abruptly stiffened and yanked himself back off.

Jared took a deep breath, recovering from the unexpected but exquisitely pleasant sensations. "Easy, stud," he murmured, caressing Irel's cheek. "That sort of thing takes practice." But even at the end, Jared hadn't felt Irel's teeth even once. Leaf and bough, he was talented. "Now, come here, you." He pulled up on Irel's arm, and Irel was quite willing to be drawn upward, until they were face to face again, lips meeting in a much softer kiss than that which had started things, but one of, if anything, greater passion. Jared curled his fingers about Irel's hard maleness, squeezed it against his own, felt the Tiki's body stiffen, fingers settling over his.

They stood like that for several minutes, savouring the contact, Jared's hand roaming all over the soft black pelt while Irel stroked his hair and twined it in his fingers. Then Jared had Irel lie down and knelt beside the bed, stroking the nearest firm thigh, reaching over with his other hand to caress the projecting black manhood. Irel shivered, then whined softly as Jared's lips slid over his glans, then all the way down in one smooth motion.

So most of Jared's practice had been on himself; it was practice nevertheless. And Irel was a much more manageable size than one of Jared's notable partners.

Strong fingers stroked his cheek, rubbed his chin, caressed his ears, as he took Irel's shaft into his mouth again and again. There was a strong, almost spicy taste to him that was quite absent in Humans, and weasel-like Kurlai tasted more of musk than spice, if the one Jared had known was an indication. This was quite fine, quite fine indeed.

He lifted his head, gasping, heart pounding. He was barely able to concentrate enough to slide his fingers along Irel's shaft, whispering words from a half-dozen languages, pushing energy through his fingertips. Irel groaned, arching up off the bed and quivering, as that energy embraced his length, coalescing into a slick film around it. Then Jared swung up onto the bed, straddling Irel's hips, gazing down upon him, lowering himself down. He felt Irel's tip between his legs, felt and saw him shudder, taking Jared's rod into his hand. Then he was pushing down, back arched, his world narrowing down to the feel of Irel's manhood as it entered him.

Things blurred after that. He just vaguely remembered bouncing on Irel's hips, thrusting onto his shaft, feeling it strike all the right places inside him, while strong fingers stroked and squeezed his own. He rode his room-mate until ecstasy surged up within him, white seed streaking black fur, and kept on going until Irel cried out and heaved up against him, filling him with his warm essence.

As their breathing slowed, Jared leaned down, lying against Irel with a sigh, his hair falling all around. Irel stroked his cheek, brushed hair away from his face, and gave him a soft kiss. "So," he murmured, "when will that stuff wear off?"

"About," Jared sighed, "five minutes ago." He leaned forward, Irel's softening shaft pulling out of him.

The archer blinked. "That's it? It doesn't last long, does it?"

"Doesn't need to," Jared murmured, kissing Irel's cheek. "Just a little bit is enough to get things moving. No, this was all us, beautiful."

Irel laughed. "You pretty little sneak. Can't even claim I was charmed, can I?"

"It'd be flattering. All the magic was at the beginning, though."

"Oh, no." Irel's fingers slid around the back of his neck. "I think this qualifies too."

Jared beamed and let himself be drawn into a long kiss. An absent gesture extinguished the lamp, and they shuffled around together to get their legs under the covers. Irel pulled the furs up, and they nestled together on the archer's bed.

It'd be dawn before very long, he mused, fingers stirring the fur on Irel's chest. Sunlight would stream in the window, warming his skin and soaking right into Irel's dark pelt where the furs didn't cover them. And tomorrow was a day that neither of them had anything they particularly needed to do. That was good; they had a great deal to talk about. There were many things Jared wanted to say, now—and many things he wanted to ask in turn.

But not now. Tomorrow would happen soon enough.

One Last Night

Time to bring it down a little. From Graveyard Greg, prolific writer of webcomics such as Gaming Guardians and Carpe Diem, comes a surprisingly emotional piece.

Two titanic slave-warriors, gladiators both, share an evening of tenderness and love in their cruel captivity.

Love of the Colossi

Graveyard Greg

Sokoro felt the tremors in the earth as his lover approached, then saw the rhino's immense form fill the doorway, the light of the little hallway lamps no bigger than his eye deepening the dark color of his skin. "Kihiga," Sokoro said as he stood up, careful not to bump his head against the ceiling. The wizards who created the quarters had not prepared for the day they would capture not one, but two massive specimens as the lion and rhino. They were of equal height, and while many agreed they possessed a musculature of prodigious proportions, no one could decide which of the two was the stronger. Certainly it would be a difficult decision, as both were undefeated in their arena matches.

None of this mattered to Sokoro as he gave the rhino a fanged smile. "Come in, my love," he said, beckoning the rhino into his quarters with a paw.

Kihiga did as requested, his lumbering, heavy tread kicking up the dust from the ground. The room, like all of the quarters, was not warded to dull the footsteps of the fighters, and so the rhino's tread could be felt from far away. "The teeth are smiling, but is the heart?" the rhino asked.

Sokoro nodded, understanding the meaning behind the rhino's question. Anyone unaccustomed to Kihiga's condition would suffer confusion.

"If the heart is sad, tears will flow," Kihiga said, insisted as he

149

placed his arms around the lion's waist, drawing him close.

"My hearrt is joyful at the sight of my love," Sokoro said, his ears folding back slightly at the sound of his speech impediment, but Kihiga paid it no mind. The rhino would gladly slur every word he could utter for the ability to speak plainly again.

Kihiga gave the lion's cheek a lick, then nuzzled the feline's neck. Sokoro tilted his head to the side, giving the rhino easier access to his throat, which Kihiga willingly took, one hand moving down to the lion's crotch, and the sheath, already starting to swell from the appearance of the large rhino, started to fill out under Kihiga's palm.

"Life is a shadow and a mist; it passes quickly by, and is no more."

Sokoro nodded again in agreement, and slowly eased his bulk onto the small sleeping mat that covered a corner of his room, slipping away from the rhino's embrace. Stretching out, he cupped his crotch, purring with pleasure at how good it would feel to have his lover touching him instead. The lion didn't have to wait long, as the rhino moved to cover Sokoro with his own bulk; the rough feel of his skin causing the lion's swollen sheath to reveal what was previously hidden. Kihiga glanced down at the emerging member, then dipped his head down to lick the tip of Sokoro's penis, prompting the lion to emit a throaty rumble as he tilted his maned head back in pleasure.

Kihiga chuckled deeply before opening his mouth to take in the growing cock, tongue sliding across the smoothness to encourage the member to grow to its full length. As it filled up his mouth, the rhino already started to feel his jaw develop the familiar ache as he struggled to keep all of his lover's length inside his mouth, but soon enough, even he had to admit a defeat of sorts. As his lips slowly slid away from Sokoro's cock, he stood up, removing the simple loincloth he wore. As the cloth pooled around his thick ankles, he stepped out of the garment, then lay down on the ground on his belly, presenting himself to Sokoro. "Let your love be like the misty rain, coming softly, but flooding the river."

The rhino didn't need to look at the lion to know the feline's reply; a moment later, Sokoro moved to where Kihiga lay, positioning himself on top of the rhino. Kihiga then felt two of Sokoro's fingers, slick and wet with the lion's saliva, exploring the tight ring of his anus. The rhino grunted a bit as those fingers slowly made their way around, then gently pushed through the ring to ease the passage for the lion's cock. Soon enough, the rhino grunted again as he felt Sokoro's length ease its way carefully into his anus. It always felt bigger than it looked, and this time was no exception as the lion slowly thrust his member into Kihiga's body. The lion's soft chuffs blew gently against the rhino's neck; the feline's fingers interlacing with the rhino's.

The rhino soon sensed his lover was nearing climax, the thrusts increasing in speed, the lion's fingers tightening around the rhino's, his breath started growing short as he tried to hold back the inevitable. Finally, Sokoro could hold back no longer, and Kihiga felt the lion's seed spill into him. It felt hot inside the rhino, only matched by the heat of the lion's exertions. Eventually the lion slowed down his thrusts, completely spent; he pulled himself out of the rhino, and moved off his back to lay next to him, panting a bit.

By now, the sun had set, heralding the arrival of night. Sokoro did not move to light the eye-sized globe set into a corner of his room, choosing instead to lay with his lover, his head resting on the rhino's chest. Sokoro looked over the rough features of Kihiga, paying a little too much attention to the fresh scars that lined his left cheek. His own features were tense, his jaw moving silently from side to side as if trying to solve a difficult problem. Finally, he voiced his frustration. "I wish I could please you the way you please me, Kihiga," he said, turning away from the rhino's handsome though scar-ridden face.

Sokoro felt the rhino's palm, rough and calloused from the years of fighting in the area, caress his cheek. "Talking with one another is loving one another," Kihiga said, slowly rising to his feet, offering a hand to the lion, who took it and was helped to his own feet. "Restless feet may walk into a snake pit," the rhino added, leading his lover out of his room and into the hallway. They wandered down the corridor, passing the rooms of the other warriors—some sleeping, some in prayer to whatever gods they worship, but all of them resigned to their lot in life. Soon, they made their way outside, and saw the countryside illuminated by the waxing moon in the heavens above them.

The night air was cool, a breeze ruffling the lion's mane and fur as they walked alongside the wall of the city, the arena behind him. Sokoro noticed the guards stationed at one of the turrets watching the two lovers from above, but they did not raise any alarm. Not that Sokoro was concerned with them or their duty to the protection of the city. Still, it was not the first time the lion wished he could smash the structure with the guards inside; were it not for the spells woven through the lion's very essence, he would have done so, and taken his lover away from all this.

He tried once, he was even able to resist the magical passiveness for a brief time, but inevitably they found a way to make him docile. That way still smoldered in Sokoro's heart, but to act upon it would simply add to the misery already collected in his soul.

Kihiga led the way to their favored spot, which was far away from the arena, but not far enough that both gladiators would feel the unyielding compulsion to return to their quarters; it was next to a stream, the waters sparkling in the moonlight with the occasional fish darting out to catch an insect that skimmed too close on the surface. Sokoro's looked over at the rhino, who pulled him down to rest beside him, and sighed. "Once they found out I had a soft heartt, and could not stand to see an innocent sufferr, I was theirrs forreverr, was I not my love?"

Kihiga leaned over Sokoro, licking the feline's cheek before replying. "Dine with a stranger but save your love for your family." The rhino's proverb, while slightly out of place, meant well. Sokoro had no lack of love for or from Kihiga, and he tried his best to put up with his jailers, the ones who thought they could own every part of him.

The lion nodded, licking the rhino's nose in return. "If it werre not forr you, I would have suffered much. What type of fate brrought us together, I wonderr?"

The rhino shrugged his broad shoulders, sliding his arms around the lion's waist and pulling his close. Resting his head on the crook between Sokoro's head and shoulder, he was quiet for some time. His thoughts took him to his first days in the arena. He had been sold by his own family, who struggled day by day just to survive. Perhaps his kin thought this would be a better life for him. He spent many a night wondering if they had been fed pretty lies about how different their son's life would be, that perhaps he would be revered as a god by the populace. Certainly in stature he was godlike, looming over even the tallest citizen in the city. New users of magic had to be brought in and trained to accommodate the rhino, as even their most damaging spell had barely managed to scratch the surface of his thick hide. Of course, this was no longer the case, as they had enough force to cripple him should they find the need to do so.

His story was unlike the lion's, whom, he understood, had been captured, but not without cost. Sokoro never said how many he killed—indeed, he rarely spoke at all about anything but the present—but Kihiga noticed several who took care of the gladiators' upkeep were never seen again. Talk of 'the bastard' and 'the devil' spread from both fighters and trainers, and by the time the lion was introduced to the other gladiators, Kihiga was surprised to see that the so-called devil was merely a lion—distrustful, angry, and hateful to those who captured him. With good reason, but the thing which frightened his captors most was the fact that their magicks, which could cripple Kihiga, failed to even be cast on the lion; it took many attempts to instill the safeguards in the feline, and all the while they had to employ the other gladiators to physically restrain him. Not an easy task, as even the rhino was hard pressed to contain the lion's fury. His fingers played across the surface of the scar across his chest where the lion struck him.

When the sorcerers finally managed to bind Sokoro to his fate as a gladiator, they were unable to predict what would happen next; the lion fell into a state of depression, and once again the gladiators had to restrain him; this time, it was to prevent him from hurting himself. Kihiga shuddered at the memory of seeing the lion, crumpled against the corner of the room, streaks of blood leading down to his head, which had suffered damage from repeatedly bashing it against the wall.

"I only wish I could have been the one to hurrt the wizarrd who currsed you." Long ago, Kihiga had been cursed by a sorcerer to speak only in proverbs, thinking that it would increase the appeal of the rhino fighter. Perhaps the sorcerer would have been found to be correct, were it not for his accidental death. During one duel, the magic user leaned too far over the edge of the arena, and when Kihiga was forced against the wall, the sorcerer fell to his death, his body broken by the fall and then crushed under the fighter's heel. Kihiga found himself under new ownership, but the curse could not be removed. Months later, when Sokoro was brought into the games, the rhino found someone who could understand him effortlessly, no matter how obscure the proverb.

Kihiga did not reply immediately, his gaze looking up at the moon above them as it was nearing it's apex. "There is no cure that does not cost," the rhino finally said, his voice almost a whisper, as if afraid of those who might eavesdrop. Like their footsteps, their voices could carry a great distance.

"It would have been worrth it, my love. I still feel a burrning shame forr theirr methods of punishing me for my unwillingness to kill." It was after Sokoro had met Kihiga, and their first tryst had been discovered. When Sokoro had defeated his first opponent, a large vulpine who did not come up to the lion's chest, the feline's owner demanded the fox's death. The lion refused, and as punishment, they removed the rhino's sex drive. For days, Sokoro avoided Kihiga, until finally the rhino confronted him, forcing the feline to realize that Kihiga loved him not for the physical act, but for his companionship, for the love he brought into the rhino's life. The same love Kihiga brought into Sokoro's life.

But with that love there came the lion's sense of justice. There were times, like now, when the lion was tense with anger over the mistreatment of the rhino. The sorcerers would rip his flesh with their magicks for even the slightest indiscretion, and Sokoro knew that retaliation would mean more of the same to his lover.

The lion was slow to learn, but even he finally relented. There was no way that he could win against the sorcerers and their magicks, not as long as he cared about the others. His own life was forfeit; the life of his rhino was not.

Kihiga, as if sensing the lion's emotions, raised his head as he brought his arms around the feline's neck. "The water, which boils, does not forget his home." Kihiga misunderstood the reason for Sokoro's tension, as the lion did not miss his former home. He had been cast out long ago for reasons he never explained to anyone. That part of his life would be a mystery, perhaps for his remaining lifespan.

"I was not thinking of that, Kihiga. I am again irrked by the glint of ourr cage." He gestured to the expanse of forest beyond the stream. The countryside, illuminated in the cold moonlight, seemed to beckon to the lion, inviting him to locales that would forever remain unknown to him so long as the wards were intact. "We arre allowed to wanderr only so farr, and cannot enterr the city." As beloved they may be to the populace, they were still considered barbaric, monstrous. To have them inside the city walls would be like inviting the predator to lie with the prey. Sighing, the lion leaned against the rhino's side. "I complain verry much, I know. I will neverr be able to accept my lot in life."

"No matter how full the river, it still wants to grow," came the rhino's reply, his arms tightening gently around the lion's neck affectionately.

Both grew silent, thinking their own thoughts to which no one else would be privy to; eventually, the cold eye of the moon reached its apex, and the glow of the city lights illuminated the surface of the stream, which to Sokoro gave the illusion that a civilization lay just under the water, that it was a better place than its landlocked twin. The lion knew this was an illusion, but he still held fast to it. Dawn would be coming soon, and if his will could slow the progress of time, then he would hold it still forever.

"I love you, Kihiga. I wish this night would neverr end."

"Thought..." the rhino began to say, then paused for a moment as if not wanting to finish the proverb. Finally, he continued: "...

breaks the heart." Then, as almost an afterthought: "No matter how long the night, the day is sure to come."

"Tomorrrow..." Sokoro's voice trailed off, and Kihiga saw the lion wiping at his eyes. The rhino tightened his embrace. "Tomorrrow, my love, I prromise you I will trry my best to fight the spell of rrage."

"A close friend can become a close enemy."

"Indeed. But if I cannot, I will at least make it quick should I have the advantage. I will not see you sufferr needlessly."

"A good deed is something one returns."

Sokoro stiffened, then slowly turned around to lock his gaze with Kihiga's. The rhino saw the lion's eyes wet with tears, and the feline saw the same thing mirrored in Kihiga's eyes. "If the heart is sad, tears will flow," the rhino said quietly, wiping away a tear that streaked Sokoro's cheekfur.

"Thank you, my love."

"Mutual gifts cement friendship."

Nothing more was said that night, the two lovers spending their last night together in each other's arms.

Graveyard Greg

The Rising Sun

When you think of the fantasy genre, shields and helmets and dragons immediately come to mind.

Cast your glance east, and you'll find that there are other cultures with stories very similar to those we're accustomed to in the west, but set in a very different world.

Mwinzi took a chance when he submitted this story. Set in feudal Japan, it follows a court bureaucrat and draws upon some better-known elements of Oriental mythology.

Where this story shines, is in the careful contrast between the strict Japanese mindset and the emotions that form the core of all living things. With a deft brush, Mwinzi paints a tapestry that mixes a few streaks of historical insight with the splendid myths and legends of the East, and tells a story of love and sorrow.

FALL

Mwinzi

As pleasant as the court gardens were during the day, Nakayama Eiji always enjoyed his nightly walks through the gardens more than any of the activities that took place on the grounds during the day. The carefully tended arrangements of rocks and plants, while very attractive and elegant, seemed to the young minister to be a bit too artificial in their exactness. Gardens, to him, were places to be in touch with nature, and with the gardens laid out so precisely, he felt they lost a lot of their mystique. The light of the moon changed all of that. There was a strange and alluring beauty to the way the moonlight filtered down through the trees and reflected off the pools and streams. Bathed in the moon's pale glow, the garden seemed to take on a life of its own at night, where everything was somehow wilder, more mysterious, and more isolated from the rhythm of the Imperial Court.

Nakayama paused on the wooden bridge connecting the cherry grove and the plum orchard and sighed contentedly. Even the bridge, unmistakable evidence of civilization that it was, couldn't detract from the natural beauty of its surroundings. The palace had been built on the edge of a vast forest, but it was only during his night visits to the gardens that he truly felt like the palace belonged in its surroundings. It was only during his night visits that he felt he belonged in his surroundings.

He'd inherited the position rather suddenly when his father died of a violent fever, leaving him as the only possible successor. After the requisite period of mourning, he was hurried into his office and left to fend for himself. Thus far, he had managed to avoid doing anything truly shameful or embarrassing, but he never really felt at home dealing with the intricacies of life at Court, and was quite convinced that the only reason for his lack of failure was his tendency to sit on the sidelines and agree with the favored majority.

Nakayama knew that the other courtiers thought him a bit peculiar because of his standoffish nature, and even more so because of his ritual walks. This didn't bother him much; privately he thought that most of the other courtiers were conceited, shallow, and altogether too interested in promoting their own agendas. Perhaps it was human nature, but he liked to think himself different. For all the luxury afforded by living at the palace, he would gladly have traded it all for a simple life with a woman of no great rank; a life in which he and his family could be themselves without worrying about propriety. Realistically, though, he knew that would never happen; he could not disgrace the family name by refusing his position, nor could he abdicate without finding a successor. His search for a partner with whom to work towards that goal had yet to yield any results.

He sighed again to himself as he resumed his slow stroll. It wasn't so much that he wanted a wife, but perhaps finding someone else at court would make him feel less out of place. Then when the pressures of court life got to be too much, they could take a walk through the garden together, and find peace in nature and in each other. Not that he minded the solitude his evening ritual offered, but it would have been nice to be able to share his pleasure with someone else.

The gardens were always empty during his walks, and he found that odd. Not just empty of people, but devoid of all animal life as well. There were nights when he felt this to be a good thing, as though the garden were being reserved just for his own personal enjoyment. Then there were nights when it made him feel even more isolated and alone. This was one such night, and so he was more than a bit surprised when he rounded a corner and stumbled over a parasol.

After regaining his balance, he walked back over to the parasol and picked it up to examine it further. It was a very simple umbrella, made of wood and reinforced paper, with an image of cherry blossoms painted delicately along one side. Definitely a ladies' umbrella, and long ago out of season. This gave him pause to wonder where it could have come from; none of the court ladies he'd met so far would have been so improper as to use a spring umbrella so close to fall. As if in response to his question, he heard a very soft and high-pitched gasp, and when he turned around, he found himself staring into the face of the most unusual woman he had ever seen.

If she were to walk into the palace, she would have been the object of much derision, as she followed none of the fashionable standards. Her face was not powdered, her eyebrows were not plucked, and her teeth were not blackened. Her kimono was simple, she wore very little jewelry, and her hair was as unadorned as a peasant woman's. All in all, Nakayama thought her incredibly beautiful, and it seemed like a great deal of time had passed before he gathered his wits enough to speak.

"I'm sorry. Is this yours?"

As his question broke the silence, she snapped to herself as though awakening from a trance, and looked away from him demurely, hiding her face in her sleeve. "Yes, my lord. Thank you so much for finding it for me; I… I was afraid I'd lost it."

He stepped towards her hesitantly, as though afraid any more aggressive moves would frighten her away, and he didn't wish to frighten her. He held out both hands and offered the umbrella to her. "It pleases me to be able to return it. I wasn't aware anyone else came to the gardens at night."

He was surprised to see her blush, and he felt his own face flush red in a curious mix of sympathy and desire that he couldn't quite explain. "It… it's the only time I can come and get some peace. The other ladies… when I'm around, they laugh… " she stammered out haltingly, her nervousness and embarrassment evident in every word she spoke.

He smiled gently at that, throwing a teasing note into his voice. "What, laugh at one as beautiful as yourself? I'm sure they laugh out of jealousy. Don't you want your umbrella back? Surely you don't intend to make me wait until the spring to return it to you."

She turned away from him at that, casting her eyes at the ground. "Please, do not mock me."

He strode up to her side at that and placed a hand on her shoulder, surprised at how warm she felt to the touch. "Forgive me, my lady, it was not my intention to make you feel uncomfortable. I say these things not to mock you, but because it would be a great pity to have to wait until the spring to see you again." He opened the umbrella and held it over her so she could see the cherry blossoms. "A beauty this rare and exquisite deserves to be seen more than once a year."

She turned away again at that, whipping around so violently that her hair slapped him in the face, and Nakayama put a hand up to his cheek in surprise. "I am not beautiful!" she insisted, her entire body as taut as the umbrella, which Nakayama dropped off to the side, wanting only to concentrate on her.

"Nonsense! Who tells you aren't beautiful? The other ladies at court?" A pause, then a sulky nod. "Why do you listen to what they tell you? You know they're just jealous." A shake of the head. He sighed. "You're new at court, are you?"

"Yes, my lord. One of the ministers made arrangements with my father for me to serve as a lady-in-waiting to the crown princess, and I only arrived at the palace yesterday."

Nakayama stared, his mouth dropping open at that statement. She's only been here a day and yet she's already been subjected to enough cruelty to elicit this kind of reaction? He shook his head, trying not to dwell on it. "The other ladies… they have not been kind?"

She shook her head again. "I am but a simple girl and know very little of the conventions that are expected of a lady here at the palace. They laugh at me for being uncultured and unfashionable, and they tell me no one will ever give me a second look. It hurts because I know that what they say is true." She closed her eyes, and Nakayama could see tears running down her cheeks.

All at once, he felt his heart contract, and he knew that he wanted to be with her in spite of all of her claims to the contrary. He lifted a hand to her cheek and caught the flow of tears, surprised again at the warmth of her skin. "You may be unconventional, but I do not think everything they say is true. I think you are the most beautiful woman I've ever laid eyes on." She buried her face into her sleeve further at that, but Nakayama didn't feel like trying to read proper signals anymore. "No, do not hide. I would look upon your face this night." She tensed up immediately at that, but slowly relaxed and turned towards him, and as they made eye contact, both of them gasped.

"You... you're minister Nakayama Eiji!"

Any surprise he might have felt that she knew his name was lost as he stared at her, captivated by her beauty. Oh yes, definitely unconventional, but he would not have traded her simple charm for ten thousand court ladies and all of their proper fashions. "I feel I am at a disadvantage, for you to know my name and for me not to know yours. A beauty such as yourself deserves to be addressed properly."

She looked into his eyes, still stunned, as though she could not believe such an important personage was taking any sort of interest in her. Just as he reflected on how odd it was that she could communicate so much through her expressions, she interrupted his thoughts by responding. "... Akiko."

He smiled at that, caressing her cheek delicately. "Akiko. Child of autumn with a spring umbrella. A delicate contrast, but so fitting. And so beautiful... " Emboldened by desire, he leaned forward to kiss her, feeling an electric thrill run through his entire body. It was the most intense experience he had had in a long time, and he didn't want it to ever end. But he saw the desperation in her eyes, and backpedaled immediately, as the two of them gasped for breath. She stared wildly into his eyes, and he felt overcome with shame. "Forgive me, my lady... I should not have subjected you to such rudeness…" But even as he apologized and tried to deny his body the pleasure he knew he desired, he felt his loins stir, and he felt flushed and overheated as never before. After only a moment's hesitation, she ran up to him again and kissed him, and as he felt the desire in her body as well, all higher thought left him and he lost himself in the sensation of being with her.

Aki allowed himself a short period of triumphant reflection as he felt the minister's reaction to the second kiss. So far, everything was going just as it was supposed to. The fox had been looking forward to his chance to be with a human for many months now; both of his sisters had already taken their mates and moved into the palace, and Ume was expecting her first child soon, according to palace gossip. Aki had been happy for her when he'd heard the news, but at the same time, he couldn't help feeling a little jealous that she was getting to experience the human world before he had his chance.

Of course, he knew that for himself, things were going to be considerably more complicated than for his sisters; court ladies were almost impossible to single out, due to their secluded living arrangements and proximity to all the ladies-in-waiting. Similarly, the servants were almost never found apart from each other or their lords. There were stories of rare cases where male foxes were lucky enough to find a woman living apart from the rest of the humans, but for all practical purposes, Aki knew he would most likely have to go after a male. This took only a little bit of adjustment—to him, as to all foxes, human males and females were equally exotic, and there was something about the way human males carried themselves that he found very attractive. Their independence, their passions, their desires and the freedom they exercised in order to achieve their desires, all of these things appealed to the wildness that ran in his blood, and he knew that when the time came, he would have no trouble being with a man.

Eventually, he knew, he would be expected to vanish from the human world to mate with a vixen, preferably one who had also been with a human, and then they could both pass on their knowledge of the human world to their kits, thereby brightening the prospects for the future of all foxes. He suspected that he would enjoy having the chance to raise kits, but he also knew that now that he had been with a human, he would never forget what it was like.

Every touch, every word, every heated breath; there was passion behind it, and longing, and tenderness, and so many other things he couldn't possibly put into words. Humans truly were the race the gods favored, and they had been blessed with many gifts. This night, for the first time, Aki felt like he, too, had been blessed with those gifts, and he could feel a stirring deep within his own body as he yearned for what he knew would soon come to pass.

He checked the magic carefully; it was necessary for him to maintain the illusion that he was a human woman and not a fox; especially not a male fox. While it was certainly not unheard of for men to mate with vixens, or even with other men, he knew that such liaisons were considered improper. He knew that most men would be too proud to allow themselves to indulge in such improper fashion even once, much less for the long-term, and he knew—oh, now more than ever before—that he would want this to be a pleasure in which he could indulge himself for a long time.

It was therefore necessary for him to devote a lot of mental energy to the task of diverting Nakayama's attention, so that the minister still saw a beautiful woman and not a male fox, so that he didn't feel the fur rubbing up against his skin,

… the touch was unlike anything the fox had ever known…

… couldn't smell Aki's musk, its potency growing as the fox felt his desire build,

… the scent of arousal was unmistakable, and he panted desperately as he craved more of that delicious aroma…

… felt the lips of a woman's sex and not the tightness of the fox's tailhole as he tore off Aki's kimono and began the process of making love…

… the high-pitched moan that escaped his throat wasn't forced in the least, and he dug his claws into the ground as the minister's caresses grew more and more intimate…

… there were so many sensations to pay attention to, so many things to concentrate on, and soon Aki, too, felt his higher thought processes fail him as he lost himself in the here-and-now.

He lay there, panting and moaning, mentally exhausted by everything that had already come to pass, and could do little more than whine piteously as Nakayama primed him for entry.

"This is your first time?"

Aki racked his brain for plausible answers, trying desperately to maintain the illusion as his concentration was stressed more than it had ever been before. "It is all right, my lord. Just… please be gentle with me."

He felt more than saw the minister's tender smile; felt it in the gentleness of his touch and in the delicacy with which his rear was spread apart. "I would never wish to hurt you, my lady."

There was a part of the fox that thrilled to hear those words; thrilled to be the recipient of such intense emotion, to know that here was one who would care for him, care about him, make him happy in every way possible, and fill his life with new and wonderful experiences. To this man, he mattered. His feelings mattered. And he knew that as long as he kept this illusion going, he would have everything he wanted.

It is all only an illusion, though. You know he doesn't want you for yourself.

The thought gave him pause, but then he was being penetrated, and an intense wave of pain hit him, followed by a wave of pleasure many times stronger.

It can't be helped. I will take what I can get, and this is already beyond everything I expected.

As Nakayama hilted himself inside the young fox, Aki shivered with delight. He felt whole in a way that he never would have imagined possible before, as though the act of coupling were a rite of passage, opening a new stage in his life. In a lot of ways, he supposed it was, although whether it was simply the sex, or the presence of the human, or something special about Nakayama himself—but then the minister began thrusting, and it was all

Aki could do to maintain the illusion. All thoughts about what the coupling meant for him were lost, and his gasps and moans rose in pitch and in volume as the thrusts continued.

The combination of intense, primal lust and delicate care overwhelmed his mind and body, and he couldn't decide what to feel. He wanted to cry aloud in a fit of passion, to lie back and sigh in contentment, to worship the ground Nakayama lay on, to clamp his jaws down on the minister's shoulder in a bid for dominance. Ten thousand conflicting emotions ran through him all at once, and before he had a chance to grow accustomed to the incredible mix of sensations, he felt a different kind of heat run through his body, with all the suddenness of a summer storm, and he knew his climax was approaching him. The physical and emotional stimuli grew to be too much for his excited state of being, and he yipped and moaned aloud as the orgasm washed over him. So caught up was he in his pleasure that he didn't realize he'd let the illusion slip.

If Nakayama had had any doubts about Akiko's virginity, they were shattered the instant he felt her sex close around his maleness. The heat and pressure were overwhelming, and he felt as though his world was spinning as he began to couple with her. The normal laws of nature didn't seem to apply anymore; all the lights seemed brighter, all the colors more vivid, each and every sensation more intense and somehow more "real" than ever before. Her delicate, gasping breaths and soft, piteous moaning soon evolved their own natural rhythm, and he slipped neatly into that rhythm as their mating grew more intense.

It wasn't long before he, too, was panting and moaning; he had been with a woman before, but Akiko was special in ways that the others never were, and he marveled that he had run into her by chance. It seemed almost too good to be true, but he couldn't deny the feel of her juices seeping down his maleness, the touch of her skin, the feel of his approaching climax, and the moans and yips his actions elicited as he pleasured her...

... yips?

167

In one fatal moment, the illusion was over, and Nakayama found himself not cradling a delicate young woman, but a delicate young fox. They were not wrapped delicately in each others' arms; he was clutching the sticky, matted fur on the fox's chest, straddling the fox from behind and had entered the fox under—his—tail. For the fox was undeniably male, and Nakayama's brain reeled with this sudden realization. Had everything he'd just experienced all been the cruel jest of a fox spirit?

But no, as the fox rode out his climax, clenching his buttocks together in rapid contractions, Nakayama realized that not everything was illusory, and as much as his mind screamed out in horror, his body was responding to the contractions just as it would have had he been with a woman. No, that wasn't true either; as loathe as he was to admit it, this time, even without the carefully crafted illusions, even without the touch of the fox's magic, this time it was more intense, more passionate, and more pleasurable. It wasn't long before his body gave in to the pressure, and the world seemed to disappear as he rode out his orgasm, clenching his teeth and throwing his head back in a mix of confusion, fear, and lust.

It seemed much longer than it must have been before Nakayama's world stopped spinning, and he lay still for a long time, still buried under the fox's tail, not trusting his mind or his body enough to make any further actions. The fox, too, lay still for a while, but it was quickly obvious that the reasons for his inaction were completely different. He swished his tail back and forth lazily a few times—How did I possibly miss his tail?—smiling to himself as his breathing slowed to a more normal rate.

"That was indescribable, my lord. I hope I didn't disappoint you…"

Nakayama clutched his hands to his head, unable to reconcile the image of the fox in front of him with the innocent girl he'd thought he was with. This cannot be happening! He stared stupidly at the motion of the fox's tail, losing himself in its graceful, fluid motions, before he realized what he was doing and thinking, and he withdrew himself from the fox immediately, scrambling away as quickly as he could.

The fox noticed that immediately, and raised himself up on his elbows to look back at the minister curiously. "My lord? Is something the mat—" The fox's voice died mid-sentence as he took in the look of horror on Nakayama's face, and the young man felt unaccountably guilty as he watched the fox's dreamy smile fade into a somber, blank expression.

An awkward silence settled over the two of them, lasting the space of several heartbeats before the minister forced himself to speak, feeling that something, anything to talk about, was better than the silence. At least then he had something else to concentrate on besides the fox's body and how much it reminded him of the illusory Akiko and the sex he'd just had. "What is your name, really?"

The fox looked back at him sadly for a few moments, his green-gold eyes seeming to reach out and pull at the minister's spirit, before stammering out his answer in a voice entirely different from "Akiko's" in pitch and tone, but somehow no less heartbreaking. "My name is Aki, my lord."

Nakayama sat back on his knees and took in Aki's appearance, his voice, his eyes. He felt something deep within him respond to the fox and his deep sadness, and even as he acknowledged that he felt terrifically ashamed of what he had done. He shuddered with revulsion and sighed with longing and as the two sides warred within him, he found he no longer knew what to think. "Do not call me that!" He shook his head violently. "I do not belong to you!"

Belatedly he realized that the fox had not referred to him in a possessive sense, but as Aki shook his head and closed his eyes in deep despondence, he knew it had been on both of their minds. He fought down the guilt and forced himself to listen. "After what we just shared… the wonderful gift you gave to me…"

"I did not give you anything! You tricked me into this! Why? Why would you do such a thing?"

Silence fell over the clearing again, both fox and man stunned by the force of the minister's harsh question. "Why?" Nakayama repeated, more quietly than before but no less insistent. Aki looked away into the distance, running his forepaws through his tail, and it was several minutes before he responded.

"You... you have so many gifts. You and all humans. So many things that we foxes can never hope to understand on our own. Your passions, your dreams, your intense emotions, your cultural traditions... They promise such beauty to life; such joy, such hope. The gods were not so kind to foxes. In order to understand such things, in order to better ourselves, we need to understand you. To be with you..."

Nakayama remained silent, and after another measured pause, Aki continued. "I regret the need for deceit, but you know there was no other way. I've been watching you for a long time, and I know you too have been discontented, restless, searching for something. I knew you, too, would understand what it is like to be on the outside, looking in." Nakayama looked away from the fox, and was surprised when he felt the touch of fur on his cheek, surprised more at how natural it felt. He turned to see the fox cradling his face in a forepaw, and felt himself falling into the fox's eyes once more. "We are not so different, you and I. I thought perhaps we could learn from each other."

It took a great deal of effort for the minister to look away this time, and he shook himself, brushing away Aki's touch as though it were unclean. "S-stop that! You're trying to entrap me again, to take me away and keep me for yourself! I—I am not yours to have!" He sat up rigidly, shivering violently, and though he told himself it was because of the cold, he knew it was not so, and somehow, he knew that the fox knew as well.

"I think you do us both an injustice here, my lord." Nakayama shuddered again at this, but he did not interrupt this time. "There is much we can learn from each other, and I know you enjoyed our time together." As Aki continued to speak, his tone grew progressively bolder, his voice carrying a great deal of conviction, threatening to sweep the minister along with its tide. "I cannot entrap you again unless you let me, and I know that even now, despite everything you say, you are more content than you were before tonight. It is not unheard of, you know, for pairings such as these to happen. If you feel it shames you, the court would not have to know."

Nakayama moaned softly to himself, the memory of what he had just done coming back to him—the true memories and true sensations this time, and he had to admit to himself that everything Aki said was the honest truth.

"You could teach me… "

He remembered the feel of the fox's body under his, the warmth of his skin and the soft caress of his fur, the feel of the his tail as it gently stroked his chest and his loins…

"I could teach you… "

… the feel of the fox's tongue pressing against his own, hot and wild and eager, the intense heat as he entered the fox…

"We could be happy together… "

… the intense pleasure of their mating, the mere thought causing his loins to stir and awaken again, and he moaned and curled himself up into a ball.

"Someone who understands you. Isn't that what you always wanted?"

Nakayama merely huddled there on the ground, trembling with fear and desire and confusion. He knew the fox was waiting for his answer, and every fiber of his body told him what answer he had to give.

"I… I can't… "

The disappointment in the air was real enough to touch, and he wasn't sure whether it was the fox's disappointment or his own he was feeling. He heard the rustle of fabric, and he knew, somehow, without looking, that the fox was getting dressed to leave.

"You have my umbrella, my lord. It would please me if you kept it. If you wish to see me again, I will know where and when to find you."

And then Aki was gone, and still Nakayama remained motionless. The garden seemed so much colder, so much lonelier, now that the fox had gone, as though Aki's departure had taken the life of the garden with him. Still Nakayama remained motionless, and he remained motionless for quite some time. By the time he stood up again, the moon was well past its zenith, and he shivered with cold and exhaustion.

He strode across the garden to gather his clothing, and as he got dressed, he turned to look at the umbrella, still lying beside the acacias. He walked over to pick it up, and was unsurprised to find that when he turned it over, he saw not cherry blossoms, but instead maple leaves, their russet color a bold contrast to the white paper.

"My lady..."

It seemed almost a dream to the minister; everything about the encounter was so surreal. And yet, the umbrella in front of him, and more, the vivid, sharp image of the fox and his plaintive, entreating gaze, had him convinced that it was real. No dream had ever been so powerful. None had ever affected him such. Fall truly had come to his life.

Perhaps the fox had been right about some things. He was lonely, and it would be nice to share his life with someone else. But could he and Aki really continue to meet? He was perhaps not the typical courtier, and certainly Aki was nothing like he had expected from a fox, but it was still unseemly in the eyes of the court. Nakayama bowed his head shamefully as he recalled his earlier advice to "Akiko." When it came down to it, he couldn't go against the court either. His family name was too important for him to be able to tarnish, even if it meant his own happiness.

Was this to be how his fall and his winter played out? Bound by duty and obligation, forbidden from pursuing his own happiness, to live and to die cold and alone? He turned the umbrella over in his arms. It was an unappealing prospect, and yet he saw no way around it. For his father and for his ancestors before him, he knew he had to bow to the dance of the court. Subject to its rules and intricacies, just like everyone else. For all the life Fall had yet to offer him, he knew he could not take it.

"For propriety and loneliness both,
We all do such strange things."

Nakayama shook his head and sighed, unable to finish. He set the umbrella down and looked at it for a long time, the autumn leaves whispering a thousand entreaties to him. Still he could not bring himself to take it with him as he left the clearing, walking slowly away to his room. As he left, he thought he heard Aki's voice calling out to him, offering a reply to his unfinished poem.

"And yet, are they so necessary?"

The words gave him pause, and for a moment he stopped, thinking to look back and hoping to see the fox. But he knew Aki would not want to see him unless he could find a way—but surely that was impossible. He sighed and bowed his head, resuming his walk and hoping to reconcile his head and his heart. Behind him, hiding unseen behind the acacias, Aki watched, knowing nothing of the minister's inner turmoil, knowing nothing of his hopes for a brighter future; knowing only that the man he had watched and come to love was leaving. Overwrought, he curled up in a nearby thicket and tossed restlessly, choking down his sobs and hoping to cry himself to sleep. The umbrella remained in the clearing, untouched, softly glowing in the moon's light.

When the crown princess came out to the gardens the next morning with her ladies-in-waiting, the umbrella was gone.

Hooves and Humping

Uncle Oakie is another returning customer; there's simply no keeping him away from FANG's gates.

His characters are lively and rambunctious, and tend not to be burdened by too much self-censorship.

The Glade is the story of a young Greek lad, name of Lippio, who, like any boy, sneaks out to where he isn't supposed to be.

For Lippio, there is no finer way to spend a day than watching the noble centaurs of the Glade, and who could blame him for thinking that?

Magnificent creatures they are, strong and graceful and free.

So what happens when one of these creatures notices young Lippio?

THE GLADE

Uncle Oakie

I grew up in a small village almost lost in the rolling hills, copses of trees, and endless horizons that define the edge of an empire. I knew nothing of empires as a boy, and to me the village seemed quite grand. It had eight fine houses in the village proper and several others scattered amongst the farms, vineyards, and olive groves around it; their chalk-white walls looked made of bone and their edges rounded as if they had been there forever. Olive trees provided shade for the houses and a place for the very young to run naked as they screeched and played, while their mothers worked the gardens or close fields. When traders came through the village offering colorful dyes from other lands, mothers and children would sing together under those trees, stirring cloth in large pots until it was hung where the soft breezes wafted it into lively rainbows. Whether owned by crafter or farmer, each house boasted painted shutters, bright red tiles on the roofs, and boxes planted with bright flowers and sweet smelling herbs under the windows.

Ours was the only village for more than a day's walk in any direction prosperous enough to boast a public house. Kratos, an actual soldier who had been in the army and seen battle in far away lands, owned that place. His bronze sword hung above the mantle whispering tales of battle and glory to dark eyed children still clutching their mother's knee. In the evenings, the men of the village would gather there under the lazy spell of chirring cicadas. They sat on long benches polished

175

smooth by generations of bottoms while they drank the sour wine that
Kratos made. There they would laugh together and discuss their crops
of grapes, or olives, or grandchildren. Later, their wives would descend like a flock of colorful harpies to harry them home. Sometimes
a stranger would pass through, and if it was late in the day, spend the
night on the floor of the public house, curled up near the hearth. In the
morning, they would be on their way, having paid Kratos in a coin or
two of hard metal. On special days, such as when the Prelate's taxman
would come to collect the annual tithes, all the men could fit inside that
one building, dressed in formal blue chitons, and their hair and beards
carefully oiled and twisted into intricate curls. Twenty men gathered
in one room at the same time! Though there was no room for more
than a favored few to sit with that many packed inside, there was still
room for the more adventurous boys to squeeze in amongst the forest
of legs, dodging curses and kicks to listen to the serious talk of grown
men and see a stranger from far away.

Were I to see that village today, with its handful of tiny cottages
and that leaky, ramshackle, wine and sweat smelling house, I would
probably shake my head ruefully and move on, hoping that another
few hours walk brought me to someplace better. However experience
shapes opinion, and to a boy with none, the village seemed a grand
place at the center of the world.

One thing truly was special about that place. One thing that neither
time nor experience have diminished in my eyes. It was a glade just
outside the village, where the roughly tilled fields gave way to wide
expanses of rolling, tree covered hills. The glade was quite broad and
the shade resting comfortably under the bordering firs, oaks and pines
seemed to make the sunshine falling into it somehow brighter and
more energetic than the sunlight anywhere else. A small brook spilled
through the meadow, neither dancing nor dawdling, it seemed to take
its time as if it enjoyed being there as well. In the spring, butterflies
drifted between wildflowers in clouds of blues and reds and yellows. In
the heat of summer, dragonflies skittered above the dry, crackly grasses
as they hunted.

It was not sunlight or brook that made that place special, however.
It was something much grander by far. That glade, you see, is where

the centaurs could be found.

Not always, but on many days, that is where the centaurs came to meet, to talk, to rest and to play. Some we saw nearly every day, for they were farmers who tilled fields beside our fathers and brothers, or the elders of the clan who settled rare disputes and kept order. Others were woodsmen who lived deep in the forest, harvesting elm and maple for building or burning charcoal for smiths to use in their forges; those we saw less often. Rarer still were the artisans and traders who spent many of their days far away from a tiny village with a grand public house that could hold twenty men and a handful of boys.

Even more special still was the tree. it stood back from the far edge of the glade, away from the village and almost lost in the woods. I don't remember what kind of tree it was, nestled there between several smaller mulberries. Its branches fell in a leafy cascade all around it, creating a shady refuge within. Shielding the interior from prying eyes, the curtain of leaves provided an easy view of a good bit of the meadow. Countless days I spent sprawled on a wide branch, gaze riveted on the centaurs going about their business in the sun. I have no idea whether that tree still stands, but that sheltered haven is forever a part of me. What happened under those branches helped to make me who I am.

Boys had been gathering at the edges of the meadow for as long as there had been a village, for the centaurs had been there long before the first man turned a clod of earth in that area. They came to watch the centaurs—the female centaurs to be more specific. Although from navel down and back they were horses, from navel up the female centaurs were women. Many of them were young and beautiful and, more importantly, all were naked. For generations boys had haunted the edge of the glade, eyes locked on sun-browned breasts swaying and bouncing as the centaur lasses lounged and played. They would watch until their brief tunics tented, their chests grew tight, and they had to wander deeper under the trees, looking for someplace private where they could bring themselves release.

Year after year, generation after generation, the boys engaged in this ritual of impending adulthood. And year after year, the centaurs smiled to themselves and pretended not to notice. Theirs was a culture that held no room for modesty about their bodies or of the functions that came naturally to them. With each succeeding generation, human mothers fretted and scolded their sons while fathers looked outwardly stern and smiled inwardly, proud in the knowledge that their boys were on the road to becoming men. They knew that the furtive spying and solo releases of the glen would soon lose their allure and be replaced by a warm, human breast in the hand...one proffered by a girl on her way to becoming a woman.

I was as guilty as any other boy of spending long hours there, even before I learned that my penis could be used for more than drawing wet squiggles in the dust. I came to see the centaurs—all of them. They fascinated me. Unlike my friends, I sought out every opportunity to speak with them until nearly all of them knew me by sight and would greet me by name. I did not want to merely gawk at them; I wanted to know them. To everyone else, there was only one reason why a boy would seek out the centaur's glade. I endured more than my share of scolding and dire threats from my mother. Having only one son and no brothers, she saw my behavior as an affront against the gods and nature. As I grew older, the half-hidden smile and knowing winks from my father wounded me much more than did the scoldings. I came to know that they were undeserved and that the truth would bring me no smiles, only the sight of my father's broad back as he turned away in disgust.

I had been watching the centaurs for years before I realized that something was wrong with me. My friends did not understand my fascination with our neighbors or my eagerness to speak with them rather than spy on their daughters and wives. Their limited imaginations were incapable of seeing the people attached to the breasts they adored. As my friends pointed and discussed the relative merits of firm, small breasts versus large, swaying ones I found that I had nothing to contribute to their arguments. My tunic did not tent at the sight of a nipple and my eyes did not follow the every rise and fall of a breast. When others rushed into the forest, lifting tunics or ripping off belts, I was content to sit in the shade and watch my beautiful, four-legged friends.

Eventually, my comrades noted my abstinence from their eternal *discussions of mammalian topography. Accusations flew that I was too young to properly enjoy the opportunities that presented themselves. I must be too young to make my sap rise, they would claim. I endured calls of "baby" and "wether" (that being the term for a neutered goat) until I proved to them that I could indeed make the sap rise. They watched in a circle to verify my emission and then started tormenting me even harder than before. Being unable to fully enjoy the bouncing vistas of the glen they could accept; a source for teasing, but understandable. Being able to and not wanting to was another thing entirely.*

It was then that I began to feel that I was truly different from my companions in some fundamental way. The following year, my hand did hold the warm, soft breast that my father had known was on my horizon. I squeezed it a few times and looked at my hopeful temptress expectantly, wondering what I was supposed to do or feel. When she reached down, cupped my limp maleness, and huffed away with an offended air, I knew that there was something wrong with me. After that, the torment from the other boys became unmerciful; my would-be paramour had felt compelled to share all with them in order salve her bruised ego. To escape their hateful barbs, I sought shelter, by myself, under the tree.

There I watched the centaurs. Alone in body and spirit, I watched. Finally, I began to feel the magical magnetism that grabbed my former playmates' eyes. I finally began to understand the vibrating tingle that saturated my body and caused my chest to tighten until I almost thought that I would suffocate. I understood the almost queasy sensation in my gut and the aching hardness between my thighs that made thought all but impossible. I finally came to understand that I was truly different.

When I was not visiting with them and talking to them, I was on my branch under my tree watching the centaurs. I did not moan when the females pranced by. My head did not even turn so that my eyes could follow them. I watched the males. The older ones were powerfully muscled, solid and proud; the younger ones, wiry and graceful. My eyes drank in every aspect of them, not just that which appeared human. I hungered for the sight of a rippling flank, or the slope of a broad rump as they walked or leapt. I devoured both glistening chests and flowing tails with my eyes. Even their verdant dung smelled pleasantly earthy, mild and somehow as if the meadow would be lessened without it providing a subtle undertone to fallen pine needles, vibrant flowers and herbs. Everything about them caused my insides to quiver. A long, hard-hoofed leg idly pawing at the sod could get me hard, and the site of a penis slowly dropping from between powerful thighs, as a centaur pissed, was almost enough to make me ejaculate without even the need to touch myself.

I watched and I dreamed. I knew that acting on that dream would cost me all that I knew and all that I loved. To a boy already feeling different and alone, that would be the ultimate nightmare—so I watched. I watched and brought myself release that was not relief, until the all seed that I spilled on the ground under that branch could have fathered a legion.

Lippio struggled to contain a sneeze as one of the thin leaves hanging in front of him tickled his nose. Moving back from the canopy a fraction of an inch, he continued to stare straight ahead while his hand eased between the bark and his belly to squeeze his painfully hard erection. Ten yards from his hiding place at the edge of the glade, a young centaur stood lazily soaking up the sun. He had been there for about half an hour, doing nothing and seemingly content to do it all day. The only movement other than the slow drooping of his shoulders and head, as the warm sunlight baked tan skin, was the slow swish of his tail as he lazily brushed away equally lazy flies.

The boy recognized the centaur as Doran, a young male about his own age. Doran was easy to recognize, being dark brown-furred except for his rump, which was white with black and gray spots, and for his lower legs, which were covered in three black 'socks' and one white. The boy would have recognized Doran from a mile away, even if his rump was not visible; the same pattern continued over the human half of his body. His skin was a rich walnut color and he had the same spotted pattern of white and gray over his shoulders and chest. A large circle of white covered the upper left side of his face except for an irregular black splat over that eye. Having befriended most of the centaur community, the boy recognized almost every member on sight and spoke with most of them at great length whenever he had the opportunity. He had never spoken with Doran though, even though he had memorized every aspect of the young centaur right down to the number of spots speckling those magnificent haunches. He had watched Doran closely for over a year—watched from afar, never daring to approach him. Even the thought of speaking to Doran made his stomach knot and his tongue grow thick in his mouth.

Doran was sleek and strong and... well, perfect. An always-ready smile full of even, white teeth competed with lustrous brown eyes to create a visage that stole the strength from the boy's legs whenever he was near. Silken, auburn hair, washed back by the breeze, flowed over the centaur's shoulders and ran down his back almost to that exquisite junction of skin and hide. Although he was not bulky like some of the massive woodsmen of his clan, nor were his legs the long dancer's legs of some of the artisans, anyone watching the ease with which he launched his equine body over obstacles as he ran, arms and head thrown back in joy, could not doubt his power or his grace.

Lippio was overjoyed to be so close to, and yet safely concealed from, the the young stallion. For half an hour he had stared, his eyes tracing every line, probing each shadow and one in particular. Doran stood sideways to the boy's hiding place and each time he shifted his weight from one hoof to another, the boy could see the centaur's sheath sway slightly. Each sway and twitch of that magic portal made him dizzy with feelings he hated but could not deny. A mantis crawled across his hand with a torturously slow gait that tickled unmercifully and he didn't dare flick it off for fear of alerting the object of his adoration.

He noticed Doran wandering over to his secluded corner of the meadow and feared that his sanctuary had been discovered. His fear turned to joy when he realized that the centaur was merely coming to nap after drinking at the stream. His joy turned to

181

ecstasy when he realized what that drink could mean if Doran stayed close for any length of time.

The boy almost groaned when his hopes came true and he saw the rounded tip of the centaur's prepuce slowly emerge from the black lips of his sheath. It was happening! It was really happening, he was going to get to see Doran's penis closer than he ever had. He clenched his hand around his own penis to keep from stroking it as he watched. Already he could feel his scrotum tightening as his adolescent testicles threatened to give up their bounty prematurely. Slowly, ever so slowly, the round bulge continued to protrude, extending itself further and further until five inches of black shaft began to droop between the centaur's thighs.

Many people thought that what they were seeing, so like a man's in shape, was the head of an equine penis. The boy had been watching for far to long to make that mistake. What was about to happen was like magic to him and visions of seeing it happen before, under other stallions, filled his head at night while his hand was busy between his own thighs.

Slowly, the smooth roundness at the end of the young centaur's exposed maleness gave way as the bell of his penis emerged—a pink wedge nestled in a collar of black suede. As if gravity, suspended until that moment, suddenly returned, the head of the equine member drooped towards the ground and began to fall, pulling a remarkable length of virility behind it. Over a foot of penis swayed under Doran's belly a short time later. Just as the markings of their coats varied from individual to individual, so did the colors of their members. Many were the ebony poles that filled the boy's dreams, and with them the creams and whites and pinks. Many were of a single color; others began one tone and changed to another at some arbitrary point. Still others almost appeared splashed with large splotches of earth-tone paints. In the boy's dreams, all of them twitched and swayed before him, lengthening and swelling into rigid poles of desire. On those nights when he awoke gasping and trembling with a sticky wetness cooling on his belly, it was always the same majestic shaft throbbing in his mind's eye. Always it was pink-headed fading to a soft cream that gave way to black in an uneven band. As in his dreams, the boy stared at it now and ached.

Doran's front legs stepped forward, stretching him until his equine back arched and his shaft waved to and fro, the tip brushing the grass beneath him. He stood thusly for several minutes, shifting now and again to send his member swinging gently. No stream of yellow emerged and it seemed from his blissful half-lidded expression that he was enjoying the feeling of warm sun and gentle breeze on what he usually kept tucked away. Eventually pleasure gave way to need and the sound of splashing water briefly disturbed the quiet of the remote corner of the glade.

Unable to stop himself, the boy's hips spastically thrust his penis into his tightly gripping hand, his orgasm already ripping through his body. Gritted teeth were not enough to hold back the groans of pleasure wrenched from him. Again and again, he felt the sticky wetness of his essence pulse over his fingers and drip onto the silvery bark beneath him. He struggled to keep his eyes open, refusing to surrender even an instant of that vision. The effort only seemed to make his climax harder and more impossible to control. In spite of himself, his eyes closed as the last waves of pleasure left him panting and shivering in his green-roofed hideaway.

When he came back to himself, Lippio saw that the rare gift that Doran had shown him was already retreating into its sheath. A moment more and he realized that the stallion was no longer still. Doran was no longer lazing in a half-doze, but had turned and was moving slowly towards the tree where the boy was hiding. The centaur's head tilted to one side as if he was straining to hear something and his tail no long swished lazily. The boy began to move back along the branch he lay upon towards the gnarled trunk behind him, silently praying that the centaur would ignore whatever had alerted him and come no further.

The gods, as was so often the case, did not listen to his prayers, or chose to ignore them. Before he had wriggled even the eight or ten feet between himself and the trunk, the centaur reached the wall of living greenery and was parting the hanging branches to step within the sanctuary. Doran looked around the unexpected grotto curiously and shrugged his shoulders. As he turned to leave, he glanced up and his eyes locked on the embarrassed, naked boy with his almost hard penis still wet and glistening and a flush of red crawling up his cheeks.

The centaur paused a moment to take in the scene, standing almost directly under the very branch that the boy had lain upon moments before. Shifting from hoof to hoof in apparent embarrassment himself, he opened his mouth to speak when something cold and wet dripped onto his shoulder. The groans he had heard, the state of the boy's manhood and the distinctive odor told him immediately what was even then leaving a wet trail down his chest.

As one, both of them spoke, "Ah! Please forgive!"

Each heard his own dismay echoed in the other's voice and suddenly the centaur began chuckling. Those chuckles built into mirth and quickly the grotto echoed with his laughter.

Perhaps it was the shared embarrassment. Perhaps it was the relief of having his worst fear realized and no longer hanging over his head. In any case, the boy found himself staring at the centaur, whose sides heaved in gales of laughter while a glob of semen made a snail-track down his speckled chest, and he too found a chuckle rising in his chest. The cacophony of guffaws doubled as his laughter joined the centaur's. When he lost his balance and fell from the branch to land with a foreboding thump at the centaur's feet, the laughter cut itself off with an 'oomph!' from Lippio and a started gasp from Doran. Then the boy saw that the little drip of semen had almost reached Doran's right nipple and once again began to laugh uncontrollably; the centaur found himself unable to help joining him.

Lungs large enough to feed the oxygen-starved muscles of a horse at full gallop also have the capacity to produce a truly impressive volume. The ground didn't quite shake and the leaves didn't quite fall from their branches, but several startled birds and squirrels fled the normally serene corner of the glade for quieter realms.

184

When the chuckles finally faded and teary eyes dried, they fell silent. Doran reached up absently to wipe away the wetness on his chest and saw the red flush return to the young human's face. Doran shrugged as if to ward it off and reached down to the boy to help him to his feet.

"Are you whole and well?"

The boy accepted the help, did a quick mental check for any injuries, and decided that he was little worse for wear.

"Yes, all of my limbs seem to work and it does not look as if I left behind a pool of blood," he said, with a shy smile. He noticed that he was still holding Doran's hand and felt the sticky wetness there, jerking his hand back in shame.

"Please forgive, Doran. I did not mean to..."

Doran got a wicked look in his eyes, an evil grin on his face, and wiped the slimy hand on the human's chest before the boy could react.

"There, now justice has been meted."

The chuckles didn't reach the point of hysteria this time, as both relaxed and realized that it was going to be okay. The boy didn't even resist when Doran's powerful arms helped to boost him onto a broad, level branch.

The centaur used the opportunity to take a good look at the young human. Although it had no beard, and so was not yet mated (humans considered male offspring to be children and made them trim their face hair until they took a spouse), it looked to be of mating age; proof of its ability was still drying on the centaur's chest and still shrinking between the human's thighs. He tried to keep an eye on the latter without being obvious about it, and felt his pulse start to race. He forced himself to return to his inventory before he got himself into trouble.

It had come up to nearly his chest when standing, so it... he— they were people, not things—must be well into adolescence, and was probably not that far behind Doran himself in relative age. Though it was sometimes difficult to tell one human from another unless you knew him or her well, this one was familiar to nearly every centaur in the area—even if Doran could not quite remember his name. This was the one who seemed to want to know everything that there was to know about Doran's people. Though he had the same black hair, cut to shoulder-length, that all of their males seemed to prefer (though not oiled as the adults wore it), the same dark eyes, sturdy build, and tanned skin of the rest of the villagers, this one stood out. An odd glint danced in his nearly black eyes, along with a pain so sharp it stung to see. As if an invisible spear braced him, his back and shoulders stood straight and square; it was as if he were poised to challenge the world. A constant look of wonder in his open expression made him shine. These last few observations, and the respectful way he treated the human village's other-than-human neighbors were the things that the centaurs thought mattered most.

A short, un-dyed tunic (little more than a knee-length piece of cloth with a simple hole cut for his head and a leather strap to tie around his waist) of woven goat hair, and the simple, leather sandals with long calf wraps indicated that the boy came from farmer stock.

Lippio! That was the name he was looking for!

The branch was not very high. Sitting on it, the boy could not see over the bushes outside the tree and into the glade. That is why he favored higher perches for his vigils here. As it was, he now found himself looking down into the face that he had adored for so long rather and craning his neck to look up at it. Seeing no cruelty or derision in the laughter that still danced in those russet eyes, he even ventured a smile that the centaur happily returned.

Doran broke the silence first, "I regret having barged in here and startled you. I am glad that you were not hurt when you fell. You are the one they call Lippio, yes? The one who is always talking to the Elders. That is you, is it not?"

"Yes, I am Lippio: the annoying human who buzzes around your people like a persistent fly. 'Twere no fault of yours that I fell, but only my own. Besides, I have fallen from branches much higher than that. You could not have known that I was here, and I should not have been watching..."

Lippio's lips clamped shut an instant too late as he realized that he had as much as admitted to spying on the centaur. He felt the flush rising again in his cheeks and wished that he could die on the spot and end the humiliation.

Doran paused and then his eyes widened as if he too had suddenly realized the implication of what the strange young human had been about to say. He had pretty much known what he would find under the tree when he heard the muffled groans; he had been counting on it. The centaur enjoyed wandering in the edges of the wood surrounding the glade and had long ago learned the significance of those sounds. In fact, the possibility of catching a human boy in the process of producing those sounds was one of the reasons that he enjoyed the wandering so much. He knew very well that the human boys watched the centaur marems, and why; so too did the centaur marems who put on shows to tease the human boys. Only then did he register the fact that there had been no centaur females in that end of the glade. In fact, he had chosen that spot because of its solitude. That meant that this boy had been watching him as he produced those moans.

He did not speak at first but looked up at the branch the boy had been on, then down at his chest, and finally out through the leaves into the glade. Not another centaur was in sight. There could have been only one target for the boy's eyes. He remembered what he had been doing when he heard the sounds and suddenly blushed deeply himself. He was not embarrassed to have been seen pissing, that was natural and not the kind of thing that a centaur thought twice about. He blushed because it made him feel a strange, but pleasant, quiver inside to discover that the mere sight of his penis could have had such an effect on the boy.

"You... um... you were watching me. Were you not?"

The boy looked down at the ground, clenched his hands in utter humiliation, and answered with a tiny nod and an almost inaudible "Please forgive."

"And watching me made you... spill your seed?"

A flinch and another nod.

"In truth?"

The boy was slow to realize that he was hearing wonder rather

187

than anger or disgust in the centaur's voice and was not sure what that meant. He could not even raise his gaze to venture a quick glance at Doran's face as he gave yet another nod in reply.

"Simply from looking at me?"

Lippio began to get irritated. Why was the centaur dragging it out like this? Why didn't he just hit him or laugh at him—anything other than asking the same question over and over again. Anger began to replace embarrassment and he lifted his gaze to look at the centaur. Prepared to leap from the branch and make a run for it, he stopped when he saw the smile and look of bemused wonder on Doran's features.

"You do not wish to strike at me? Or laugh? You do not find me vile?"

"No. We all know why the young humans visit the other end of the meadow, and it gives me a strange sense of pride to know that simply staring at me so could cause you such pleasure. They know that the boys watch and what they watch, they always have. We mostly think that it is amusing so long as the boys do not pester the marems. You need not worry, I will say nothing of this to them."

Doran seemed not to see Lippio's discomfort and continued his questions, "You used to be over where the other humans gather, but you are rarely seen there these past two years or more. Have you been here instead? By yourself?"

Lippio did not want to answer but could not refuse after being caught spying, "Yes, here or simply wandering the forest. I do not fit in with them, and they do not welcome my company. All that they care about is teat shows. Many do not even see your folk as true people!"

Doran tried to suppress a flinch; only moments before he himself had been thinking of this insightful, proud, lonely, and resourceful youth as an 'it'. He grew quiet as he pondered Lippio's answers and decided what they must mean in light of present circumstances. He crossed his arms over his chest and lowered his own gaze as he asked his next question. He was unconscious of the fact that his hind hooves were shifting and tapping at the ground, a sure sign of nervousness in a centaur.

"Do... uhm... do you watch... all of the centaurs? Or just the ones like... like me?"

Lippio felt the first tear trickling its way down the side of his nose. He had to swallow several times before he could force a whisper past the lump in his throat. His life was over and everything he cherished was now lost. The secret shame that he had been carrying with him for years was out and now it crashed down upon him. Even if the truth brought him the inevitable banishment from his father's house and every door closed against him, he would not lie; it was he who brought shame on himself by his actions, not the centaur.

"Not all. Just... just the stalls."

"You too?"

Lippio had prepared himself for many reactions and stumbled over such an unexpected one.

"I... I..." he jerked his head up to look Doran in the eyes, "What? Does that mean that you..."

Doran blushed and bobbed his head, "Yes, it does. I apologized for startling you because that is actually why I poked my head in here. I enjoy catching the human boys at the other end of the glade when they go into the woods to do that thing with their penises or do it to each other. When I heard the moans in here, I thought that maybe I might see one doing it. I am shamed."

For an endless time Lippio was too stunned to answer. Not only was he not going to be banished or killed, he was no longer alone. Even if there was only one other soul in the world who shared his secret, he was no longer the only one. The relief was so profound and flowed so deep that it took him many long seconds to realize that Doran was waiting, trapped in the same limbo he had just been suffering. The centaur was probably waiting for and expecting censure and derision.

"They watch your marems, Doran. I think that it is only fair that you get to watch them," he said.

The smile that broke out across Lippio's face was so open, and so genuine, that the centaur could not help smiling back in obvious relief.

With their innermost secrets revealed, other walls seemed to evaporate and the two young males quickly found themselves discussing everything under the sun. They shared thoughts, feelings, and dreams as an instant friendship sprang up between them to replace the loneliness of not belonging that had been their fate until then. By the time Lippio remembered that his tunic still hung from the branch overhead, he also realized that it no longer mattered and forgot about it.

Dusk was falling before the flow of words and laughter even started to wane, and the two agreed to meet under the tree again the next day. Putting on his tunic, Lippio slipped through the leaves and even gave his new friend a playful swat on the rump as they both headed to their respective homes.

The night that followed was the longest of Lippio's young life. Again and again, he woke with a strange feeling that took long moments for him to identify as happiness. He could not know that, under the trees not so far away, Doran earned several rebukes for disturbing others with his constant shifting.

The sun was still under the horizon, and the dawn star still prominent in the sky, when Lippio rolled up his mat and softly padded outside to hurry through his morning chores. When his mother, usually the first one awake, rose to braid up her hair and stoke the fire, she found the large, earthen jug already full of warm goat's milk. She looked out into the rosy-purple of the pre-dawn to see the piles of weeds at the edge of the vegetable plot, and the goats quietly munching grass on a nearby hillside. She even discovered one of her own chores already finished: a neat bundle of wood, with one of her favorite flowers resting atop it, sat beside the fireplace. Failing to find anything to scold her early riser for, she began preparing the morning meal and quickly forgot about him.

Past the far side of the village, at the furthest edge of the glen, Lippio was sitting on a low branch, swinging his feet and wondering if Doran would show up. The last of the stars had just faded and the first of the birds had just begun its morning song.

He smiled as he listened to the lively tunes. The songs sounded so much like a celebration of joy, but the centaur elders had explained to him that all birds sang the same two messages: "Come here! Look at me! Come here!" to prospective mates, and, "Go away! I will kill you! Go away!" to just about everyone else. As he chuckled at the merry threats in the trees above him, he heard a distant thudding that grew closer and closer.

He watched the still shadowy glade as Doran galloped towards the tree. As he watched, Lippio's heart thudded with the pounding of Doran's hooves and he could almost feel the wind in his hair and the earth flying under his feet. He sighed deeply, realizing that there were some feelings he could never know, and then smiled at his new friend when the branches parted.

"May the morning's blessing fall on you, Doran!"

"The gods bless you, Lippio! Why the mournful sigh?"

"You could hear that sigh from out there, even over the sound of your own hooves?"

"Yes. We centaurs have better than fair hearing. I, as you well know, am particularly practiced at hearing sighs and moans."

"That seems to be so. I, as you know, am especially skilled at producing sighs and moans."

The both laughed and immediately settled into the ease that they had felt upon parting the evening before.

"I was thinking of how it must feel to run like that," said Lippio, "And then sighed when I realized that there are some things that humans will never know. How does it feel? What is it like to run as fast as the wind? It must be almost as grand as flying!"

Doran tried to explain the sensation and the feel of the wind and the giving firmness of the ground under hoof, but fell silent when he saw that Lippio, without any frame of reference, had no way of truly understanding.

Both were briefly disappointed, but soon the jubilant nature of the youths returned and they fell to joking and laughing. They spent much of the day wandering the woods around the glade. Doran pointed out trails that led to where centaurs had erected simple, but semi-permanent, shelters and explained that the human should probably avoid those areas. In return, Lippio pointed out the best spots to find boys in the process of pleasuring themselves.

During that summer, the two of them frequently convinced mischievous marems to put on shows for the not so well hidden human boys. Doran would hide himself near a spot Lippio suggested, and then "happen upon" many of the boys in the act of fertilizing the ferns and bushes with their seed. Doran returned the favor by pointing out to Lippio a field of grasses that would develop heavy, smooth seedheads in late summer; he explained that stalls enjoyed standing among those waving grasses with their penises dropped so that the grasses could brush away any uncomfortable crusting that may have built up there.

Autumn came and went almost without notice. Even in winter, only the coldest and wettest days kept them apart. Spring brought with it bright colors, birdsong, morning mists, and hearts suddenly so infected by the new life around them that they felt ready to burst.

On one such morning, Doran heard a winsome sigh from Lippio even before he came into sight of him. The centaur realized that it must be the sound of his hooves that elicited such a sigh. It dawned on him that Lippio was wondering the same thing that he had that morning almost a year before; he had probably wondered about it most days since. Doran only then saw how not being able to understand haunted his beloved friend.

He turned and was gone even as the human came into sight, hooves thudding into the distance before Lippio could ask where he was going.

Doran was back almost as quickly, sides puffing but not overly breathless. He walked to where Lippio was sitting on a fallen log in front of their special tree, motioned for Lippio to follow him through the green curtain, then stepped in behind him.

"The others are all still at the other end of the glade; I had to go half the distance before I could even see them. I do not think that any of them are likely to come this way until at least mid-morning. If I answer your question, will you answer one of mine?"

"My question? Which one?"

"The one you have been wondering about every time you hear me run. If I let you know what it is like to gallop with the wind, will you answer a question for me?"

Lippio nodded his head, confused but agreeable, "You need not make a bargain of it. Ask me any question you wish and I will happily answer it if I can, with no thought of getting anything in return. If you can help me know what it is to be that free I will, of course, accept with joy."

"Good. Now you must make the most sacred vow that you know that you will never speak of what we are about to do to anyone. I am about to share a closely guarded secret of the centaurs and will be expelled from my folk if it is ever discovered that I shared it."

"I vow by the earth that feeds us, the sky that shelters us, the stars that teach us and the health and hearth of those I hold dear. But, if this is so secret, maybe you should not tell me."

"I want to. We already know each other's deepest secret, and I feel right about sharing this one with you. Get on my back."

"What?"

"I mean it. Swing your leg over my back and lower yourself gently onto me."

Lippio was at once excited, confused, and frightened. Being from a poor village where foot was the way men traveled, he had never seen a mounted rider, nor even a horse not meant for the plow.

"I might hurt you! I am pretty heavy."

Doran stifled his amused snort, "Lippio, have you seen the logs that the woodsmen carry strapped to their backs when they return to the glade? Have you not seen every spring as one of us draws your father's plow while he guides it through the furrows? We are strong, very strong. Some of us have let humans ride us in the past: very special humans, under special circumstances. That is the secret. We do not let anyone know that we can do this because there are some men who would try to make us slaves, beasts of burden with the brains and hands to do human tasks as well.

"Now hurry!" said Doran, "The others will start moving soon and, if we are caught, I could be banished or worse."

Lippio was still unsure but sensed his friend's urgency. Frightened, but unwilling to miss this magical opportunity, he climbed to a higher branch until he could lift his leg and drape it over Doran's back. He began to slide from the branch onto the centaur. The excited youth tried to be careful, but slipped the last foot, thumping onto his friend's back and almost falling off. Only a quick grab by Doran kept him from going over.

"Maybe you should grab me around the waist. Ow! Not so tight! There you go. I will not let you fall... I hope."

"You hope? You hope! What do you mean 'You hope'?" Lippio looked down and realized that the ground seemed very far away, even though he was lower than he had been a moment before on the branch.

"Please be calm. This is new and strange to me as well. Do not forget to duck. Remember, you are as tall as me now."

As the centaur turned and began to move, Lippio's arms tightened in a deathgrip around Doran's waist. They left the green refuge and stepped into the meadow proper where Doran began to lengthen his stride. As he felt the roll of muscles gliding under his legs and the warmth under him, Lippio quickly forgot to be afraid. He looked over the centaur's shoulder and unconsciously shifted position to accommodate his friend's rolling walk. The mane of black hair pressed against his cheek and tickled his face; he inhaled deeply the warm, earthy, equine scent that permeated it.

The transition from walk to trot was exciting. Already they were moving about as fast as Lippio could comfortably run. He watched in wonder as the forest wall moved past them. His balance shifted easily to the rolling bounce.

His breath pounded out of him in rapid 'whurfs' and his butt felt bruised when his friend shifted into the jolting canter that has always been the bane of novice equestrians. He could not stay connected to Doran's back long enough for him to get his balance and only his grip on the centaur's waist kept him from falling.

"Slow down! I am going to get bounced off! Doran! Please! I

am falling!"

"Hang on! It will get better in a second. Trust me. I will not let go!"

Only then did Lippio realize that Doran's strong hands gripped his arms as tightly as he was holding onto Doran. Even then, he felt himself slipping sideways and knew that he was about to drop to the ground and be trampled under the centaur's pummeling hooves.

Then, between one hoof leaving the ground and the next one touching down, the bouncing was gone. There was no jolt, no panic, just a smooth flow of up and down. He regained his balance and his body moved easily with his friend's as they galloped over the meadow. He saw the blue-green blur of trees rushing past him in the dim, morning light. The gallop was so smooth, the impact of hooves on turf so much a part of them both, that he felt as if they were flying.

He was flying! The wind did not rush through his hair. It ran with them. Laughing and tugging playfully at his tangled locks. The ground flowed like a green river beneath them and the smell of morning dew, crushed grass and fresh turned earth filled the air. He could feel every beat of his friend's heart beneath his hands and between his thighs, every breath between his legs, and every hoof-beat in his spine. He was a centaur and he flew! He was the wind! He was freedom!

All too quickly, they had gone half the length of the glade. He began to panic again as he felt his friend lean under him and begin to turn without slowing. He need not have feared; the glade was wide, and the turn gentle. Soon they were racing the way they had come. As they reached the end of the glen and Doran started to turn for another circuit, Lippio became drunk on excitement and found himself laughing and calling, "Faster! Faster! I am the Wind! Faster!"

Legs churning, heart thumping, Doran obeyed and they literally leapt forward as the centaur put his all into the run. The world became a blur. The world became nothing but a centaur under a boy. The world became nothing but the warm weight of a friend on a centaur's back.

Near the tree that once had been Lippio's sanctuary lay the log that Lippio had been sitting on a short while earlier; remains of a once mighty maple brought down by lightning so many years before that neither could remember it standing. Many times Lippio had watched Doran and other centaurs leaping such obstacles as effortlessly as birds flew.

As his friend began to slow, he cried out, "Jump it! Jump it! I am the Wind. I can fly!"

Doran needed no encouragement and gathered himself for one last burst. The ground fell away. Such a leap as he made that day would earn praise from even the most stingy judge. He cleared the log with almost a length of leg to spare before the earth rose back up and his forehooves again thudded on terra firma.

Suddenly Lippio's world became a pinwheel of blue and green, sky and grass. Then blackness and stars.

"Lippio! Lippio! Can you hear me?"

"Oh no! Oh, please Lippio. Do not die! I will be right back. I am going to get help!"

The centaur turned and began to race towards where the rest of his clan still gathered when he heard a moan from behind him. Turning again, he raced back to his bloody friend.

"Lippio? Can you hear me? Lippio?"

"mnh..."

Carefully folding his legs under himself, the centaur knelt next to his friend and gently brushed the hair and dirt from his face, "Lippio, can you hear me? I need for you to answer me. Now, Lippio. Please open your eyes, Lippio. Open your eyes."

The young centaur almost sobbed with relief when the boy's eyes flickered open. They remained glazed and unfocused for a few seconds and then seemed to find Doran's face. A moment later, they filled with recognition.

"Wha... ha'nd?"

"What was that, Lippio? You are doing fine. No, do not close your eyes. Stay awake! Talk to me!"

"Wha... what happened?"

196

"You fell, Lippio. I am sorry. I tried not to let you fall but I could not hang on. I am sorry. Please forgive. Are you badly hurt?"

"No. Help me up."

"Not yet. Lay there for a few minutes before you try to move, but stay awake. If you hit your head, it is dangerous to sleep. Keep talking to me."

As he coaxed his friend back into awareness, the centaur tried to check him for serious injury. The boy's face was a mess that turned out to be a simple bloody nose. Although he had a large bump on his head, it did not appear to be too serious, and Lippio remained awake and aware.

After ten minutes or so, Doran helped his friend to his feet and then held his arm as they made their slow way back under the tree.

Once he was sure that the boy was safe to leave alone for a moment, he asked to borrow Lippio's tunic and went to the stream to wet it. A careful cleaning and another inspection revealed no serious injuries and fewer bruises and scrapes than he expected.

By the time the sun had risen another hand in the sky, the youths had mostly forgotten their scare and were recounting the ride.

"It was like magic! It was the second most wonderful thing that has ever happened to me! Thank you, Doran. I shall never forget it."

Doran grew curious, "You look to be so filled with joy now that I must ask. May I know the first?"

Lippio grinned at the centaur and leaned against him before answering, "Getting caught by a centaur with excellent hearing and a painful secret. I am sorry for telling you to jump the log; I became a little too excited."

Doran squeezed the young human tight and had to work down the lump in his throat before he could answer, "That is okay. I did not stop to think about how having the extra weight would throw off my balance. I was very excited as well, I would not have attempted it otherwise. I am glad you were not badly hurt; it looks like your tunic came out of it worse than you did."

They both laughed. Lippio's tunic hung on a branch to dry. Even after several attempts to clean it in the stream, the bloodstains on it were still obvious and the large tear down one side would be impossible to hide.

"I will tell mother that I fell out of a tree. She has been telling me since I was three that someday I was going to fall and break my neck. She is always happier when she gets to prove that she was right about things like that."

Doran chuckled and said, "Mine as well."

Neither had thought to bring anything to eat with them, and before noon both of their bellies were growling like feral dogs. They wandered a bit deeper into the woods. Doran collected a variety of roots and mushrooms and berries while Lippio climbed trees to collect great armfuls of early season fruits. Soon they had an ample feast laid out under their tree and shared a meal.

The centaur smacked his lips noisily as he finished his twelfth plum. They were not quite ripe, but they were delicious and juice ran freely down both their chins, "These are wonderful! You humans are lucky. You can climb up to where the fruits are. We can only get to the low stuff and then have to wait for the rest to fall."

The centaur farted loudly, "I may have eaten too many of these; I am sure to be trotting into the woods all night."

"Ick! As big as your ass is, that will be a lot of green apple squirts!" said Lippio.

"I am sorry. I forgot. You humans shit spice and fart rose petals," Doran pressed the heels of both hands to his mouth, made a loud, wet, farting sound; then he wafted his hands towards his face, inhaling deeply and sighing loudly with obviously faked delight.

Lippio laughed and threw a plum pit at his friend, and lunch deteriorated into a storm of leftovers.

Still later, they rested in the shade. Not talking much but still enjoying each other's presence. Lippio sprawled out on the branch that Doran leaned against.

"Doran, did you really mean it earlier when you said humans were lucky?"

"Oh yes. There are so many wonderful things that you can do

that I cannot. Like climb trees and swim; mostly climbing though. It must be wonderful to be up high and to be able to look out over the land. That is closer to flying than galloping is."

"I never would have guessed that a centaur would envy a human anything. I would give about anything to be a centaur. Besides, I have climbed trees and now have galloped, and I am telling you, beyond any shadow of a doubt, that galloping is much more like flying."

"That is only because you had never done it before. If you grew up doing it your whole life, like me, then it would not be so special."

Lippio thought about this for a while, "That may be so. Still, I think that you got the fat end of the bone. I have heard that the cliffs beside the sea are as high as the clouds. Standing atop them and looking out over the blue sea must be like looking down on the sky. I promise that, if I am able, I will help you get there some-day so that you can experience climbing too."

"I do not think that I will ever reach such a place, but thank you. There are other things that humans can do that I can not and wish that I could."

"There are? What kinds of things?"

The centaur grew silent for a long time and Lippio began to think that he was not going to answer when Doran asked in a qui-et voice, "Lippio, do you remember your promise this morning?"

"Of course. I would never break that oath or ever tell what we shared, even without the oath!"

"No, not that one. I know that you would never tell about that. I mean the one before. When you promised that, if I told you what galloping was like, you would tell me what something else was like."

"Yes, I remember. What do you want me to tell you about?"

"It is difficult for me. I feel shameful for asking and it makes me afraid."

"Doran, we are friends. You know my darkest secret. You can ask me anything in the world and it will not upset me."

"In truth?"

"I swear a sacred oath to all the gods that you can tell or ask me anything without fear. May each god curse me if I prove false to this vow."

"Lippio! You should not do that! It is dangerous to make frivolous oaths to the gods!"

Lippio stared into his friend's eyes, meeting his gaze squarely, "It was not a frivolous oath, Doran. I meant it. You are my one true friend. I do not want you to ever fear to share something with me. I do not expect you to share everything, only that you never withhold sharing out of fear."

Doran stared back for a minute, saw the sincerity in Lippio's eyes, and was suddenly shamed for doubting him. He leaned across to hug the human tightly, "Thank you, my friend."

Doran took a deep breath. "There is one thing in particular that humans can do that we cannot. I think that it must be one of the most wonderful things in the world and want you to tell me what it feels like."

"What is it?"

"You know how much I enjoy catching the human boys doing... Well, you know... Giving themselves pleasure and release."

Lippio nodded, "Of course I know. I have helped you set it up so that you could catch them. You still hesitate to ask your question."

Doran sighed again and then asked his question as quickly as he could, as if to force it out before he could change his mind, "What does it feel like? It must feel wonderful from the sounds you humans make, and because you spend so much time doing it."

"Do you mean that you can not? You never..."

"Oh, we can... a bit, but not like you can. We can clench and relax our penis it to make it slap up against our belly. Although, if we do that enough, it may trigger a climax, it usually does not. It feels wonderful when it does, but I think that the feelings of getting there are different for you humans. It must feel better your way; otherwise you would not spend as much time doing it as you do."

Lippio giggled, "It was that difficult for you to ask such a simple question? And how do you know how much we do it."

"I know, from how the boys I catch react, that it is a shameful thing to be caught; thus might be taboo to ask. As for the other, I can smell your seed on you almost every morning when we meet, and I have seen the same boy head for the bushes near the marems many times in one day."

Lippio felt himself blush when he discovered that Doran knew it virtually every time his human friend masturbated. It had been hard for Doran to ask his question and Lippio didn't want to give him any reason for regretting it, so he pushed his own embarrassment away as well as he could, "Do not worry, Doran. It is not taboo, nor is anything taboo between you and me, it is just the being caught is embarrassing... Like farting at an inappropriate time. Mothers chastise boys for doing it because they think it shameful. Fathers subtly encourage it because they think of it as a step towards manhood. Can you really smell that on me? In truth? I usually do that on the way home, or late at night when the rest of my family is asleep, and you can still tell?"

Doran nodded his head, "My nose works nearly as well as my ears do." The centaur's tail hung limp and his hooves shuffled in a way that Lippio had learned meant discomfort or shame.

Realizing that he had not yet done anything to answer his friend's question he thought hard about how to go about it. He was embarrassed, but determined to keep his promise. Unfortunately, just thinking about doing it, especially with Doran standing right there, was making the object of discussion start to wake up and take note. He blushed and leaned over to try and hide his reaction even as he tried to figure out how to answer the question.

He began by realizing that treating something as natural as an erecting penis as shameful was certainly not going to help Doran feel any easier about asking his question. He sat up and moved his arms, no longer trying to hide the softly bobbing mound under his tunic. "Yes, it does feel good. It feels so good that, as you can see, just thinking about it has made my member start to grow. Next to the gallop this morning, I would say that it is the best feeling in the world. It is kind of hard to explain, but I will try."

Lippio thought about where to begin, "Uhm... I have seen a couple of you hard once or twice from a distance." Remembering those rare occasions was enough to wake Lippio's maleness from half-mast to a full, so hard that it almost hurt, erection. Enduring his own embarrassment to lessen Doran's, he continued, "Is that because they were aroused? I mean do your people feel a kind of aching need and sexual stimulation that makes you grow hard and feeling as if you must find relief or explode?"

The centaur shifted a bit and nodded, his eyes wide and his ears taking in every word, "When their marems are in season, the stalls will feel these things, and any mated pair will sometimes tease each other into such states of arousal for the sake of sharing pleasure. At other times, a stall's penis may drop for many reasons ranging from discomfort to blissful relaxation. When dropped, either thoughts or something physical may trigger it to harden and the stall might masturbate then." He fought to keep his eyes on Lippio's face rather than staring down at the boy's lap, as he longed to do.

Doran nodded as he now had an idea of how to continue, "Okay. When that happens to us, if we are alone, and no one is likely to catch us, we play with it. Usually we will grab it lightly between our fingers rub them up and down to make the skin slide back and forth over the tip."

Doran nodded again and stamped a rear hoof; knowing that Lippio's penis was hard and visible under the cloth so close to him was making it harder to follow the words. It also caused his own penis to extend from his sheath until its full length drooped towards the ground, "I have watched some of the boys doing it from beginning to end. But how does it feel?"

"It makes you feel all tingly. Especially down there but just inside. The feeling keeps getting stronger. A ball of it slowly builds at the base of your spine and climbs up your backbone. The tingling in your penis grows too and reaches your eggs, making them ache in a way that feels good. A pressure builds inside as if you need to spill urine, but is different from a full bladder feeling too.

All of this slowly builds and builds until all at once it explodes like a giant sneeze."

Lippio stuttered to a halt as he realized that he could not adequately explain the way it felt. He could explain how to do it, but not what doing it felt like in a way that would make Doran understand. He could see the confusion and disappointment in his friend's eyes and knew he had failed. He had made scant repayment for the incredible ride that morning.

He knew what he needed to do, "Doran?"

"Yes?"

"We are true friends, are we not?" asked the youth.

"Truest of friends, I swear it!"

"And friends trust each other, right?"

Doran nodded, with a befuddled expression.

"And friends will do anything for each other, or so I have been taught," continued Lippio.

Suddenly, awareness of where the questions might lead began to shine in Doran's expression. With the awareness, came a mixture of fear and excitement. He was almost afraid to nod his assent.

"When I asked you what running felt like, you showed me because words could not express it. Some things need to be experienced to be understood."

Doran seemed helpless to do more than nod, although now he was trembling slightly as well.

"If you will trust me too," said Lippio, "I will show you what words cannot explain."

The trembling centaur nodded yet again, his whole face filled with an expression of eager anticipation as well as morbid fear.

Knowing the joy that he would soon bring his friend, Lippio had confidence in his decision.

When Doran stepped back from the branch to give Lippio room to climb down, the boy sighed loudly as he saw the centaur's fully erect penis bobbing under his belly. His own penis throbbed in time with his heartbeat as he lowered himself to the ground.

Placing a hand on Doran's equine shoulder he looked up at his friend one last time to make sure that it was still okay, and then he slowly dropped to his knees.

"It is going to get really hard for you to concentrate or remember anything by the end, but try really hard to remember that I am down here and do not move around too much. I do not want to be stepped on or worse."

Doran realized that his hind hooves were dancing a bit and concentrated to make them stand still. His rapidly twitching tail still showed his extreme nervousness, "I will try. You be very careful with that down there. I would hate to have it get broken before I have had the chance to use it properly."

Lippio turned away from his friend and scooted back to look under the young stallion. Doran's excitement had apparently turned to nervousness, because there was no longer any sign of his erection. With even the tip of the prepuce retracted deep within the centaur's penile pouch, none of his penis was visible anymore.

The boy understood the centaur's reaction. He was so nervous himself that he was trembling now even worse than his friend was. That was okay, though. He took a deep breath and thought about his ride that morning and about the pleasure he was about to introduce Doran to. Determined to make this as special as the galloping in the pre-dawn light had been to him, he decided to take his time rather than get it over with to spare his own nervousness. He placed his hand on his friend's side to steady himself and leaned forward.

With his other hand, he lightly stroked the centaur's slightly rounded belly; the skin there trembled and jerked as if Doran were trying to twitch off an annoying fly. He almost giggled. He too had been so worked up, or nervous, that he became hypersensitive and ticklish. He applied more pressure and the stroke became a rub. Back and forth over the belly of his centaur companion, his hand roamed in large, slow circles. The short coat felt wonderful under his palm, smooth and silken as he rubbed one direction, and then becoming stiff so that the short hairs tickled his palm when he rubbed another. He did not allow his hand to travel anywhere near Doran's genitals yet. He wanted his friend used to being touched and relaxed enough to enjoy what was happening. After all, he had said that he had experienced climax before. It was the human experience of getting there that he wanted to know about.

As his left hand continued its slow circles, his right began lightly scratching slowly down the centaur's haunch. He took the opportunity to examine a view he had always wondered about but had never had the chance to see up close. Once he saw them, he wondered how anyone could possibly miss his friend's enormous testicles. Held up closer against his body than the boy's own were, the pair of oval shaped balls should have been impossible not to notice. Either one would be large enough to fill both of Lippio's cupped hands. As he watched, they rolled slowly, one lifting as the other descended further into the soft, black scrotum. He stared at that hypnotic dance for a long time as his hands continued their ministrations unheeded.

With a start, he came back to himself and realized guiltily that he was supposed to be doing something special for his friend, not for himself. Knowing that he would be getting much more familiar with the beautiful orbs soon enough, he turned his attention back to what his hands were doing. Carefully, he changed the rubbing to a light stroking and barely brushed the hairs of the centaur's coat. This time there was no twitch or jerk. Good, Doran was relaxing a bit. He checked again but there was still no sign of the centaur's proud flesh. That was okay as well: he planned to try all of the things that he enjoyed when he had the time and privacy to take himself to the highest peaks.

Kneeling lower, he shifted until he was directly under his friend and stretched both his hands back and up, behind his head until each of his fingertips pressed into the warm hide of Doran's equine chest. Curling his fingers, he dug his nails into the musky coat and dragged them slowly over the centaur's chest and belly. About a hand span before the opening of Doran's sheath, his hands spread out to pass either side of that portal without touching it. When his fingers had reached his friend's haunches, they began dragging down the front of the centaur's hind legs, not stopping until the reached the hard material of his hooves. Pausing but a second, they retraced their journey, slowly dragging back the way they had come. Every time his face passed Doran's sheath or testicles, he could not help but inhale deeply, filling his head with the rich, pungent, and, above all, male muskiness.

When his hands were once again at his friend's chest he started the process all over again, this time rubbing with his fingertips as he went instead of dragging his nails. Over and over, he repeated the process, frequently varying pressure and speed. On the fifth pass, Doran's chest heaved as he uttered a sound halfway between a sigh and a groan. By the tenth pass, the groans and were constant and Lippio even heard the occasional whimper. When he again reached the centaur's hooves, he scooted out from under his friend and moved behind him. This time, his fingers traced their way up the backs of Doran's legs and, when they reached his haunches, flattened out until his palms rubbed up over his rump, out and around his thighs and then back over that glorious expanse of flesh to finally trail back down his legs. The second time he found himself rubbing the centaur's spotted rump his own groan echoed those of the centaur.

His arms, hands and fingers began to ache, but he did not mind, and would have been happy to stand there all day rubbing the rear end of his first and only friend. He would have, if not for that fact that he was here for Doran and not for his own satisfaction. Becoming bolder now he allowed his hands to work themselves closer together, so that the next time he rubbed down, his fingers traced the inward curve of the centaur's buttocks, coming together a bit beneath the stallion's tailhole and parting again just before reaching the top of his scrotum. Doran gasped and tensed for a moment, and then sighed and relaxed. Lippio noticed that the centaur's tail lifted just a bit and smiled to himself.

When he had the leisure to masturbate for sheer pleasure rather then for urgent relief, Lippio frequently used one hand to lightly stroke from the base of his penis, over his tightly clenched rectum and back as he stroked his penis with the other. Since he had started his ministrations, neither of them had spoken, but now he found himself forced to break the silence.

"Doran, if anything I do makes you uncomfortable or does not feel good, let me know. I know what feels good to me but it might not be the same for you. And if you want me to keep doing something after I stop, let me know that too."

"Okay, Lippio."

Feeling more confident now, the boy continued rubbing the centaur's rump, no longer continuing down the legs. Each time his fingers traced deeper into the cleft between the stallion's buttocks, they came ever closer to the base of his tail and the puckered opening beneath it. Each time he did this, his friend's tail lifted a little higher. Again he could not help leaning in and inhaling equally powerful, but subtly different musk of his friend's hindquarters. It did not smell at all dirty, in fact, Lippio found himself wondering what that glorious expanse would taste like. Shaking his head, he resumed his careful ministrations. Finally, his fingertips brushed over the rim itself.

Lippio jumped back with a start when one of Doran's rear hooves lifted and stamped back down as the centaur uttered a sound somewhere between grunt and squeal.

"I'm sorry, Doran!"

"No! It is okay. I just was not expecting it to feel that... strong. Everything you have been doing to me has felt wonderful. Is this how it is for you?"

Stepping back up to his friend, his fingers once again beginning their stroking massage he answered, "I do not know. But if it feels very good and makes your stomach feel odd and rolly, and your head buzz like it was full of bees, then I think so."

The centaur's only response was a drawn out moan as the boy's fingers once again delved into the musky crevice between the stallion's buttocks. He traced his fingertips in slow circles around the puffy rim of his friend's anus before brushing them over the opening itself. This time there was no surprise in the groan that issued from deep in Doran's throat, just pleasure.

So far, he had only explored the area from the centaur's tailhole down. Now that he was able to see under the tail itself, he noticed a long, tapered triangle where no hair grew; it ran a little over a hand down the underside of the tail. On impulse, he scraped his nails up the length of this area.

"Ooh... Yes... yes... please more!"

Lippio did it again. "Here? You like this?"

"Oh gods, yes. Do that some more! Please?" the stallion's request was almost a whimper.

Lippio was happy to oblige and began to scratch and rub the area in earnest. He had to brace his shoulder against his friend's rump as the stallion lifted his tail even higher and pressed back against him. Soon the centaur was panting and moaning steadily. While one hand teased his friend's tailhole and base, he lowered the other hand to begin lightly tickling the back of the velvety soft scrotum. Doran forced him to move his feet back and lean against the centaur even harder when the stallion's hind hooves began to dance again. Feeling the happy rush that administering such pleasure gave, he did not even think to ask his friend to be still.

Before long, he was cupping and lifting the huge testicles in his hand, only able to accommodate one at a time. He glanced again under his friend and was disturbed to see that there was still no sign of his penis. As he straightened back up, he saw that Doran was looking back at him with a demoralized expression on his face.

"I am sorry, Lippio. Everything you have been doing has been so wonderful. I am feeling things that I never dreamed possible. But, no matter how hard I try, I cannot drop."

"How hard have you been trying, Doran?"

"Very. I am sorry. I guess this is not going to work. But, thank you for trying so hard."

"Oh, we're not finished, my friend. Especially now that I know what the problem is."

Lippio stepped around from behind the centaur and moved to face him, "Just let yourself feel what is happening. Do not think about it. No, that will not work. Trying not to think about something will just make sure that you think about it. Wait just a moment, I have an idea."

Turning from his friend, he walked to the long, drooping branches that surrounded their enclosure. After a moment's inspection, he deftly snapped off a branch little thicker than a nail but about five feet long with long, narrow, blade-shaped leaves paired down its length.

Nodding with satisfaction, Lippio carried it back to his friend and handed it to him. "Turn and face the branch that I was sitting on. Good. Now, how high can you count?"

"I can count to sixteen by your way of counting. Why?"

"I want you to start counting out loud. Every time you reach sixteen, I want you to pluck off a leaf and lay it on the branch. Each time you have sixteen leaves lying on the branch, I want you to push the leaves off and start over. Can you do all of that?"

"Yes. I can do it, but why?"

"It is a trick I learned when I was being punished. Sometimes mother will force me to stand facing a wall without moving until she forgets why she was angry with me in the first place. It can be torture. I start counting lines in the wood or speckles in the rock, whatever is on the wall that I can focus on. Before long, I start to daydream. It helps make the time go by. It seems like most of my daydreams involve me doing what I have just been doing, and so I usually end up with what you are worried about not getting. Understand?"

"Yes, I do. You are very clever."

"Thank you. Now start counting."

"Okay." Doran's head bobbed a bit but he made no sound.

Lippio waited a moment, "Out loud."

"Oh. Sorry. I forgot. One... two... three... four..."

Lippio moved back behind his friend and began again by rubbing his hands over Doran's rump. Once again, he worked his way inwards towards the tailhole and the magic area above it. He did not touch that spot until Doran was had pushed his first pile of leaves off the branch. Soon after, he heard the centaur moan and struggle to remember what came after twelve. The boy would have helped him out, but his own counting skills stopped at ten.

When he saw the second small pile of leaves flutter to the ground, he moved his way around his friend's side and once again knelt under the centaur's belly, facing the supple and heavy looking sheath. This time he could see his friend's penis nestled back between the folds of skin. Knowing the effect a light touch could have on his own foreskin, he reached up and trailed his fingers down either side of the opening. Lippio shivered as he watched the centaur's penis advance infinitesimally. Feeling that he was on the right track, he continued stroking just the dry, velvety rim of the sheath, hardly daring to breathe as the enormous tube of flesh inside began to slide forward. He reached back, cupped his friend's balls in both hands, and then slid them forward, running them up both sides of the sheath, feeling the slowly swelling girth within.

He was no longer aware of whether or not Doran was still counting and it no longer mattered. The black hooded tube of flesh now protruded from the sheath and the tip was beginning to open like a flower, revealing the pink blossom within. He did not yet touch the centaur's penis itself but instead continued to tickle and tease at the rim of his sheath, all the while watching the magnificent member descend. He marveled at the pink and cream flesh, and ached to feel the texture of the shaft under his fingers, but forced himself to wait. Finally, when his friend's maleness was fully exposed and beginning to bob slightly as it thickened, he reached back and dragged his hand over the now hot scrotum, along the sheath and finally down the length of that mighty organ.

He twitched and whimpered as his fingers finally felt the warm, living suede-like texture and the growing firmness within. He did not even notice his own reaction as his penis drooled evidence of his passion onto wet the dirt between the centaur's feet.

He noted the ring of skin a bit more than halfway down the centaur's glory. It looked similar to Lippio's own foreskin when it retracted. Wrapping both hands on either side of that point, he stroked the length in both directions and then back to meet again. Doran's reaction was immediate and, in the space of a single heartbeat, the mighty pole hardened and jerked upwards to slap against the stallion's belly with an audible smack.

Nothing could have prepared Lippio for the feeling of holding eighteen inches of hard, pulsing maleness in his hands as a whimpering centaur gasped and swayed above him. In an instant, he was no longer even aware of his friend; his whole world had compressed and focused itself on the rigid, iron-hard organ that burned in his hands. Now that erection was no longer the goal, he began stroking the entire length over and over again. As one hand reached the base of the enormous penis, he would draw it quickly back up to rub over the huge glans and start its journey anew while the other continued it on its own path downward.

Every beat of the centaur's mighty equine heart made that shaft throb and grow harder. Lippio guessed that the heart in Doran's human chest must be beating even faster. Each time that Lippio thought the huge penis could not get more solid, the next heartbeat proved him wrong. Above him, Doran uttered an unending string of huffing grunts as his haunches began to thrust forward of their own accord, pushing his pole through the boy's hands. Rather than warn his friend to be careful, he joyfully gripped the shaft in one hand letting the stallion thrust into it. With the other, he grabbed the swollen head of the lunging member to try and keep it from thrusting too far.

No sooner did he squeeze the spongy bell, than Doran squealed loudly—an almost animalistic sound of primal lust. His rear hooves stamped into the loam of the forest floor in a staccato beat of urgent need. Beyond thinking, learning and adapting on instinct alone, Lippio began to squeeze the head each time the equine pole drove forward. Slick, clear fluid ran freely down his arm as the precursor to the stallion's impending climax jetted into his palm. His hand grew slippery with the centaur's natural lubricant and he began rubbing his palm over the hardening bell and stubby tube jutting from it; his other hand gripped the rampant member as lightly as he could and stroked up and down, faster and faster.

Doran cried out short, soul rending sobs of ecstasy. Finally, both of his hooves left the earth to slam back down, driving his haunches forward with an almost fearful forcefulness. Lippio was staring at the flared glans in his hand as it instantly swelled to twice the size and became as hard as stone. The small tube that protruded from the lower side stiffened and opened as Doran screamed.

There was no initial spurt of semen—no warning. The flood of pearlescent seed that gushed forth in a solid stream stung with its unexpected forcefulness. The first torrent caught the boy in the chest, immediately drenching him as it splashed up under his chin and ran down his belly and thighs. It coated the inside of his arms and splattered his legs. Still the centaur screamed, tail bobbing, hooves dug into yielding earth as he drove his weight forward and a second eruption jetted into Lippio's face, stinging with the force of its venting. The hot, sticky emission stung his eyes and burned its way up his nose. His mouth filled with the driving wave of the stallion's sperm. He swallowed as much of it as he could before it overflowed his mouth and was wasted; still most of it escaped to hang from his lips in long ropes. The next cataract soaked the boy's hair, drenched the stallion's own chest, and spattered his forelegs; the next two jetted into Lippio's lap.

When the mushroomed head of the stallion's penis grew spongy and the shaft, still hard but losing its raging tumescence, no part of Lippio's front remained un-drenched. A thick, warm coating of semen dripped its way down to his lap, where he realized it joined his own seed. Seed that Lippio did not remember spilling. As it flagged, Doran's penis continued to ooze a steady stream of sperm that ran down the boy's arm and dripped onto the fallen leaves below. Lippio could not move, could not think, stunned by the immensity of what had just happened.

Finally, he looked down at himself and the huge globs and streams of semen that coated him. He swallowed and tasted the essence of his friend's masculinity. Slowly he became aware that the wracking, heaving sound he was hearing was the sobbing of his centaur friend. Not knowing why, but unable to stop it from happening, he began crying as well.

Salty tears mingling with salty seed, he crawled out from under his friend and moved to face him. Neither said anything but both opened their arms and collapsed against each other hugging tightly. Each sobbed, but somehow each knew that it was okay.

When they had both quieted and stepped back from each other Doran looked down at his friend and asked, "Are you okay?"

"Yes. I am wonderful. How are you? Are you alright?"

The centaur nodded, "It was so... big. It was everything. I never dreamed that anything could be... so much. When it was finished, I was crying but did not know why."

"Me too. I suddenly realized that I had made you feel that special and could not stop crying either."

Doran pulled the boy into his arms again and nodded into his wet, sticky hair, "I am so glad that it was you who gave me this gift. It is too big to have been shared with anyone else."

Lippio looked up and smiled. Then he looked down and laughed. Stepping back, he spread his arms and, when Doran looked, the centaur began laughing as well. Seeing the sticky smears that covered his chest and belly and feeling the semen matting his coat, he grinned.

"And to think, last year a single, tiny blob of spilled seed nearly made us panic. I think that we had better hit the stream and clean up before this dries."

Lippio laughed and nodded, "Maybe we should take the long way through the woods. If anyone saw us, it would be kind of hard to explain."

Still laughing, they left their grotto and headed into the forest. The sun was still high. Their dawn ride was only hours, yet a lifetime past.

The seasons determine the pace and nature of life in a farming community. To a young man discovering life and himself with the first true friend he has ever known, a single summer can seem to last a lifetime. Nevertheless, in spite of my wishes, the seasons continued to turn. Doran and I spent every possible moment together that summer, and the day of that magnificent ride was not the last time I felt his powerful back between my thighs or his equally powerful member in my hands. Freed from guilt and shame when we were together, we explored each other and ourselves and discovered new ways of sharing pleasure. Mouths, hands, and exploring fingers elicited many happy sighs and groans in that secluded grotto under our tree.

Our camaraderie was not merely sexual. Together we drew as much excitement from exploring the world as we did from exploring each other. Walking or riding deep in the forest, we truly felt alone and free in the world and laid many elaborate plans for our futures. We sought out the secret and forbidden places. On the shortest night of summer, we hid side by side near a small valley sacred to the satyrs, and listened as they played their pipes, danced their dances, drank their wine, and found sacred joy in sharing their bodies with each other. While the satyrs celebrated life and lust with each other, the sounds of their passion served to muffle our own.

The leaves were already bright golds and scarlets before we were even aware that they had started to turn. Suddenly the seasons thrust us back into the measures and restrictions of our lives. Less and less time was free to devote to each other as harvests needed to be gathered and stored, farmsteads made ready for the rains of autumn, and lives made ready for the season of rest.

We met when we could, but it grew harder to manage.

Winter was the season of courting. Young women were presented at quiet family gatherings. Young men were kept home where they could meet said young women under the protective supervision of the adults. The women gathered to discuss this match or that while the men bartered dowries. That winter, my younger cousin, Oedipus, found a wife and moved in with us (taking my loft and banishing me to sleep on the floor by the hearth) until the men could help him put up a home of his own in the spring. The fact that he was younger than I was seemed to spur my mother on, and she introduced me to every eligible girl in the village, as if I had not seen, talked to, and played with each of them most of the days of my life before Doran. When matchmakers noticed that no furtive smiles, warm glances or stolen kisses resulted from these meetings, they decided that I must be a "late bloomer", or that maybe I should be taken to spend the next winter with family in another village. They assured my mother that next winter would surely see me settled and happy. My father, however, seemed to watch me more closely with something of confusion and fear in his eyes after that.

Doran had his own problems to deal with, as his clan went to as much effort (albeit by different methods) to see him settled down with a marem of his own.

Eventually, cold wind and rain gave way to spring, and the winter pastime of mating sons and daughters gave way to the matings and birthings of livestock, and the plowing and planting of not so tender fields. I learned that spring that I was no longer considered a boy. Without a wife and a holding of my own, I was not truly a man, but Pa expected me to do a man's share of the work that went into tending a farm and raising a family. I had little time or freedom for the pursuits of boys. Through that spring, I plowed and sowed the fields, re-thatched roofs, and hauled rocks and stumps as we cleared new fields. When there was not enough work to keep me busy at home, my father loaned me to other farmers rather than grant me any freedom.

It was my father who collected the fruits of the labors I performed for the other farmers. They usually gave me a tool or bag of seed, sometimes even a coin or two. None of these profits did I hold longer than it took to carry them from my latest labor to my father. My work was not fruitless, however. In many ways, I was a man in truth, even if my father or society preferred not to recognize it. My lanky limbs filled out and swelled with newfound muscle. I no longer had to crane my neck to look into my father's eyes. By the time summer finally rolled around again, I would tilt my head down to kiss my mother on the forehead before heading out to the fields.

As I said before, life on a farm is inseparable from that of the seasons. Summer is lazy. Not totally free of labors, as hay needed to be dried and put up, livestock moved from meadow to meadow lest they overgraze, outbuildings repaired or built. The work was not constant, and the days grew long enough that completing chores was a simple matter. Putting up houses included the home built for my cousin and his wife and their impending child. I was glad when we completed it and I got my loft back.

The quickening of his wife's womb was a sure sign that the gods blessed their union. It seemed that, with the swelling of her belly, my

*father's glances at me held more and more concern and the first glim-
merings of anger. My mother seemed diminished and lonely after they
had gone and her glances at me were, for the most part, confused and
disappointed. I did not know which hurt more, but maybe, with my
cousin out of the house, the glances from both might stop.*

*Between the periods of intense labor were long days of leisure where
I was finally able to slip away to be with Doran.*

*He too had changed in the year that had passed. His graceful
form had filled out to become muscular and powerful without being
bulky. He was also quieter and a hint of fear seemed to have taken
up residence behind his eyes. On one of the rare days when we had
the freedom to wander the land together, he confided to me that he
had been receiving a lot of pressure to "not spend so much time with
the humans". It seemed that his people too were beginning to attach
unwelcome significance to his "late bloomer" status. Though we each
felt the fear, neither of us could bring ourselves to admit that our time
together might be drawing to a close.*

*That fear became an underlying current to our brief visits together,
lending them a sense of urgency and need that had not been there
before. When we shared our bodies with each other, it was no longer
with an innocent playfulness, but with desperation, as if we feared that
the only other things in our lives that mattered might pull us apart at
any moment.*

Lippio had learned long before, that having his friend's penis in
his mouth when the centaur ejaculated was a good way to break a
jaw or drown. Therefore, when Doran's balls pulled up tight and
the centaur began to stamp his hooves, the young man quickly
pulled his mouth away and pointed the mighty phallus at his chest
while continuing to stroke madly. Just as he had been the very first
time, Lippio was amazed at the force and volume of the torrents
jetting over him. It was difficult for him to maintain his grasp on
the pole as it bucked and jerked in his grasp. When the third wave
had washed over him, he quickly lowered his mouth and took as
much of his friend's swollen glans into it as he could. The final
surges of semen flooded in and gushed down his gulping throat.

When he had drained all that Doran had to offer, he finally released the equine member, slid his hand down his slimy chest to coat his own erection with Doran's semen, and pumped himself eagerly. He could not wait for Doran to use his mouth to grant him release. It had been too long since they had been able to share this joy. The feel of his lover's gift on his skin made it impossible for him to hold back his climax. Lost in their passion neither heard the shuffling in the weeds outside their sanctuary. It was only when he tossed his head back as the fires flared up from his groin that Lippio saw the face watching them.

Unable to stop the tidal wave crashing through him, Lippio stared into his father's eyes as his seed jetted between his centaur lover's legs. By the time the last of the spasms had washed through him, his father was gone. The parting look they shared told him that all had ended.

The young man and the centaur fled into the woods; the youth upon the centaur's back and the evidence of their passions drying on their skin. They fled in shame but even more so in fear.

Seasons may define a farmer's life, but so to did tradition, predictability, and knowing that all was as it should be. Everything had its place and a role to play. A tiny secluded community like Lippio's had no room for anything that refused its assigned role. Farmers tilled fields and raised sons and daughters. The sons and daughter married and tilled their own fields and raised children of their own. Goats made other goats. Horses made other horses. A ram that refused to cover his ewes became a wether, then dinner. A ewe that refused to be covered became a roast and leather. A son that refused his role betrayed his father, his home, his community, and the gods. One that betrayed that role in such a perverted way was an abomination must be banished or destroyed.

Several years earlier, Lippio's father, along with several other prosperous farmers, donned his formal toga, oiled his hair and beard, put on his bronze bracers and earrings, and went to a neighboring village. Lippio did not know the details at the time but had put bits, pieces and rumors together to learn that it had been for a trial. Neighbors in the other village caught one of their own doing with young girls what should only be done between husband and wife. As was proper, they did not try him themselves but asked for men of good standing to come from other villages to stand in judgment. Lippio's father was one of the judges who condemned the man. He was also one of the executioners who hurled the stones that killed him.

There was no room for those who refused to follow their roles or the laws of nature.

Doran ran until his sides were heaving and his legs trembled. Finally, he came to a halt and Lippio slid from his back. Together, they held each other and cried their fear and loss. Eventually fear and grief gave way to numbness and the two stood silent as they tried to make some sense out of what their world had become.

"What are you going to do, Lippio? Will you be able to go home?"

"I do not know. I do not think that I will be able to, but I think that I need to try. What is going to happen to you?"

"Nothing," Doran said, "My people do not feel quite the same way about these things as yours do. They will disapprove of me. They will probably mock and humiliate me for a time. The elders will forbid me to see you again, but they will not banish me. They would see you riding upon me as a threat due punishment... Even death, but the pleasure we share will only be viewed with mild contempt."

"That is just one more reason of hundreds for me to wish that I was one of your people instead of mine."

Lippio had uttered the mournful wish in a sense of helpless futility, but raised his head to look at his friend when Doran uttered a startled gasp.

"What did you say?" asked Doran.

"I said what you have heard me say many times, that I wish that I had been born a centaur."

A tiny glimmer of hope began to kindle in Doran as he looked down at Lippio and once again wrapped him in his arms. "When you said. 'If you were one of my people', it made me think of something."

218

"What? Tell me!"

The centaur slowly dropped to his knees and then all the way to the ground. He held out his arms, and Lippio sat down with his back against his lover's chest and felt those arms close tightly around him. It might have been the protective feeling of a lover's embrace or the hope he heard in Doran's voice, but he felt the fear receding just a tiny bit.

"My people do not feel about many things the same as your people do. I think that they would be more disturbed by the fact that you are human than the fact that you are male."

"In truth? Why would you think that?"

"Well, there are some centaurs, I am thinking of two of the woodcutters in particular, who choose a mate of the same gender. Now that I think about it, I will bet that two of the marem traders are mates as well. It does not happen often, but when it does, the clan just accepts it as being right for them. After a time they do not even really notice that both partners are stalls or marems."

Lippio uttered a wistful sigh, "Then it is too bad that I am not a centaur."

"Maybe you could be."

"What! What are you thinking? You think that if we pray to the gods hard enough that I will suddenly sprout an extra pair of legs and a tail?"

Doran flinched at the anger in his lover's voice and rocked him gently for a while before speaking again.

"Let me try to explain this. I am not really sure if I am right and am trying to make sense of it for myself too."

"Okay, Doran. I am sorry that I cast my anger at you."

"It is okay, Lippio. I know you are scared and are not really angry with me. I love you too."

The young man crumpled in the centaur's embrace. It was the first time the words that both had known were between them had been spoken out loud. Between his wracking sobs, Lippio managed to say, "Oh gods, I love you. I love you so much. I do not want to live without you. I do not want to die, but I would rather be stoned to death than be sent away from you."

"Do not say that, Lippio! Never, ever say that. I could not live without you either."

For a time, the two rested silently in each other's arms letting their words of love cover them in a protective blanket.

Eventually, Doran began speaking again, "Actually, it is my love for you that made me think of this."

"Go on, Doran. I am listening."

"Well, my people and yours do have some things in common. One of them is marriage. We do not do it the same way your people do, but when two centaurs become mates, it is for life. They are inexorably bound, one to the other. Not even the will of the whole clan can break the bonds of that union if it is properly consecrated. If they are from different clans, as is usually the case, they will choose one clan to be part of and the mate from outside becomes part of that clan. It is law. The new member is just as much a part of the clan as if he or she had been born into it."

Lippio nodded against his love's chest, "It is mostly the same with our people except that it can take awhile, sometimes years, before an outsider is fully accepted as part of the community. And everyone always remembers that they originally came from 'outside.'"

"I have seen that happen with your people. They used to pretend that Tamrin's wife did not exist. She was merely an outsider until after the birth of her first child. I think that, with your people, it is the continuity that the child represents that makes the bond between newcomer and community. With mine, it is the bonding between the mates that creates belonging."

"That has the ring of truth in it, but it does nothing to help us." said Lippio, "We should be trying to figure out what is happening right now and how we are going to deal with it. No matter what happens, I am not going to let them take me from you."

"And I am not going to let you go. Be patient. I told you before that I am still trying to figure this out myself, but part of me is practically screaming that there is an answer in here somewhere."

Lippio nodded again and settled back to go over everything Doran had said so far, "So, when two centaurs are mated, the mate from outside automatically becomes a full and true member of the clan."

"Truth, and as I said before, that even applies if both of them are stalls or both are marems."

"But, I still do not see how that applies to us. I mean, you have already said that your people and my people are different. It is not like you and I can become mates or anything." Lipio sighed as he came face to face with a dead end.

Doran did not answer and Lippio looked up at him, "Right? I mean you and I could not... there is no way for us to be mates or it would already have been done."

"I do not know, Lippio. I truly do not know, but I think that there may be a way. Let me think about it some more. I am starting to get stiff. Let us move while we talk. Do you want to walk or ride?"

"You know me, Doran. When have I ever refused a chance to ride? But, do not jump any logs today, okay?"

Lippio reached for Doran's arm as he stood to mount his friend but faltered when the arm wasn't there. He looked at Doran and saw a far away blank look in his eyes that slowly blossomed into a glorious smile. He was startled when Doran reached down to grab his face in both hands and proceeded to kiss him soundly.

"That is it! You are wonderful, my love! You have just hit upon the missing piece!"

"What? What did I say? Tell me! Stop standing there like a stubborn mule with that goofy look on your face and share it with me."

The centaur smiled down at his human lover beatifically, "Our first ride. Our first ride may be what saves us. The questions we asked each other opened the door for our love and now may save it!"

"Lippio, remember before I had you climb on my back that first time I explained to you how secret that this ability was? That only a very few special humans had ever been allowed to do it?"

"I do. But what does that mean to us, here and now?"

"Well, what is it that made those particular humans special?

Our stories do not mention them doing great deeds for the clan that would warrant that privilege before they were allowed to ride a centaur, although several of the stories retell some of their great deeds with their centaur partners after that honor. What if it was not the human but the bond the human shared with the centaur that made them special enough to ride?"

"You mean 'bond' like between mates?"

"I do not know. It feels right though, does it not? What if relationships like ours have happened before? In all the stories, the centaur and human are of different genders but that should not matter because the clan will accept bonded pairs even of the same sex."

"Are you sure about this, Doran?"

"No, I am not sure of anything, but it makes a kind of sense. Even great human heroes who have done incredible service to the centaurs have not been granted the right to ride. Why would some humans who never did any great service get that honor instead? It makes sense, Lippio. It is the only thing that does!"

"But does that means that a human and centaur bonded as mates?"

Doran nodded, "I think it does. It does not happen often, and the clan has done a job of keeping that it has happened very quiet, but I think it must have. We cannot be the first to have found the feelings we have for each other."

"Do you think the clan would let us?"

Doran remembered the admonitions to stay away from the humans and dropped his head, "No. Probably not."

"Then it is not really a solution to our problem. Well, you tried, Doran. We tried and I love you for it."

"Lippio?"

"Yes."

"They probably would not allow us to become mates. But they could not stop us if they did not know."

"What?"

"We do it differently than you people do," said Doran, "Usually, when a stall and marem exchange oaths they do it before a communal gathering of one or both clans. The clans witness their first mating to celebrate and bless it. I think you watched a couple of those ceremonies from the bushes."

Lippio blushed to remember his days of skulking and spying but nodded.

"But it does not always happen that way. Sometimes a couple is away from the clan when they exchange their vows and mate for the first time. It is the oath and mating that binds them... not the ceremony. Once two oathbound centaurs have mated, they are mates for life. All that comes after is a celebration of something that is already fact."

"That means that if you... and if I... if we..."

"Yes, Lippio. I think that it does."

"But we can not mate can we? Is it enough to make the oaths?"

"No. It is the oaths and the mating that make it binding." Doran flipped his tail up and down a couple of times, "And you can certainly mate me."

"I... could? But how? Oh! You would let me do that? To actually be inside of you?"

"Let you? Lippio, you dense, little man, I have dreamed of being mated by you since almost the first day we met. I have yearned for it. I just never said anything because of what mating means to my people. Before now, I never thought of what it could mean for us."

"Doran, you oversized donkey! Every time my fingers tickled under your tail and worked their way into you, I dreamt of it being another part of me sheathed in that way."

"You did?"

"By the gods, I did. So, that is all it takes for two males among your people, an exchanged oath, and for one to mate the other?"

Doran's head drooped and his hooves shifted nervously, "Uhm... not exactly. Uhm... you see, the planting of the seed is symbolic. And because there is no chance of fertility between two males... well, they kind of have to plant the seed in each other."

Lippio's eyes grew wide and he felt his anus clench as he realized what that implied.

Doran's voice dropped to a hoarse whisper, "I am sorry. I did not think of that part until just now. I guess that is why there has never been a mated pair like us. I am sorry, so very sorry, my love. I did not mean to get your hopes up for nothing. I never should have said anything until I had thought it all through to the end."

"Hush! I love you. You love me. We are partners. We promised that very first day together that we would never be afraid to say something to the other. Besides, do not give up now when we have come so close to a solution. Let us figure a way around this instead. Even if it is not possible, look at what just imagining it did to me."

The centaur looked down, saw the young man's erection bobbing proudly before him and chuckled.

"Lippio, thinking about anything seems to do that to you."

"No, only thinking of you does this to me anymore, my love," His voice dropped to a hesitant whisper, "Doran?"

"Yes, Lippio?

"How much would it take for it to count as a mating?"

"What do you mean?"

"I mean do you just have to spill your seed inside me there? Or would you have to be... you know... like all the way inside me?"

"Just inside you, not all the way. Even half would suffice for the symbolic union. It does not matter though because there is no way that I could put even part of myself inside you. It would never fit."

"Doran? I have a confession to make."

"What, Lippio? What do you mean 'confession'?"

"Well, after the first time I put a finger all the way inside you and saw how good it made you feel, I started doing the same thing to myself."

"Yes, go on."

"Well, I told you that when I am doing it to you, I think about what it would be like if it was my penis instead of my finger."

Doran's only response was a pleasant shiver as he thought about it too.

"Well, after that, when I had a finger inside myself I would pretend it was your penis inside me."

Doran and Lippio both chuckled at the stretch of imagination it would take to turn a boy's finger into a stallion's phallus.

"After awhile I found something better than my finger. The wheelwright had some scraps behind his shop. One of those scraps was a rod of black wood that was very heavy. It saw how smooth it was and noted that it was over two hands long. Like any other spoke, it thickened at the middle and thinned down at each end. Since I found it in the scrap pile, I asked the 'wright if I could have it. He said that it was left over from an experiment for a new kind of spoke that had not worked out and that I was welcome to it."

Lippio saw Doran nod and continued, "The dense wood took a long time to shape and finish, but I eventually managed to carve one end into a knob that I could keep a grip on, and polished the whole thing until it was as smooth as butter."

The centaur's eyes flashed amusement, interest, and a bit of admiration for Lippio's daring, if not for his sense, when he guessed where the story was leading.

"I used lard to make it slippery."

Doran could not quite muffle his snicker.

Lippio's head ducked in embarrassment when he heard the snicker, and so he missed his lover's warm smile when the centaur realized just how far his young human had gone to fulfill his fantasies.

"It took a month before I could get more than the tip inside me. Like most wheel spokes it was thicker in the middle than at the ends. It took over three months before I could fit the thickest part inside me comfortably. After another four months of trying, I could take the entire length. All of it except the knob I used to hold onto it with, I mean. Every time I used it, I pictured that it was you inside me."

"Lippio, was it as big as I am?"

"No. It is a little thinner than you were when we first met, and not as long. Now it does not even make me feel stretched and does not hurt at all. I think that I might be able to fit something bigger in me now."

"No, dearest, I will not take a chance of hurting you like that. I might tear you apart. I could kill you. Do not ever ask me to risk something like that, my love. Please!"

"But can you not see? If we will not try, then you are going to lose me! I am going to lose you! What in the world could hurt worse than that?"

"Please, Lippio. Do not ask me to hurt you! Please, never ask that of me!"

"I am not asking you to hurt me! I am asking you to trust me! To make love to me! To save me... us! You said yourself that you do not have to put all of it inside me. I know better than you do how much I have learned to take there. I know how much I ache for more when I dream of you. I want to try! I need to try! I do not care if it hurts. It cannot possibly hurt more than losing you would. My cousin's wife cried beneath him on their wedding night and left her maiden's blood upon the sheet. Why cannot I do the same for the one I love?"

"No, Lippio! I will not take a chance that might kill you. I cannot and you should not ask it of me."

"Then I will not ask. I will beg. I will beg you in the name of the love that I have for you to trust me. I can do this! I swear to you that I will stop if I think that there is even a risk of you injuring me. Please! Please, my love, let me try," said Lippio, "If we do not try, I am doomed. I cannot live without you. I will not try. No matter how you might ask, beg or threaten me."

Doran's tears dripped off his cheeks as he once again took his lover's face in his hands, "But, Lippio. Even if we did this, there is still the chance that I am wrong. That it will make no difference. The clan may not accept us no matter what we do."

"That does not matter, Doran. It will make a difference! To us! It does not matter if the clan will not recognize it. If we do this then we will be mates. For life. No matter what else happens, no one will ever be able to take that away from us!"

Doran's resistance crumbled. The thought of being bound to his love in the most intimate way possible, of sharing an eternal union that could not be broken pierced even his fear.

"You are right. Even if we are the only ones who recognize it, we will always belong to each other. We will do this, not for them, but for ourselves. If others do not honor it, we will go our own way, but we will do it together."

For the rest of the afternoon, they spoke of the Oath and other aspects of the bonding ceremony. Just then, neither was quite ready to face the actual mechanics of the mating that would follow. They decided to include human traditions in their private ceremony as well, such as the exchange of gifts. Each gift should be something of the self, given to the other. After long consideration of their limited resources, Lippio hit upon the idea of braided collars woven from each other's hair. Lippio used his belt knife to carefully shave away a large swatch of hair from the side of his head and then helped Doran harvest long hairs from his tail and mane.

As each sat braiding his own hair into the band that would later encircle his mate's neck, Doran kept glancing over at Lippio and cocking his head. Finally, Lippio could not stand it anymore, "What? Am I bleeding? Is a second head sprouting from my neck? Why do you keep looking at me like that?"

"It is strange. When you head moves in a certain way, the change between shaved head and the long hair on top almost makes you look like you have a mane."

Lippio reached up to feel his scalp and hair then shook his head and whinnied. They both laughed and returned to their braiding, but Lippio still noticed the centaur looking over at him with a bemused expression from time to time.

It had been late morning when Lippio's father discovered them. By the time that they finished weaving their mutual gifts, it was late afternoon. There were still several hours of light in the summer evening ahead of them but they realized that they had better prepare for the coming ceremony. Both agreed that they needed to do it that night. The longer they waited the greater the chance of discovery and if that happened, their dreams would come to naught. By then, Lippio's father would have sent out the call for judges from nearby villages, and may have even sent out hunters to search for them as well.

They chose the meadow where the satyrs had danced on midsummer's night the year before, knowing it to be blessed by at least one of the gods. They thought that Pan, of all the gods, was most likely to bless their union.

Because Lippio was likely to be attacked, detained, or worse should he be seen, it was Doran who sneaked back to pick up some needed supplies, including lard or butter to ease their mating. They agreed to meet at moon's rise on the hillock they had hidden behind the year before.

The centaur was already there, pacing nervously by the time Lippio arrived and grabbed his lover in a relieved embrace before getting a good look at him. Only when he had reassured himself that Lippio was truly there and safe did he notice what the human had done to himself.

Letting his lover's feet settle back to the ground, he release his soon to be mate and stepped back from him, "Oh, Lippio! You are beautiful!"

Lippio could not speak with his throat closed so tightly by the joy in his partner's eyes. He had stopped by a still pool on his way to the meadow. In the last light of the setting sun and using the pool as his mirror, he had shaved his head removing all the hair on both sides. All that remained was an unbound flow running from his forehead, down his neck and past his shoulders: a mane fit for his mate. Instead of speaking, he tossed his head and pranced for the centaur.

After both finished crying and managed to end their embrace, they grew solemn. Hand in hand, they stepped into the meadow that was to become the start of their new life.

The ceremony itself was short and simple. The two avowed their enduring love one for the other, and then each fastened the ring of their own hair around the neck of his chosen mate. Calling upon Pan and all the gods to witness their vows, they bound themselves together until the end of time. They stood silent under the rising moon for a long while sending forth silent praise and prayer to Pan, thanking him for giving them that place for that one night.

As they listened to the night, each of them mused that they heard a faint, merry laughter and the sound of pipes.

Returning to the supplies that Doran had brought with him, Lippio was delighted to see, among the other items, a bota of wine. He uncorked it, spilled some on the ground in honor of Pan, and then drank deeply. When his belly sloshed, he held it out to Doran who also spilled a libation to the god they had been praying to. The centaur drank deeply as well, marveling that Lippio had managed to find and bring wine to their ceremony.

The bota passed between them several times. Both tipped the bag to spill another offering into the soil before corking it and putting it away. As one, they turned to each other and kissed. That kiss, so gentle and sweet, took flame and soon their mouths pressed together hungrily. Tongues darted and tasted each other. Fingers tangled in each other's manes. Their impassioned moans filled the night as each forgot his fear and realized that the time had come to mate.

Moaning and gasping into Lippio's mouth the centaur begged, "My love, take me. Mate me. Make me your own. From now until the end of time."

"Doran, I am your mate. You are mine. From now until the end of time."

The young man drew his lips away from his love and nuzzled the hollow of the centaur's throat. They had each feared the possible harm to Lippio too much to truly look forward to their first mating as much as they might have hoped. They intended for the mating to be quick and obligatory, leaving lovemaking for the sheer joy of it for a future time when they were comfortable enough to put fear aside. Instead their veins filled with fire. Lippio's hungry lips burned as they closed upon one of Doran's nipples and he pinched it lightly between his teeth. His tongue flicked back and forth across the trapped nub until the massive centaur squirmed and begged helplessly. He delighted in his mate's pleasured whinny and began to tickle the juncture of skin and fur where the centaur's torso merged into his equine chest.

He felt Doran's hands caressing his shaved scalp and clenching in his dancing mane as he licked and devoured every inch of his lover within reach. Soon the stamping of hooves drummed a counterpoint to their moans and gasps of pleasure.

With a laugh, Lippio danced away from his lover, turned and ran back to leap upon the centaur's back and roll off the other side. When he hit the ground, he rolled under the stallion to caress his balls and plant a kiss upon the roundness protruding from the centaur's sheath. Another roll between the stamping hooves and he stood to face the centaur's rump. Every beat of his heart seemed to fan the flames in his blood higher and higher and it was with an urgent need, rather than the tentative awe of their first time, that he caressed the broad expanse of his lover's hindquarters.

His fingers now knew the way and quickly found the secret places that could make Doran wriggle and dance with pleasure. They delved deep into the musky crevice between the stallion's buttocks and soon the centaur's tail flagged high and his puckered ring twitched and winked. The young man twined his fingers in the waving tail and clamped his teeth on that sensitive spot that Doran loved so well. The centaur squealed loudly in the night as teeth and tongue explored that naked area. Lippio's fingers caressed, probed and tickled the opening that would soon sheath his maleness and join them forever.

The buzzing in his head drowned out thought, and he did not wonder at it when his mouth fastened on his lover's twitching rectum to kiss and devour it. When it opened under his tongue, he did not hesitate to plunge it inwards, exploring and tasting the musky secrets that would soon be his. His hands reached under the stallion to squeeze and roll his heavy balls and to reach forward to grip the base of the huge penis jutting from between the stallion's thighs.

Part of Lippio had been aware of his lover's impassioned cries for some time before their meaning took shape and he heard the words that the stallion called out to the moon.

"Take me! Mate me! Fill me! I need you, Lippio! My love! Mate me now!"

Using the centaur's tail as a rope, Lippio pulled his lover back to where a rock protruded through the green carpet of the meadow. His feet found purchase there and soon his belly pressed against the rump of his mate. The centaur's tail pressed against his chest, the long hairs tickling and stroking his burning flesh. They lashed at his nipples and snapped under his chin as he took his member in hand and pressed it to the wet opening beneath. Doran was wet and ready, but Lippio's penis was dry and pushed the tight ring of the centaur's anus deep before parting it to slip inside for the first time. As he sunk himself into the tight embrace of the centaur, their cries joined together and climbed into the night.

"I am yours!" screamed Doran.

"You are mine!" echoed Lippio.

Lippio could not have slowed his hips as he sank forward only to draw back and plunge into Doran's depths again and again. Far too quickly, he felt the pressure rising in him and sobbed with joy knowing that he was about to fill his mate with his seed. His hands gripped the protruding bones of the centaur's hips as he pulled them back and ground his maleness ever deeper into the backside of his first and only friend, the love of his life, and his reason for being. The world became the pulling and plunging of moist heat over his penis and the wet, sucking sounds of their lovemaking. The ragged gasping of breathy passion exploded from a heaving chest. The stamping of hooves and cries of joy became an inferno that consumed the world until he felt himself dying and flowing into his mate.

The young man came back to himself slumped over a sweaty and trembling rump. His penis slipped from his mate, but it no longer mattered. The mating was forever. He was inside Doran now. His essence was forever a part of the stallion. He looked up to see Doran's head slumped, chin on his chest, bobbing slowly as his breath slowed from its ragged heaving. When he could breathe again and felt that his wobbly legs would once again bear his weight, he stepped off of the rock and, pausing to grab the bota, approached the centaur with a warm embrace and warmer kiss. He smiled at Doran's blissful look of utter contentment.

"How are you, my mate?" asked the boy who had become a

man.

"Oh, my love! I am wonderful! I feel as if I am glowing inside. You have made me happier than I ever dreamt was possible to feel. I can still feel you inside me. I think that I always shall."

"And I shall always feel you around me, embracing me, drawing me ever deeper into you. I can feel that part of myself that is in you still. A part of my soul is now carried by you."

Together they drank the rest of the wine and regained their strength. Their touches were now warm and gentle rather than hungry and urgent even though each still felt the fire in their veins. Banked, it awaited only an invitation to again become a raging inferno.

Finally, Lippio kissed his mate softly, looked into his eyes and smiled, "My mate, my love. Will you take me now? I am ready to become yours."

"Lippio, I am your mate. You are mine. From now until the end of time."

Doran picked up some items from the ground and together they walked towards the tree that they had chosen for this purpose. When they arrived, Doran had Lippio stand and lean against the trunk of the tree while he moved behind his mate.

Lippio felt his lover's breath in his hair and his fingers stroke and knead his back. He felt his lover's lips upon his neck and ears and feather-light touches upon his buttocks. His fingers clenched the rough bark of the tree as he felt his centaur mate explore and taste and tease his flesh. Strong hands gripped his waist as the centaur knelt behind him and, in reverent silence parted the globes guarding his mate's virginity, revealing for the first time the treasure hidden there.

Lippio's groan of ecstasy said all that needed saying as he felt Doran's breath wash over his cleft and, for the first time, a tongue taste of his most secret place. Legs spread and trembling, he felt the centaur's tongue dance lightly and tentatively across his expectant orifice and then wash over it with force and hunger.

Again, he felt the fire building in his veins and a heat building under his lover's tongue. He felt himself open and nearly fell to his knees as Doran's questing tongue probed his inner recesses. Only Doran's strong hands kept him upright while he whimpered and moaned, and the centaur devoured him. Those hands turned him around and pressed him back against the tree as his lover's mouth devoured his manhood, stripping it of the essence of their previous lovemaking. His head thrashed as he felt something cold and slippery press between his cheeks and then with an exquisitely burning sting push into him even as the centaur's throat milked him urgently.

He cried out as the finger buried in his rectum and found a spot that made him explode inside. He reached down and clenched Doran's flowing hair in his hands as the finger inside him began to withdraw only to plunge back into him again and again. Each penetration pushing over that magic spot until he was pushing down on the questing finger as urgently as it pressed in.

His panted "More! More!" was hardly more than a gasp, but his lover heard. Lippio's cries carried no pain when a second finger joined the first. They stretched him, explored him, opened him, and set him on fire. When Lippio ground his hips down onto the fingers, forcing them even deeper inside himself, he did not have to ask to feel a third finger spread him open. His lover's fingers, stretching him, loving him, were opening him up for what was to come. The centaur's mouth urgent upon him, sucking at and pulling his testicles until they ached so sweetly that he thought he must explode.

Now he understood Doran's urgency. He could not wait to be opened further. He could not wait for the fourth finger that they had planned. He needed to give himself to his love. He burned to surrender himself fully and utterly to the centaur's ultimate embrace. He needed to feel himself taken and made another's. He had to give himself, all that he was, to the one he loved more than life itself.

"Now! Now! Take me! Mate me! Make me yours!"

There was no fear. Only fire. A flame of passion and love. As the centaur stood, Lippio dropped to his knees, feeling the cool night air enter his well stretched orifice. He dug his hand into the small keg of grease that Doran had brought and lifted his hands up to the equine phallus bobbing strong and proud before him. His mouth engulfed the leathery head of his lover's tool and was filled with a strong jet of his emissions. He swallowed the offering, feeling it fan the flames inside him. He brought his hands up to the length of that mighty shaft, and stroked and massaged it until it gleamed wetly in the moonlight. Finally, he pulled his mouth away and continued his ministration on the spongy head. Part of him wanted to kneel there all night, worshiping that rod of flesh. The other need was even greater. The need to surrender. To be taken. To be mated.

Rising to his feet, he brushed his slippery hands across his lover's chest. He gnawed and sucked hungrily at the centaur's neck, leaving bite marks that would be dark bruises by morning, while working a large handful of the grease into his rectum.

"I want you, Doran. I need you. I must feel you inside me. I have to have you. Take me, my love. This is right. You cannot hurt me. I am yours."

"You are mine, my love. Turn now and be mated."

It was well that they had discussed how to accomplish the actual act earlier because neither could think clearly with the fires filling them. Lippio turned away from his love and stepped beneath a low hanging branch. He placed one foot well in front of the other to brace himself and waited. He heard the shifting of hooves then a grunt.

Then he felt the weight of his stallion lover descend upon him.

Doran reared up and grabbed the branch overhead. He flung his forelegs over Lippio's shoulders as he lowered himself onto his lover. His mate. He held as much of his own weight as he could from the branch overhead but knew that he was still an awesome weight upon his beloved's back.

Lippio reached behind himself and grasped the pole pushing at his buttocks and leaving wet trails across his back. With groaning urgency, he forced the member down until it slid through the cleft of his cheeks and he finally felt the shaft press against his opening.

"Yess..." he hissed, "Yes... Now!" and was taken.

At first there was only pressure, a pressure that grew and grew. Pressure that became burning and a burning that became pain. A pain so exquisite that it was indiscernible from ecstasy... but still left him closed to his lover. Unable to surrender his love, unable to forgo his need to be one with Doran he cried out, "I am yours!" and pushed back upon his need.

His lover was inside him.

Doran trembled as he struggled to remain still atop Lippio with only the head of his shaft lodged in the guts of his mate even as every instinct in him screamed to plunge in, to take, to breed, to fill him with his seed. He sobbed as he heard Lippio's cries of pain and in them the joy Lippio felt in giving himself to his love.

"Lippio! Lippio! I cannot do this! I am hurting you!"

"No, Doran. I want this! I need this. Please! Stay inside me. The pain fades and leaves behind a joy I have never imagined. Oh... to feel you inside me... to give myself to you in this way. This is right. I am your mate."

The incredible, aching, overstretched feeling did not fade, but the stinging burn of his abused portal began to make way to pleasure as he felt the enormous head of his lover's shaft pressing against that special place somewhere inside him. With the easing of pain came the renewal of need. Of hunger. With a sob that was joy rather than fear, he pushed himself back further upon his mate. Slowly but inexorably that pole of flesh speared deeper and deeper into him. He could feel his insides being pushed aside to make way for the massive invader. With one hand wrapped around the quivering base of the centaur's maleness, he forced himself back until he could force no more.

He was full. Totally. Utterly. Completely full. He had taken Doran. Doran had taken him. Both paused in astonished joy. Both felt the tears streaking down their cheeks. Tears of love, of joy, of surrender.

Finally, the stallion could fight no longer and slowly began to withdraw his shaft until the flared rim of his head tugged at Lippio's tight ring. A pause without daring to breathe, and then a mutual groan as the living sleeve of flesh once again slipped up the length of him. Fully half his length buried itself in Lippio's flesh. Feeling resistance, he stopped and let Lippio rest before withdrawing to plunge in again.

Lippio gasped and sobbed under hard mountain of flesh heaving and gasping atop him. His legs trembled, the muscles bunched and straining to support the weight of his lover. His eyes glazed and a trickle of saliva drooled unnoticed from his lips as he lost himself in the surrender of being mated by the stallion so hot and urgent on his back. The churning deep inside him as the huge, wedge shaped head plowed into him pushing all before it aside as it took him, mated him, fulfilled him. The feeling of being stretched so fully. Warm fur pressing against his back, rubbing back and forth with the increasing force and speed of the centaur's churning hips. The bucking hips starting to brush the outside of his thighs. The slick, wet sound of the enormous phallus being pulled out of him and the wetter, flatulent sound of it inexorable decent back into his depths. The pressure that was almost pain when that shaft tested his deepest recesses and withdrew before the pain could truly manifest. His own penis flopped loosely between his thighs but he could not conceive of being more aroused, more aware of himself sexually than he was right now under and surrounding his true love.

The pounding that rocked him and stabbed into him grew heavier and more forceful as his centaur lover approached the climax that would seal them together beyond even the gods' ability to sunder. He no longer noticed that more of the equine flesh filled him with each long stroke, or that his anus stretched to almost obscene dimensions as he began to accept the thicker base of Doran's penis, now fully three quarters buried. The time was approaching. Soon his lover would truly fill him, flood him, and invest him with his holiest gift. Sobbing, he pushed back to meet the stallion's thrusts. Desperately he cried out, "Yes! Take me! I am yours! I am yours!"

Faster and faster Doran pounded into him, grunting and groaning until he pulled back to the very limit, until only the hungry pull of Lippio's ring kept him inside his love. The centaur's tail bobbed once, twice. The head of his mighty shaft swelled into a fist of iron and he thrust himself deep into Lippio with a final scream. The gates opened. His seed spewed into the tight channel that sheathed him. He pulled back and ground himself into his mate again and again. Each desperate plunge jetted more of his equine sperm deep into the trembling human's guts. Still again and again, he plunged inward to fill his mate until there was no room for more and the torrent squished out around the massive pole to spill down Lippio's thighs.

Finally, the stallion was still above his lover. His aching arms, still gripping the branch overhead, held him steady and kept him from falling onto Lippio while his pounding heart, heaving chest and trembling hind legs settled enough for him to safely dismount. While he waited, his mind drifted in a dreamy haze of feelings too wonderful to have names. Coming back to himself, he whimpered in distress as he realized for the first time that so much of his penis impaled his lover. He felt Lippio sobbing beneath him and almost pulled himself out before it was safe until he heard that what Lippio was sobbing was "yesyesyes" over and over again. He finally felt himself begin to soften, the head of his pole spongy rather than stone. Slowly, carefully, he withdrew inch by inch until, with a final tug, his penis fell free with a wet plop to dangle, wet and glistening between his thighs. Easing himself off his lover, he grabbed Lippio as the young man collapsed.

"Lippio! Lippio! Please! Come back to me! I am so sorry! Come back to me, my love."

His joy knew no bounds when his mate opened his eyes and smiled a dreamy smile, "Why be sorry, my mate? You have made me complete."

"Oh, Lippio! I thought that I had hurt you. I lost control and pushed too hard. Are you okay? Did I hurt you badly? Should I get a healer?"

"No, my sweet. You did not hurt me. Even in your passion you never went farther than I could take. Even when you were lost to me, you kept me safe and cherished me. I need no healer. Only you."

The mates, human and centaur, held each other on the grass of that meadow under the tree that had helped them to make their bond and were content in the completeness each had found in the other. When Lippio finally allowed Doran to check him for injury, the centaur found that Lippio's anus was swollen, red and still gaping open. There was some blood mixed with huge amounts of semen still flowing from Lippio, but not enough to cause either of them concern. Finally, assured that he had not hurt the one he loved, Doran kissed his mate again and again. His smile was bright enough to make the stars want to hide their pale glimmerings.

Lippio looked up and his mate and smiled a wicked little grin, "You have checked and rechecked and must now admit that I took no real harm from our lovemaking. Do you know what that means?"

"What does it mean, my love."

"That you do not have any excuse to make our first time the only time. With a lot of practice, someday I might even be able to take all of you inside of me."

The centaur smiled down at him and said, "If that is what you truly want, then I will make sure that you have all the practice that you can handle."

After a time, how long neither could have said, the centaur rose and extended a hand to help Lippio up, "It is time, my love. We should return to the glade now while the evidence of our union is still apparent. The elders may doubt our word, but cannot doubt their eyes."

Lippio blushed deeply. This too, was something they had planned but the human did not have the centaur's lack of modesty about such things and was sincerely embarrassed by the idea. Still it was a small price to pay for a lifetime with his mate and so he did not object.

Seeing his lover's bow legged, wincing gait the centaur did not offer to let Lippio ride, but walked beside him with one hand upon his shoulder.

As they left the meadow Lippio turned to Doran and chuckled,

"I do not know what was in that wine, but I sure am glad that you brought it. It turned something frightening into a gift beyond price."

Doran stopped and looked down at Lippio, "That I brought? I thought that you brought the wine."

The two lovers turned back to look out over the meadow. In the distance, they thought that they might have heard laughter and the sound of pipes. With a smile and a shrug, they turned and stepped into the forest. Side by side. Heading for home.

We arrived at the glade in the early morning hours. We chose not to wake the clan, but waited for them to stir. It was Doran who had the idea to have us wait with me astride his back. It was not comfortable; I still ached deep inside with a mysteriously wonderful emptiness. Still, those quiet hours as the moon set and the sun began to rise as I sat atop my mate's strong back, my arms wrapped around his chest and my cheek resting against his broad back, are some of my most cherished memories.

We had intended to make an impression and cause a stir. Within a single minute of the first early riser, nearly the whole clan surrounded us. Each of them yelling and threatening us, and several trying to pull my from my mate's back until his flying hooves and fists forced them back. Finally, they waited in a ring around us; glaring at us, seeming to be angrier at Doran than at me. The circle broke as the Head Elder approached us. I had known him almost my whole life and had always counted him friend. If I had expected any warmth from him that morning, I would have been disappointed. His glower was as icy as the rest, if a bit more controlled.

After he restored the clan to respectful silence, he asked the meaning of this abomination.

In a voice that carried clear and firm over the glade, Doran declared that there was no abomination and presented me as his mate.

The pandemonium that broke out at that announcement took a very long time to quell. A meeting of the clan elders was called for noon and Doran was told to wait with his parents. Another argument ensued when we refused to be parted. Finally, Doran was allowed to carry me to his Stall'na and Mar'na. They respectfully asked me for permission to speak with their son alone, and seeing confusion, fear and love in their eyes but no anger or animosity, I agreed. I could not hear their words but saw the frequent glances my way and that my mate never bowed his head in shame or remorse. He met his parent's gaze squarely and proudly.

When they returned to me, I had no idea what to expect, and was caught off guard when his Mar'na pulled me to her and clasped my head to her bare breast. His Stall'na clapped a heavy hand on my shoulder and I was welcomed into their family.

When we were ordered to present ourselves before the council, Doran and I stood together, and his parents stood by our sides. Things did not go well at the council. Doran had been correct about the laws and traditions of his people, but they did not like feeling as if those traditions had been manipulated and used against them. There was a core group of the clan that seemed bent on refusing all evidence that our claims of union were legitimate. They even tried to throw doubt on the evidence of our mating, claiming that we were already known to engage in bizarre acts and that the semen inside each of us could have been put there by any number of means.

The arguments raged on for hours. The tide seemed to be steadily growing against us when a pair of stalls stepped out of the woods and into the glade announcing that they had received a message telling them that they were needed. It took more time to tell them the whole story all over again and then for it to be repeated yet again when a pair of marems galloped into the glade, sides heaving and clotted with foamy sweat. They too had received an urgent message telling them that they were needed.

It turned out that the pairs were the mated woodcutter stalls and trader marems that Doran had referred to the day before.

No one knew who had sent them the message, but when all was said and done, they stood behind Doran and me along with Doran's, and now my, Stall'na and Mar'na.

As humiliated by the thought as I was, I offered for Doran and I to repeat our oathbond and mating before the clan. Even that was *refused by the opposition who claimed it was just a trick to get the clan to legitimize something that had never happened. They pointed out that it would be meaningless without the mating that was so obviously impossible in spite of our 'faked' evidence.*

When I demanded to prove their accusation lies, I was ordered to shut up in centaur council. At this, the marem pair, the stalls, his... our parents and, finally, he and I turned our backs on the Elders and the clan. If I, who was now a centaur even if they refused to acknowledge it, was not permitted to speak, then we would not hear any of them. It was a grave insult and a dangerous move, but it worked. My voice would be heard.

Throughout the day the numbers behind the opposition grew steadily while only a few of the clan moved to stand behind us. The actual decision rested in the hands of the elders but they were unlikely to act against the will of the whole clan for a young stall and a human. Things would probably have gone against us if not for the final stranger to step into the glade.

Another uproar ensued at the appearance of a satyr in clan council. Through the outburst, the little goatman stood calmly, drinking now and again from his bota or casually scratching at his genitals. At one point, he smiled and waved to the stall and marem couples behind us and we understood who had sent the message, if not why. Finally, he called on the pact between centaur and satyr that allowed either to sit on the council of the other where matters affected their own people as well.

When asked how the satyrs were involved in this matter, he calmly replied that the satyrs stood as witness and then laughed merrily. Lifting his bota he turned to Doran and me and asked us if we had enjoyed their wedding gift. The gratitude and love in the smiles we gave him must have been payment enough for his generosity because he began dancing in place, his tiny hooves skittering on the turf. It turned out that we had been wiser than we knew in choosing that memorable place for our union. Calling upon Pan in that sacred place brought the satyrs who had hid and watched us, just as we had them the summer before. They witnessed our Oath and our Mating and declared them to be Blessed. The satyr even swore to it on behalf of his people by The

Grape and The Vine, clutching both his bota and his male member. It was the most sacred oath a satyr could swear and even our staunchest opponent could not present a reasonable argument as to why the satyrs would perform blasphemy on our behalf.

The rest, as they say, was just details.

I wish that I could say that the excitement was over after that, but there was one more crisis yet to come that day. All during the council, centaurs had patrolled the borders of the glade refusing admittance to all humans and chasing off the ever-present boys. When the border opened again, a delegation from the village stormed in almost immediately. They demanded my surrender to lawful authority for trial and punishment. My father's glared hatred would have shredded me even a day earlier, but that day it could even not touch me as I stood beside my mate and my new family.

The Head Elder announced that there was no human, named Lippio or otherwise, among the clan. When the villagers screamed and pointed at me, he glared down at them from his full height and in a regal voice announced that the being they pointed to was Lippio, a centaur and member of the clan, mate of Doran and, as such, beyond human law. He went on to announce that, as a centaur and full member of the clan, I was protected not only by the clan but by the centuries old treaty between the two races, and that any attempted harm perpetrated against me would be met with swift and irrevocable retribution.

The human delegation, suddenly realizing that scores of large, powerful, and very angry centaurs surrounded them, slunk out of the glade and stomped angrily back to their village.

After that day, the clan became my people. The glade became my home. If my new people occasionally noticed that Doran's centaur mate lacked equine hindquarters, they did not hold this accident of birth against me. For a while, it seemed that every time Doran and I made love, one or more of the clan 'just happened' to wander by. I was mortified at first, but Doran just chuckled about it and said that, although they believed that we had mated, they were still curious about how we managed it. I guess that you can get used to anything, because eventually I no longer even noticed the inevitable spectators. Doran and I did it so often that, eventually, everyone had a chance to satisfy his or her curiosity.

In time, Doran and I chose to leave the glade and explore the world. He finally got his chance to stand far above the sea and look out over an endless horizon. That view took my breath away, but I still think that galloping is better.

I do not think that we ever did great deeds, despite what the stories written about us claim. Always, it seems to me, we did what was necessary to stay alive and ran away from danger whenever possible. It is strange to me how a poet can make such simple things sound heroic to someone who was not there.

So, we listen to the songs and stories and chuckle and snort into our cups, each of us knowing that our greatest adventure was as two youngsters under a tree discovering a friendship that would last a lifetime.

Oops!

Stephan von Krieger's name is known to some. A prolific and enthusiastic author with numerous contributions to Yiffstar.com, Stephan clearly has great fun in his writing.

In this story, we see a young tiger doing his chores, cheerful and careless, who makes a tiny little mistake that winds up plunging him into the afternoon of his life!

Daydream Gone Wrong

Stephan von Krieger

Kiva hummed to himself happily as he swept his uncle's laboratory. The lean tiger was daydreaming, his body on autopilot while he fantasized about grand adventures and fighting fearsome monsters.

The feline knew that he would never actually partake in such things. He wasn't nearly big enough to walk around in a suit of plate armor like all his heroes did. Even with a heavy exercise program, he couldn't get the proper strength behind his sword swing. He was a bit near sighted, so archery was right out. Nor could he cast a single spell, unlike his uncle.

Viran was your typical mage, all mysterious and such in a hooded cloak, puttering around in a tall tower with a shop full of strange gewgaws. The elder tiger had had quite an adventuring career in decades past, and proudly displayed souvenirs and spoils of victory from his escapades. Kiva could sit in his uncle's lab and stare at the shelves full of curiosities for hours, making up stories to go with items that didn't already have a tale accompanying them.

Kiva pivoted and jabbed the broom-handle through the heart of an imaginary monster. He moved with inherent feline grace, spinning and twisting, using the broom as a quarterstaff, warding off the blows of make believe attackers. His tail however, wasn't quite as nimble, upsetting a dusty crystalline statue from a nearby shelf. It hit the floor with a dull 'thunk', breaking in half, the top spinning away under a nearby table.

The tiger yelped, dropping the broom and darting after the bit that rolled away, quickly seizing it in his paws. His facial fur fluffed up in a blush as he placed both broken bits of the statue back on the shelf, trying to arrange them so they didn't look broken.

The statue wasn't shaped like much of anything, sort of like a drill bit but shorter and thicker, with a big knobby bit at the top and two flatter pieces spreading from the top. It was an opaque pinkish-white in coloration, though Kiva was almost sure that it was a little bit lighter in regard to the pink tint than it had been before he'd broken it.

He looked it over from several angles; you couldn't see the crack at all from anywhere in the room. Kiva didn't think his uncle would notice, after all, it had been covered with years' worth of dust and grime. The young tiger was rather glad that this was only the apprentices' lab, where Viran came to teach his pupils about the workings of magic. The things placed here were all for show and had very little, if any, inherent magical power. Nothing that would explode if looked at cross-eyed. The thought that breaking the statue might have some sort of effect on him never crossed his mind.

As Kiva checked the statue for visible damage, he could see a passing resemblance to some kind of winged snake creature. Maybe it was some kind of award for healing? The tiger recalled a symbol like a winged snake curled around a staff somewhere in one of his uncle's books.

Or maybe it was made to represent some kind of snake-creature? The bit at the top was kind of bulbous and elongated, resembling a serpent's head with a few knobs and bumps that were perhaps meant to be horns? The feline wondered if it was meant to be some sort of demon... He couldn't think of anything else serpentine that has wings and horns.

Kiva went back to work, his humming resuming where it had

left off. Rather than resuming his fantasies of fighting monsters, after all he didn't want his errant tail to knock over anything else over, he imagined what the creature the statue was supposed to represent.

He hadn't seen any legs, so he supposed that it slithered around on the big, long, serpentine tail that was curled around the central column. The creature would obviously be reptilian in nature, with large dragon-like wings, and with dragon wings came dragon horns.

It would be a big and powerful creature, probably a male since females tended to be smaller. In his mind the beast looked like a rather fearsome creature, heavily muscled and menacing. The creature's handpaws sported only three digits, each tipped with a long, tapering claw, perfect for rending the flesh of meddlesome adventurers.

The tiger decided that it would be more likely a demon, rather than something with dragon's blood. Statues of religious figures like that were more common. Kiva was rather pleased with his mental creation, it would be a fearsome foe to face in his fantasies.

He finished sweeping the lab within a few minutes, making sure to clean up the tiny chips from the broken statue. He dumped the dustpan out in the garbage can, setting it and the broom in their places in the closet.

Walking down the hall, Kiva stopped for a moment to enjoy a luxurious stretch. Sweeping had been his last chore of the day, and now he looked forward to the last few chapters of an adventure novel and a long warm shower.

Still humming, he slipped into his bathroom and flicking the light on as he stripped. He wasn't wearing much, just a simple tunic and shorts. He paused to look himself over in the mirror.

He had golden fur, a touch more yellow than orange, with a pattern of thick black stripes, a few of which ran onto the creamy white fur of his underbelly, radiant fur covered lean muscle, his mane of brown hair was always slightly mussed. He reminded himself that he really ought to make his way to the village barber and get it trimmed as he pulled a lock down in front of his eyes. It was a bit longer than he liked.

Kiva checked to make sure he had towels. Last week he hadn't had any, and had a rather embarrassing walk to the closet at the end of the hallway while fully naked and dripping wet. His sisters were still laughing over the sight of him stomping angrily down the hall. Thankfully today there were several towels stacked neatly inside the closet. Kiva pulled one out and hung it on the rack near the shower.

He paused as he slid the shower door open, a soft hissing sound reaching his triangular ears. Kiva scowled, curious as to what exactly the sound was. He leaned his head against the wall, wondering if it was the pipes. That was probably it, someone running the water up on the next floor.

The tiger sighed as he turned the water on, waiting a few moments for it to warm up before stepping under the wonderful heat. He closed his eyes, letting the jets of water stir up his fur, washing away the sweat, dirt, dust, and grime of the day. He grabbed the bottle of shampoo, rubbing the comparatively cool goo over his fur. He rubbed the sweet scented lather deeply into his fur, relaxing sore muscles as he did so.

Kiva backed away from the flow of water as he bent down to lather up his legs. His fur lathered up, he let it sit for a while as the soapsuds tingled gently. The feline leaned against the cool tiled wall and purred happily.

His face slowly broke out into a grin; it was time to get out all the stresses of the day. A few hours of hard work and exercise always got him riled up, and Kiva took some time each day to relieve some tension in the shower. It was the single place he was guaranteed not to be interrupted while he pleasured himself.

He stepped back into the cascading stream of warm water, rinsing off his fur and hair. Kiva reached his paw up and adjusted the showerhead slightly, directing the flow straight down, rather than out and back.

The tiger sank to his knees, he leaned forward and placed one paw on the wall for balance, the other snaked over his thigh and between his legs. Kiva slipped a single finger inside his sheath, gently rubbing the head of his feline member. In response, his big, black organ slowly slipped free of its confinement, eager to be played with after a day of monotonous chores. The tiger wrapped his paw around his slick shaft, stroking himself slowly. He closed his eyes, and let his mind wander. As he did during the day, he began to dream and fantasize, imagining that it was not his own paw stroking his maleness, but rather some rescued damsel or captured creature eager to bargain for its freedom.

Kiva imagined a tongue caressing his manhood, a smooth hot tongue tickling the head of his cock. It was a rather strange feeling, two tiny points tracing over his member, a forked tongue maybe? Some kind of serpent.

The tiger thought about what his dream lover would look like, but he was drawing a blank. He moved onto the scenery, but could only think of darkness. A few more details crept in, the air was warm and laced with a strange smell.

He sniffed the air curiously, drinking in the wonderful scent. It was sweet and musky, like how he imagined a female in heat to smell, but different somehow. It was intoxicating, each inhalation seemed to travel right to his groin, enhancing his lust and desire.

Something shifted around his body; his arms were pulled roughly over his head and bound there like they were held in some untouchable force. Something coiled around his chest and legs, immobilizing him.

The restraints were hot, smooth, and scaly. A serpent's tail wrapped around him. Holding him still, a captive prisoner for whatever the creature holding him desired. Scaled paws began to caress his thighs, slowly sliding around to cup his buttocks. With the tongue on his shaft it was obvious that what this creature wanted was sex.

Why though? What would be the lead up to this? A rescued slave, thanking him for his bravery? A fallen foe begging for a second chance? No, he was a sneaky little cat that had freed a powerful force from captivity. Ages after being trapped, it was free again, ad had Kiva to thank.

The tiger purred, this was quickly becoming one of the most interesting fantasies he'd ever had. The creature, whatever it was, took Kiva's cock slowly into its mouth causing the captive feline to gasp. It was hot; very, very hot. It almost burned his tender flesh.

Kiva felt a clawtip slowly circling his tailhole. He shook his head, eyes clenched tightly shut. He didn't like that. Why had that act appeared in his little daydream? He'd never even thought about the act before. He yelped and wriggled in the serpent's coils, trying to stop the invasion of one of his most sensitive areas.

The young tiger yowled as the creature's long, tapered claw slid deeper into him, followed by a single scaly digit. Kiva growled his displeasure at the beast, he didn't like this at all. The tiger opened his eyes but found only blackness. This was feeling too real for comfort; it was much too real.

A deep laugh filled Kiva's ears. "You belong to me now, little kitten." the voice growled, and then added insult to injury with a hiss, running his tongue across Kiva's shaft again. "So delicioussss..."

"What's going... Mmmph!" Kiva began to say, but was cut off as his muzzle was suddenly clamped shut as something hot and scaly wrapped around his head.

"Silence, slave!" the creature growled, digging his claws lightly into the captive feline's left buttock.

"You released me from my crystal prison. It has been so long since I have fed, and it is only fitting that you are rewarded for your efforts." The beast said as he resumed sucking off Kiva.

The young tiger fought to free himself, but serpentine coils that held him captive belonged to a creature much stronger than himself. Growing tired of his prey's struggles, the beast tightened his grip, nearly crushing the breath from Kiva.

He couldn't move at all, only lay still and let the serpent demon have his way with him. Kiva moaned softly as the snake-beast slid a second finger into his tailhole, slowly and gently fingering him.

The scent in the air grew heavier, thicker, more enticing as the creature continued to toy with Kiva, sucking him off and violating his rear. The snake release his grip around Kiva's chest, letting the tiger take in several deep breaths. That wonderful fragrance seemed to flow inside Kiva, the tiger began to feel more relaxed.

He lay in the demon's coils for a moment, feeling kind of dizzy. His cock was aching with need, growing worse each time the tiger inhaled. He felt his resistance melting away with every breath.

He let out a soft, almost involuntary purr, letting the sensations of being pleasured overtake his rational mind. Male, female, did it really matter what this creature was? It wasn't hurting him, and it had more than enough opportunity. Kiva's dream-monster seemed interested only in pleasuring him.

The demon's lips moved up and down Kiva's shaft with almost agonizing slowness, he was tormenting Kiva, and the tiger didn't like it. The dream-monster seemed to sense Kiva's frustration and increased the speed of his efforts.

The tiger moaned loudly, beginning to enjoy the serpent's ministrations once again. "My, my, my, is my little striped kitty enjoying this?" the demon said, mocking him.

Kiva didn't care. Right now the only thing he wanted was to blow his load right into the demon's taunting mouth. He didn't know how long he had been like this, forced to submit to the serpent's desires. But it felt like forever. The sweet tingling pressure inside him kept building and building, needing to be released.

The coils around Kiva's middle loosened slightly, allowing the tiger to move his hips. The creature unwound his tail from Kiva's head, allowing the tiger's tongue to loll out of his muzzle as he began to pant.

Kiva thrust rapidly against the demon's mouth, his cock nearly throbbing with the need to cum. "Oh yeah… oh yeah…" he gasped between breaths. The demon's hand slid around, no longer caressing his backside, though the other hand still toyed with his tailhole in a manner that Kiva, in the midst of his delirium, had started to find to be one of the most delicious sensations he'd felt.

Kiva's captor wrapped his scaly paw around the tiger's cock as he sucked it, the mix of saliva and precum rendering it very slick. The feline nearly howled at the sensation of smooth scales rapidly stroking his hot, hard shaft. He did howl however, in protest as the demon pulled his fingers from the young tiger's tailhole.

251

The snake only chuckled. "Don't worry my lustful little slut-cat, I'll fill you up again quite soon." The demon hissed, as he increased the pace of his stroking. Kiva could feel the familiar hot pressure building inside his cock as he neared climax. He was so close, just a little more... a little more...

Suddenly Kiva felt something hot, hard, and wet pressed up against his backside. The creature's cock felt nearly as big around as Kiva's arm! The snake rubbed the head of his massive member teasingly against the tiger's tailhole.

"Oh no! Oh please no!" Kiva begged, gasping for breath.

"Oh yessss..." The demon hissed, his shaft oozing a thick stream of precum against, and into, the tiger's tight little hole. "You're ready now my kitten." The serpent cooed, ramming his member deep into Kiva.

The tiger threw back his head and roared in a mix of pain and pleasure, every muscle in his body suddenly seeming to go rigid as he climaxed. Kiva thrust forward as hard as he could, his cock spurting jet after jet of hot cat cum into the air.

It took all the willpower he had to make his body relax. Kiva opened his eyes and blinked in confusion. The blackness and the warm embrace of the demon's coils were gone; he was no longer bound. He found himself kneeling on the cool porcelain tile of the shower, one paw against the wall for balance with the other wrapped around his still spurting manhood.

Kiva's jaw dropped as he peered down between his legs. The pool of hot seed that lay there was far more than he was used to seeing. The strange, overpowering dream had given him the best climax of his life. And Kiva wanted more.

He stood slowly on shaky legs, turning the shower's now cold spray on the evidence of his climax. It all had felt so real, but it couldn't possibly have been. Kiva was confused; normally he wouldn't have thought up something like this.

The tiger shivered in the chill that was coming off the icy water. He shut off the twin taps and began to dry himself with the towel he had hung up earlier. Kiva had thought about what sex would be like with another male a few times and had even dreamed about it as he had now, but never that vividly, or with that much detail.

Ignoring the novel he had made plans for earlier; Kiva dimmed the lights and walked over to his bed. The tiger let the towel fall to the floor and slipped into bed naked. He lay in the darkness, pondering the strangeness of the powerful sexual experience he'd just had.

Perhaps there had been some kind of mind-altering drug concealed in that crystal statue? Maybe Kiva was developing some kind of magic at a late age? Maybe today had been more tiring than he thought and he'd actually fallen asleep in the shower for a moment?

Kiva often had strange sexual dreams that felt real. Most often they involved Kiva sucking himself off. Those had been particularly strong dreams, and Kiva almost always awoke with copious amount of his own seed on his belly and thighs.

Or maybe, just maybe, the dream was exactly what Kiva's serpentine captor had said, a reward for freeing a captive sex-demon, imprisoned in the crystal. Though the creature had been rough, he hadn't seemed overly violent. If it had been a demon, it wasn't much of a plague on the world... a friendly menace at worst.

Kiva yawned and pulled his covers up over his shoulders, snuggling into his pillow. He thought about the last option for a moment. Supposing it was a real demon of some sort, would it come back? Was he linked to it forever, the creature invading his fantasies every time Kiva felt the need to pleasure himself? Would it drag him into that dark place where he had been and toy with him whenever the beast pleased, leaving Kiva stroking his cock in a zombie-like trance? Or would the creature only come when bidden, when Kiva desired its caresses? The young tiger hoped to find out. For tonight at least the creature was welcome in his dreams. Kiva had been given the time of his life at the creature's hand, and tongue, and lips, and cock.

He purred as he began to drift down into sleep. The serpent had given Kiva the most mind-blowing sensations of his life, the tiger thought it only fair that he at least attempt to return the favor.

First Day on the Job

Here we come to the last story in this volume of FANG, and we're signing off with a reminder of what fantasy, for most, is all about.

The wonder of magic, the marvel of a world so long gone that we can imagine it a stunning place, with rules and freedoms we can only breathlessly gawk at.

This story follows a young, newly initiated wizard claiming his place in the world.

Dedication
of the Tower

Drenthe

Dakkon awoke to a pungent smell and a splitting headache. He was damp. Has it rained, he wondered, or did I miss the ground when I puked? He cracked open his eyes and blinked back the dimness of early dawn, sparing himself a look.

His throat was scratchy and raw, acidic even, but he found the breath to groan his despair when he saw the damage done by his disquieted stomach. "My new robes!" Half-missed was the ground. Half-hit were his Master's robes, the gossamer fabric stained with wine-tinted bile down the left side, ending in a fetid puddle where part of the cloth had lain.

He staggered to his feet and attempted to sit up on his chest of belongings, sparing himself another look. While the morning dew had settled into the his spotted tabby coat, it looked like the stain had had plenty of time to set. He was going to have to buy a new set, the very morning after he had replaced his old ones! With his head still aching from a hangover, he decided to take advantage of the early-morning darkness to look around a bit. Once the sun came up, it would be hellish trying to see with his pounding headache.

Dakkon seemed to be in the middle of a slightly overgrown road running through the Salisbury plains, next to a small stone tower. The plains of the British countryside were awfully yellow in September, and Dakkon far preferred the green carpet that covered this countryside every spring. But as he surveyed the landscape, he noticed that his view was obstructed by a stone... well, a stone obstruction. He craned his head upwards to look at the dark gray tower that seemed to have sprouted out of the countryside before him like a weed. The tower. His tower!

The memories came back to him in a rush: being congratulated by his Guildmaster on surpassing Journeyman rank, having Bedlam recognized as an important spell. Then the wine, then the laughter, then more wine and then the scroll of Teleport he'd read to end up here, the transportation sickness that had blown through him like a gale, the lurching feeling of his stomach turning upside down, trying to leap out of his throat...

He scrambled to his feet, ignoring the unsettling stain and his recollections of the evening for the moment, and padded over to the tower door. Moving to push it open, his paws touched the oak and inadvertently triggered a spell. The door was filled with magic, and he could tell it was no mere apprentice who cast the spell. He felt a compulsion to say who he was, and barely held his tongue as he felt his fur rise up as the energy surged through him, to eventually subside as it drained back into the numinous ether. Testing the door, he found it was held with a force unlike any mere lock, removed his hand, and spoke aloud on a guess.

"I am Dakkon Scribe, Master in the Mages Guild. This tower is now mine," he spoke the words firmly, and pressed against the door again. It swung open soundlessly on oiled hinges, which meant... The tower was his! He grinned giddily, his hangover forgotten, and moved to inspect his new home. With a slight lean on the tips of his toes, he peered inside curiously, kitty cat ears swiveling as he listened for any noise. It was only tall enough for three stories plus the roof, and had ladders connecting the various floors instead of stairs. Spacious it was not, but it was his, as was the land around it. New Masters were expected to fund the expansion of their own facilities with their accomplishments. Giving new Masters a cramped little tower was an economical way for the Guild to nudge them in the direction of profit, along the line of desire. Dakkon knew this, but he'd been working his tail off for the last few years trying to reach Master. He could use a day off, relaxing.

He shucked his soiled robe inside his new tower and looked around, feeling the rough, gray stone walls and the sandy, dirty stone floor. He was imagining what he would do here, the energies he would release and the powers he could bring to his command. With power comes wealth, and possibilities for experiments, unraveling mysteries he had yet to even discover. Wealth and power enough to solve mysteries of the universe would bring fame, which could lead to all sorts of interesting... personal acquaintances. Dakkon had developed a bit of a xenophilic kink to him, one which he had nurtured and fed with the spoils from being an industrious voyeur. A harmless little fetish, it now demanded his attention as he pondered the kind of renown that would have Guildmaster Fornman offering his daughter's hand in marriage—and his son's, when that failed. Dakkon dreamt of the fame that would bring potential candidates to him from all across the world, the awe that would hold them spellbound at a mere scent of his aura, the desperation that would drive young apprentices to extreme lengths just to study under him. Speaking of lengths, a draft cooling down his heated erection reminded him to shut the door. He thought about dragging in his chest of belongings from outside, but decided they would be safe outside until he finished. Few stole from mages lightly.

He sunk down to his knees as he stroked the taut muscles under his downy spotted coat, imagining his own private fantasies of apprentice prodigies traveling here, just to meet him. They all wanted the same thing: vying for a place under the Legendary Dakkon Scribe, willing to do anything to be accepted into his tutelage. There was one his mind kept focusing on, a strange exotic giraffe-like hoofer with a confused jumble of brown and white stripes over its lower body and arms. It was—He was called an okapi, and clad only in a small loincloth. Okapi were usually short, this one shorter than average, and underage by a year too, which

Dakkon found interesting in his daydreams. His mind's eye laid out the familiar fantasy scene as his paw stroked softly over his testicles, tugging his sheath and sensitive orbs downward to expose his shaft to the empty tower. He moaned quietly and began whispering the strange words of a spell, interleaving reality with fantasy as the images of his mind took shape in the empty tower. A glamour spread through the air. Oily words tumbled down his supple feline tongue, escaped his lips, manifested his will.

Through lidded eyes Dakkon saw a ghostly image of himself standing next to the okapi before him, while his paws glided over the spike of cat flesh rising up from his paws. One claw nimbly located a loop of enchanted platinum through the flesh, and Dakkon hissed his pleasure to the two new figures. Older, wiser, more confident, palpably powerful, the phantom Dakkon was sitting atop a marble throne glowering at the nearly naked herbivore begging before him. The scene began to play out as Dakkon sat in a trance, a tiny bead of precum oozing down his shaft into the fur of his knuckles. As he whispered to the spell, which was now cast, the okapi repeated his words in a high, almost frantic tone, smudged with an exotic savannah accent.

"Butsir," he cried, "I have given up everything to journey here. I sold my horses, my scrolls, my lands, my spell book, even the clothes off my back. If you turn me away, I will have nothing left!" His face was damp with tears and he was bending over in supplication, far enough to profile the taut mounds of his well muscled rump, sprinkled with small brown stripes that seemed to draw the eye between them. What wondrous things Dakkon's eyes beheld!

"Nothing left, you say?" the ghostly Dakkon observed with some warmth in his voice, lust tempered with indignation at the uppity behavior of this petitioner, "You claim to have nothing, but you have plenty to sell even now. I have no time for games, boy, and no need of apprentices who value other things higher than magic." He gestured to the okapi's small loincloth, and narrowed his eyes, "Return when you are serious." His paw waved in dismissal to the ghostly young man, who wailed his sadness.

"Please! I would do anything for this opportunity... If I must give up every last thing, then I shall." With that he stood up, untied his loincloth and dropped it at the feet of the marble throne. His muscled legs and skinny belly blended into petite striped hips and a not-quite-so-petite white sheath. The very tip of a shy ebony glans caught the seated feline's eye, and he relaxed into his throne to adjust his robes while the okapi blushed, holding his paws to the sides of his hips, looking nervous. With his head downcast, defeated, he softly lamented, "I have nothing else. Please teach me, master, I beg..."

The elder ghost smiled darkly, enjoying his game with the exotic little creature, "Nothing? Oh, come now, boy. Horses? Lands? Clothes? These things are the unnecessary attachments to a society full of mere men; they have nothing to do with the study of magic. You lose nothing by giving them up; don't look so deprived." His robes were slightly misshapen by a rising erection that seemed to grow firmer with each pulsing heartbeat, encouraged by the paw with which he stroked himself delicately, sensually. He continued, "It is the sacrifices a mage makes, of magic and for magic, that allow him to become great. Your apprentice's spell book and scrolls were a step in the right direction, a single step, but for the wrong reason. Perhaps living naked on the streets will carry you further in the right direction, in a few years time..." His voice trailed off, and the naked okapi was about to plead his case once again. The slender forest giraffe's muzzle was open, poised to assert his good qualities to the stubborn master who would not accept him. Years on the street? It was unthinkable!

But Dakkon's voice boomed suddenly from his more aged form before the gentle herbivore had a chance, "I have no need for an apprentice who today clings to his own weaknesses, and is too stupid to realize what they are! Your most precious magical tool is yours alone, but you don't even know what it is, do you?" The mage got such a thrill out of dominating young hoofers into doing his bidding. The smell of sex wafted off his shaft, filled his nose and suffused his lustful illusion, deepening the blush that had crept under the okapi's brown and white face fur, and through his delicately expressive ears.

The small being shrank away, turning and granting a splendid view of his rump to both the phantasmal feline and the kneeling mage in doing so. He looked like he was going to run for his life, for his body shook so violently. He held his tongue, petrified by his desire to stay and his instinct to leave, and couldn't even glance back. Eventually the elder prodded him with a soft purr, "I asked you a question... Do you wish to answer it?" He casually gave his erection a stroke through the shimmering, nearly translucent fabric that made up his clothes. A wet spot had seeped through them, and stuck to the head of his shaft, outlining an unusually shiny tip.

The okapi nodded his head shakily, "M-my... soul, Lord Dakkon?"

Dakkon's apparition considered this as if taken aback, while his mood softened. He nodded, "Why, yes, you are correct... Technically. However, the magic involved in giving up such a thing is considerably beyond your level—and it is forbidden to practice in any case—so that you will keep." He rose from the chair, stepped over the forgotten loincloth, and approached the shorter, younger male with an outstretched hand. The naked young creature turned towards him but stepped back fearfully, approaching the tower's far wall. As his warm, striped bottom touched the cold, rough stone, he yipped in surprise. Cornered, he allowed his jaw to be petted gently as he was enlightened by the illusion of Dakkon Scribe, who seemed to enjoy having his prey between a rock and a hard erection. "A mage calls magic with his voice and his will, and shapes it with his body. Calling power is simple: chant long enough and you yield a practically endless supply of the stuff. Shaping is the tricky part, because the body naturally conserves itself, and if you can't form magic into a useful state, it fades away... or blows up.

"We grow in our ability to shape power by demanding more and more from our bodies. Left to our own devices, we become content with the power we have, we stop growing. However..." he paused as the paw on the okapi's cheek was slid down over his short, silky chest hair, across his skinny abdomen, lightly grazed across the boy's scrotum, and then cupped his testes possessively, as he whispered into the youth's ear, "However, if someone else owns our bodies, we are held to a stricter standard. We are forced to meet their demands; forced to grow because we have no choice. That is why my apprentice must give his body away to another."

Dakkon's cock was already aching for release from watching this little scene play through to the end a dozen or more times before, but in its own way, this fantasy had its purpose of testing his own endurance. This was still the foreplay, after all, and a mage had to keep his concentration no matter how... distracting a situation might be. Another drop of feline precum fell off the metal ring it clung to, and joined the puddle between his knees as he knelt, no longer touching himself. It was unnecessary at this point, as long as he watched "himself" caress that nubile male flesh, watched his muzzle lap at the boy's cute ears. It had been too long since he'd enjoyed the company of a willing apprentice.

The young okapi was elated to hear his master might accept him, but still nervous at speaking up. He somehow found his voice, raised it, and breathed, "Take it, my lord. I will do—whatever you command! I will be your apprentice..."

Dakkon's phantom smiled, nodded, and pressed his muzzle to the okapi's lips while soft wet noises escaped the seal of their muzzles. His paw gripped a striped buttock and forced their bodies together, grinding until... "Zephyr," the illusory cat commanded, "to my closet please." With that his shimmering robe pulled itself away from him as if silently tearing to pieces, then gathered itself in the air and floated through the wooden ceiling, casting a dim glow across the three figures on the tower's ground floor.

Okapi had a number of intriguing features that Dakkon found exciting, such as the striped ass and the black maleness that looked like it was now grinding into his likeness's leg. Others included the tiny horns that crowned the heads of the males—handles provided by a randy savannah god, perhaps?—and their exceptionally long tongues, long enough to lick their forehead, their eyes, or the entirety of a spotted tabby cat's sheath.

The smaller's male's paw closed around the newly exposed, jutting erection of his master, awed by the sight as his horns were tugged down firmly by an insistent cat's paw. He lowered to his knees and studied the shiny metal loop through Dakkon's engorged flesh, faithfully reproduced in his illusion.

"Master, why—" began the okapi as he studied the dripping piercing, only to be interrupted before he could ask of its purpose.

"Apprentices," the cat hissed at him, annoyed that his muzzle was not already put to better use, "assist with research according to their master's wishes." He rubbed his seeping cock tip against the lips of his new understudy, "The glans was one of many locations tested, but the only one that was... useful, when my master's research was performed."

A few agonizing seconds later, every muzzle in the tower, real or figment, hung open as the long okapi tongue was applied to kitten cock, circled the drooling girth, and drew inches of pulsing hot flesh forward. The illusory precum was slurped off by the sinuous stroking and flat herbivore teeth nibbled at the platinum jewelry between them, tugging slightly and eliciting more tabby juice from the elder male.

A minute of oral teasing passed before the spaced-out mage suddenly sat up a little bit, splitting half his concentration away from the cocksucking he was supposed to be directing. Dakkon realized that he'd forgotten to say the okapi's line immediately before the blowjob. He wondered if he'd entranced himself—then quickly reminded himself that that was merely a myth. He put it down to his hormones, today, and brought his attention back to the scene, wishing that okapi were native to Britain.

The nursing on the erection resumed as Dakkon focused his full concentration on the task at hand, with the okapi making slurping noises and the owner of the fine shaft groaning quietly as his claws dug into short, giraffe-like horns. He bucked his hips to kiss the poor lad's tonsils with his glans, and the hoofer nearly gagged. But with his will focused on not displeasing his new master, not letting him down and being turned away after coming so close to that which he had paid so dearly, he persevered in his servitude. His eyes watered. His jaw shook and trembled, exhausted from the strain. Still, he took the firm stabs into his throat and swallowed every second to fight his gag reflex.

The illusion of Dakkon growled, gritted his teeth, and pulled back to rapidly massage the first two inches of his shiny, wet, cat dick inside his new apprentice's muzzle, jerking off between tongue and palate. Moments after, the Dakkon made of fur and flesh grabbed his scorching hot, engorged erection, stroking frantically to stoke the coals of lust into orgasm, starved by neglect, kept hot by desire.

This was the test of his control! He had to hold onto his concentration! How he ached to hold onto those tiny horns instead! His claws unsheathed from his empty left paw as involuntary spasms traced a line through his spinal chord, a line which curled through his seed-laden testicles and up the crooked blood vessels of his primed maleness, waiting for the shower of sparks that would set him off like a cannon. Inside his head, he screamed for focus despite the torturous vision of his elder self in the throes of orgasm, as the flood of seed spilled from the straining muzzle that sought to contain it, to swallow it. Dakkon panted under the unbearable, heavenly stimulation of his paw with his eyes staring blankly at what his figment did next, paralyzed as he held onto consciousness by a single golden thread: the thread which he used to direct his illusion.

Now spent, thanks to the ministrations of his apprentice, the spotted tabby cat withdrew his shaft from the sticky muzzle he had just enjoyed, purring as he unwound a tongue which had threaded itself through his platinum piercing. He drew his fingertips along the underside of the boy's chin and moistened his claws in the fluid which had missed its mark, gathering up some of the mess on the ends of two fingers to spread it across the boy's forehead. Carefully, he formed his spilt essence into the symbol of the Scribes, a goose quill pen, and purred calmly—ignoring the feline spell caster in the corner, whose cum was finally spraying out like a waterfall onto his tower floor. "You," the calm phantom stated, as his sharp nail formed the point of the quill pen adorning his slave, "are mine."

And that was the last of Dakkon Scribe's illusion. The marble throne, the sexy little apprentice slave, the older, wiser, more powerful version of himself, even the pool of cum that had flooded the boy's mouth were gone, like they had never existed at all. The tabby cat wizard slumped to the ground, breathing unsteadily as his orgasm faded, fluids oozing out from around the platinum ring in his urethra. He rolled over onto his back, ignoring the dirt that stuck in his fur as he sprawled naked on the stones, and laughed exhaustedly. He exulted in his success, he'd held onto the spell! His self-gratification successful, he ran the scene back through his mind and felt a shiver, an echo of the powerful orgasm he'd just had.

As he lazily studied the mess he'd created in a line from one inch to six feet away from him, he was struck with an urge to duplicate the last part of the scene on a larger scale. A wizard's research laboratory is every bit as important as the assistants who do the research, after all. Moving to sit next to the middle of the puddle he'd created, he began drawing a large symbol, similar to the one placed on that lovely okapi's forehead... In a few minutes he was done, and he spoke sharply in a language that sounded of forked tongues, interminable lives and saber-sharp teeth while the quill pen-shaped stain turned black as soot, and sunk into the grayish stone permanently. Nothing but the faintest tingle of magic bleeding away could be felt as he stroked the lines once more, and he knew he would be spent until he rested for several hours. Still he called to the empty air expectantly, purposefully.

"*I am Dakkon Scribe,*

and this tower is mine."

Afterword

There you have it, folks. Years in the making:
FANG Volume 3.

Your humble editor admits to shedding a tear or
two as I send this off to press. This will most likely
be the last volume of FANG produced under my
auspices, and it's been a wonderful ride. I'm proud to
have brought some fine authors to print, and getting
a lot of furs to pick up a damn book for a change. I
thank you for buying this book, and I sincerely hope
you enjoyed it.

Of course, it's not over yet. Ben Goodridge joined
the team and is now in charge of FANG's sister
anthology, ROAR, whose pages collect the finest non-
erotica to be found in the furry fandom. Volume 1
is already done, and if I can get him to stop working
on his own damn novels long enough, Volume 2 will
soon follow.

FANG's torch, meanwhile, passes to a new edi-
tor. Cinnamon DeWolf, who dragged himself out of
retirement and rolled up his sleeves to join Bad Dog
Books and keep FANG going.

Given his background in furry erotica—you
should read some of his stories!—and that fact that
he's almost stricter than I am in his demands for
quality, FANG Volume 4 is bound to shatter the suc-
cess of the first three volumes.

Looking back, FANG has become what I intended it to when I set out: a who's who of furry fiction. Kyell Gold was a published author before he submitted his stories to the first volume, and his bibliography has only grown. Teiran Dragon, whose story I had to reject from this volume, now has his novel gracing BDB's catalogue.

I'd like to thank all the authors who submitted their stories and endured the editorial process, and were patient when things too longer than expected. I'm proud to put their work to print.

But, as I said, the story isn't over yet. If you happen to write the odd story yourself, do take a glance at www.baddogbooks.com and check out the submission guidelines, and maybe down the road your name can be found somewhere between FANG's sleek black pages.

And if you don't write, well... you might want to visit the site anyway and see what else we have for you!

Sincerely,

The Editor.